Abby Clements is the author of three previous novels, *Meet Me Under the Mistletoe*, the bestselling *Vivien's Heavenly Ice Cream Shop* and *Amelia Grey's Fireside Dream*. She lives in north London with her husband and son.

The Heavenly Italian Ice Cream Shop

Abby Clements

**SIMON &
SCHUSTER**

London · New York · Sydney · Toronto · New Delhi

A CBS COMPANY

First published in Great Britain by Simon & Schuster UK Ltd, 2015
A CBS COMPANY

3 5 7 9 10 8 6 4 2

Simon & Schuster UK Ltd
1st Floor
222 Gray's Inn Road
London WC1X 8HB

www.simonandschuster.co.uk

Simon & Schuster Australia, Sydney
Simon & Schuster India, New Delhi

A CIP catalogue record for this book
is available from the British Library

Paperback ISBN: 978-1-47117-683-8
eBook ISBN: 978-1-47113-704-4

Typeset in Bembo by M Rules
Printed and bound by CPI Group (UK) Ltd, Croydon, CR0 4YY

For my nieces, Penny and Eloise

Prologue

Friday, 7 November, 1.30 a.m.

Imogen was in a deep sleep, nestled into Finn's chest, two duvets and a wool blanket covering them, when her mobile went off. The harsh ring cut into her dreams – she'd been night-swimming in warm seas, surrounded by the firefly-like scattered lights of phosphorescence, as if the starry skies were being reflected. For a while, she'd been back in Thailand – and, as she put a pillow over her head to silence the sound, she tried to go back there. The endless white-sand beaches, the fish and birds, the place that made her feel most alive, and where she'd been inspired to take the photos that had launched her career. The phone was still stubbornly ringing. Reluctantly, she removed the pillow and sat up. The frost on the bedroom window reminded her she was in Brighton, in the beachside house she shared with Finn, in the middle of a cold English winter, and she wrinkled her nose at the cruel reality.

She reached down to the floor, clumsily padding around with her hand. Squinting, she saw her brother-in-law Matteo's name on the screen. A picture of her sister, Anna, came into her mind – tall, with long chestnut-brown hair, her willowy figure unbalanced lately by a large pregnancy bump – and her heart started to race.

'Yes?' Imogen said, taking the call.

'It's Anna,' Matteo said. He quickly filled her in, his usual laidback demeanour replaced with a slightly panicked tone.

'We'll be there,' Imogen assured him, awake now and full of excitement. She hung up and nudged Finn awake.

'It's happening,' she said.

'What's happening?' Finn asked. His sandy hair mussed and voice husky with sleep, Imogen felt drawn to him. In any other situation she would have been seriously tempted not to leave the bed. But this wasn't any other situation – and the bolt of adrenaline rushing through her veins reminded her of that. This was her only sister – on the brink of the life-changing event they'd all been waiting for.

'It's Anna,' she said breathlessly. 'The baby's coming.'

Finn raised himself up to sitting, and rubbed his eyes. 'You're serious?'

'Of course I'm serious,' Imogen said, getting up and hastily pulling on her jeans and sheepskin boots. 'Get up,' she said, throwing a sweatshirt in his direction. 'That was Matteo. They need help.' She tied her light-brown hair, sun-streaked from a recent trip away, up into a ponytail.

'Right . . .' Finn said, a concerned look on his face.

'Not delivering the baby,' she said, shaking her head. 'At least that's not the plan at the moment. They need a lift to the hospital. Apparently, the cab they called refused to take her.'

Imogen put some things into her handbag: some snacks, money, bottles of water – then saw that something was missing.

'Have you seen the car keys?' she asked Finn.

He seemed rooted to the spot. 'The thing is . . . I thought Anna's due date wasn't until December?'

'I guess when it's time, it's time,' Imogen said, with a shrug. 'Where are the keys? We need to get going.'

'The car. I put it in for an MOT yesterday.'

'You didn't,' Imogen said, her chest tight.

He nodded.

'Oh, God! Anna's relying on us to pick her up.'

'There is one other option.'

'You're not thinking . . .' Imogen said, reading his mind, her heart sinking.

'It's still here, from when we repainted it.'

Imogen raised an eyebrow. She looked out of the front window and saw the vintage ice cream van parked just a few feet away from their house, the pistachio-and-pink paintwork visible in the glow of a street lamp. She'd bought it for the shop – Vivien's Heavenly Ice Cream Shop – that she and her sister had inherited from their grandmother and which Anna and Matteo now ran together. Imogen had left to focus on her photography, but she still helped out at the business from time to time, covering the occasional shift and looking after the van. The van might have become a popular feature at local food festivals – but Imogen was pretty sure her sister wouldn't be pleased to see it that night.

'It's better than nothing,' Finn said.

Imogen shook her head. 'OK, let's go. But Anna's going to kill us.'

Imogen and Finn drove up the seafront in the early hours, the vintage ice cream van rattling as they gradually picked up speed. Ahead of them, the road was clear, sparkling with the frost that had gathered overnight.

'Could you check that text?' Imogen said, pointing at her mobile buzzing on the dashboard.

Finn read it. '"*Contractions two mins apart. Where are you?*" That last bit was in capitals, by the way.'

Imogen thought of her sister, waiting there for them to arrive. Anna, her older sister, always calm, controlled and together – she was heading right into the unknown. Anna had always been there for Imogen, with wise words and a listening ear while Imogen emerged from another drama. Now, Anna was the one who needed support. Imogen put her foot down on the gas, and the speedometer creaked up another two notches. She could see her sister's apartment building in the distance, an imposing Victorian block overlooking the sea. 'Tell her we're almost there.'

'Done,' Finn said. 'Smiley face?'

'I don't think so,' Imogen said.

A few moments later, Imogen and Finn pulled up outside her sister's building. Anna and Matteo were standing in the main doorway, a large bag at their feet. Matteo, tall and dark, with a thick coat to guard against the cold, waved over. He put his arm around Anna's shoulders as he led her carefully down the stairs. She had one hand resting on her bump, and her face paled when she saw the van. Imogen opened the door and hopped out.

'We're not all going in that,' Anna said, shaking her head.

'No, of course not,' Imogen said. 'We won't all fit. Finn can meet us there, right?'

'Sure,' Finn said.

'But I'm afraid *you* are,' Imogen said. She put out a hand to help her sister into the passenger seat. 'Come on, let's get you to the hospital, so I can meet my new niece or nephew.'

'No way, Imo,' Anna protested, her eyes bright with fury. 'Matteo – tell her.' She fell silent and drew in her breath.

'Uhhhhhhhh.' With the pressure of another contraction, Anna gripped Matteo's hand tightly.

'Anna, love, I think we should get in,' Matteo said.

'You're in the right place,' the midwife reassured Anna. 'And, the way everything's looking, it won't be long till you meet your little one.'

'Right,' Anna said, her cheeks flushed pink, and her hands gripping the side of the hospital bed in her private room on the labour ward. Her brown hair was tied back in a ponytail, damp strands clinging to the sides of her face. 'That's good. I think.'

'Of course it's good,' Imogen said, meeting the midwife's eye. 'Keep going, Anna. You're nearly there.'

'Do you have a birth plan?' the midwife asked.

'Matteo,' Anna called over. He was standing over by the window on his mobile phone.

'*Sí*, Mamma . . . in the hospital.'

'Matteo . . .' she said, more insistently this time.

He covered the mouthpiece. 'Mum wanted to know if you'd tried the pineapple. I told her that was what got this all started.'

'The birth plan,' she hissed.

He said something in Italian, then put the phone on the side. 'Yes,' he said, rifling through the hospital bag and taking out the folded sheet of paper. He passed it to the midwife. 'Here you go.'

A female voice called out from his phone, and he picked it up again. 'No, Mamma . . .'

'*Hang up the phone,*' Anna said firmly.

He held up a finger to signal he needed a moment.

'Tell him to stop talking to his mother, or I will kill him,' Anna whispered to her sister.

'I think you'd better put the phone down,' Imogen said.

Matteo put the phone away. 'Sorry. She's just excited, that's all.'

'Oh, Christ!' Anna said, straining and holding her back now. 'Can I have some pain relief?'

'Are you sure?' Matteo said. 'I brought that lavender along. Or I could give you a massage? Like you wanted?'

Anna gave him a steely glare. 'No lavender,' she said, shaking her head. 'And don't you *dare* touch me.'

Imogen was startled at seeing the sudden change in her polite, gentle sister.

'OK,' Matteo said. He got closer to his girlfriend and held her hand tightly in his, kissing her gently on the head. 'I'm a bit nervous, I guess,' he said.

'*You're* nervous?' Anna said.

'Are you getting her some kind of pain relief?' Imogen asked the midwife.

'Not much point now,' the midwife said. 'I can see the baby's head.'

Imogen took her sister's hand, and held it gently. Anna

looked at her, her warm brown eyes wide, and – for the first time that Imogen had ever seen – full of panic. Imogen desperately wanted to be able to take the pain away, to swap places with her sister and go through it for her.

'I can't do it, Imogen,' Anna said, her eyes brimming with tears. 'I really don't think I can do it.'

She gripped Imogen's hand tightly.

'You can,' Imogen said to her, calmly and softly, stroking her hair back from her face. 'Anna, you can do it. Let's meet this baby.'

Tearful, Anna nodded.

The midwife spoke to her firmly. 'Anna, it's time for you to push.'

Isabella McAvoy-Bonomi was born at 4.30 a.m. After the necessary checks, the delivery room emptied out and Anna and Matteo had a moment alone with their new baby.

As Anna held her daughter in her arms, she felt a surge of love. When she'd met Matteo two years before, she'd thought that it wouldn't be possible to care about anyone more than she did about him. But this little girl, her hands and feet curled and her cheeks pink, was so complete and perfect, ready to start her journey in the world, full of potential. Her blue eyes were open wide, as she looked towards her mother and father. She was theirs. If not for ever, then for a while, at least.

Then a new wave of emotion came, catching Anna completely off guard. The sense of responsibility felt overwhelming. Exhausted from the labour, she could barely think straight, let alone plan how to care for Bella. What if she messed it all up?

Matteo put his arm around Anna's shoulder and kissed her cheek, seeming intuitively to sense what Anna was feeling.

'We'll always be there for her,' he whispered to Anna.

'Do you think we can do it?' Anna said. 'Be the parents she needs?'

'Of course we can,' he reassured her.

Anna brushed her tears away but more came. 'I don't know why I'm upset. I guess I didn't expect to love her this much,' she said. 'Not right away.' A smile made its way through the tears.

Matteo touched his daughter's face gently. 'She's beautiful,' Matteo said. 'I'm so proud of you, Anna.'

Jan and Tom, Anna and Imogen's parents, arrived, and Imogen and Finn returned with coffee, the family bringing a flurry of activity and chatter to the room. The quiet moment between Anna and Matteo was gone, but, when Anna looked over at him, talking animatedly with her mum and dad, the intimacy between the two of them, the feeling of a shared adventure they were embarking on, was still there.

'You did it, love,' Jan said, beaming. 'I told you you could.'

She gave her elder daughter a gentle hug. 'How are you feeling?'

'OK,' Anna said, her cheeks flushed. 'Tired – but happy.'

'Nothing can really prepare you, can it?' Jan said. 'When
I had you, Anna . . . well, it might have been thirty years ago,
but I can still remember every moment of it. Proudest day of
our lives, wasn't it, Tom?'

Anna's father nodded.

'Thanks, Mum,' Imogen said, teasing.

'Oh, it's still quite nice the second time round,' Jan said.
'But there's something special about the first.'

'Anna was amazing,' Matteo said, smiling at his girlfriend
proudly and kissing her head.

Tom looked into the glass cot, his expression softening.
'Our granddaughter . . .' he said quietly. 'She's finally here –
I can hardly believe it.' He paused. 'Is it just me . . .?' he said.

'No, Dad,' Anna said, smiling. She knew exactly what her
father was thinking. Bella's mop of dark hair was jet-black,
like her Italian father's, but her eyes and mouth belonged
very much to Anna's side of the family.

'Her eyes,' Tom said, his voice soft.

'She looks just like Granny V,' Anna said. Her eyes met
her dad's.

She pictured her grandmother, her silver-grey hair pinned
back, and her blue eyes bright, enhanced by a line of liquid
eyeliner. She was smiling, dressed in a burgundy dress, a

cream cardigan, and T-bar heels, her dachshund, Hepburn, by her side.

Anna felt a sharp pang of regret that Vivien couldn't be there to share the moment, but, just as soon as it had come, it lifted – she was still there with them, in their thoughts and memories. Even now, Anna felt spurred on by her granny's words of encouragement and pride. She always would.

Part One

Part One

Chapter 1

Monday, 8 February (fifteen months later)

Rain lashed against the windows of Anna and Matteo's top-floor flat on Marine Parade, the bright lights of the Palace Pier shining blurrily through it. Bella was sitting between her parents in her high chair, chewing on a rusk, her dark hair curling around her temples and her cheeks still rosy from sleep. Hepburn, the black-and-tan dachshund who had once been Vivien's dog, and now belonged to Anna's family, darted around under Bella's high chair, snatching up crumbs.

'Cannoli,' Matteo said, a dreamy look in his eye. 'We should add cannoli to the winter menu at the shop. Sweet pastry with fresh cream. Perfect with coffee for days like these.'

'OK, sounds good,' Anna said.

Anna remembered the delicious pastries she'd shared with

Matteo over breakfast in Florence, where they'd met on an ice-cream-making course, and fallen in love. It felt like a life-time ago now. The landlady at their *pensione* had brought them out to the terrace – warm from the oven and irresistibly comforting. Now, since parenthood had taken over, if she and Matteo had a chance to grab a cup of tea before heading out to open the shop, it was a good day. The year had brought them together – when Anna saw Matteo singing to and laughing with their daughter, the love she felt for him was even deeper than before. And yet, also, with the fractured nights' sleep, the pressures of juggling parenthood with run-ning the ice cream shop, and the piles of laundry and washing-up that seemed to fill their home, the romance of those days when they first set eyes on each other seemed like something that belonged to a distant past, one that they wouldn't be revisiting.

Bella flung the rusk down onto the floor and started bang-ing her hands on the high chair, shouting gleefully.

'We'd better get ready,' said Anna. 'We've only got twenty minutes.'

She lifted Bella out of her chair and tried to persuade her fidgeting feet into a pair of shoes.

'I'll call Carolina and get the recipe,' Matteo said, getting his phone.

'What recipe?' Anna said, distracted by the Velcro on Bella's shoes.

'The cannoli,' Matteo reminded her.

'Oh, yes. Right. Good idea,' Anna said.

Matteo's sister-in-law, Carolina, kept the book of Bonomi family recipes with her at home in Siena. 'How is Caro, by the way?'

'Good,' Matteo said. 'She and Filippo have just had a swimming pool installed, Mum said. Apparently, sales at Filippo's company have been the highest ever this year.'

'Wow!' Anna said. 'Impressive.'

Anna's gaze drifted to the framed photo of Matteo's family on their kitchen wall. All of the family, bar Matteo, lived in Siena, where their family business, a large ice cream shop, was located. Long-established, it drew customers from all over the country.

Carolina, a chic Italian woman in her mid-thirties with waist-length black hair, was standing next to her brother, with their parents – Elisa and Giacomo – just behind. Carolina and Matteo were close, just a couple of years apart, and had spent a lot of time together when they were growing up in Italy. They were both tall, with the same dark brows and deep-set eyes. Elisa was a little shorter than her children, her hair dyed a deep red-brown and her face heavily made up. Anna had tried so hard to get on with her demanding mother-in-law – she really had. But she'd gradually accepted that their relationship would be healthiest if kept to small doses.

Matteo's father, Giacomo, was tall and grey-haired, a hard-working man who generally kept quiet while the rest of the family chatted animatedly over the latest drama.

Next to Carolina was her husband Filippo, a self-made millionaire in the olive-oil business, a charismatic man who tended to dominate the room. Carolina seemed to hold her own in the marriage, but Anna had wondered recently if her confidence had dipped since she gave up her job to concentrate on running the household.

'At least someone's going to be able to keep our parents in their old age,' Matteo said, with a wry smile. 'We've got a minute, right?' he said, scrolling down on his phone.

'Not really—' Anna started.

'Caro!' He began chatting in rapid-fire Italian.

Anna raised an eyebrow and pointed at the clock.

'One minute,' he mouthed back.

Anna looked at Bella – her face still covered in biscuit crumbs, one shoe on. She needed to be dropped at Imogen's before they opened the shop, and time was rushing by.

'*Sí, sí . . .*' Matteo said, cheerfully, going through into the living room to talk to his sister.

Anna was tempted to insist that they go, but stopped herself. She got to talk to her family almost every day – while Matteo's were in another country. His moments catching up with them were precious, and she and Bella could go ahead of him if need be.

'Now, Bella,' Anna said, half to herself, looking around the room. 'If we ever make it out, we'll need your coat. It's tipping it down out there.'

'There!' Bella said, pointing to the back of the door.

Anna smiled in surprise at the reply.

There it was, Bella's tiny yellow anorak hung just where it should be, on the coat hook. At least one person in the family was on top of things.

Vivien's winter specials:

Warm waffles with praline and whipped cream
Spanish churros with thick hot chocolate
A selection of crêpes with indulgent ice cream

'Two chocolate-ice-cream-and-hazelnut crêpes,' Matteo told Anna as he passed the freshly made dishes to her that afternoon. 'Extra hot chocolate sauce.' Anna carried the laden plates across the ice cream shop to the waiting customers.

'Fantastic!' A young woman and her friend took the crêpes gratefully. 'Just what we need on a day like this.'

Brighton was still wet and blustery, but Vivien's Heavenly Ice Cream Shop, under the arches, was a haven, sheltered from the chill south-coast wind and rain. The pale-pink-and-pistachio interior, large mirrors and retro 1950s bar stools and booths had all been put in by Imogen and Anna when they'd first started the shop, giving it a vibrant, vintage look. In the summer months, the pistachio-and-chrome counter had customers crowded around it.

The past year, as autumn came and the nights drew in, Anna and Matteo had decided to make a few seasonal changes. Anna had warmed up the interior of the shop, hanging hand-sewn drapes at the window and putting fairy lights along the walls, scattering cushions in the booths and lining the bookshelves with paperbacks and board games. Locals had continued to come during the usually quiet winter months, and the changes had attracted new customers to the family-run shop. In her three years of running the shop, first with her sister and now with Matteo, Anna had learned that she could never stand still. Innovating and adapting – adding new recipes to the classic ones on their menu – was what kept the café full, and meant people were always talking about it.

Anna glanced back towards the counter, watching Matteo get plates ready, taking his time over the presentation, frowning slightly in concentration as he swirled on the chocolate fudge sauce. When Matteo had arrived in England, insisting that he was still thinking of her after their time together in Florence, and that he was willing to move to England to be with her, Anna knew she was taking a risk. But it had paid off. As much as she loved Imogen, working together in the early days, after they'd inherited their grandmother's rundown shop, had pushed their relationship to breaking point – they'd navigated past near-bankruptcy and bad reviews, finally emerging with a strong business, but both slightly frayed.

Imogen's ambitions had always been elsewhere – and when she left to go travelling with her boyfriend Finn, committed to building up her portfolio of nature photos, it had seemed a natural progression, and in some ways a relief for them both, when Anna took the lead. Now Anna and Matteo – with their shared passion for creating gelato and sorbets with the most enticing textures and indulgent flavours – ran the shop together, and, aside from the occasional good-natured complaint about the weather, Matteo seemed happy with all aspects of his new home.

With a brief burst of cold air, Imogen entered the shop. 'Hey, sis,' she called out cheerily. Her light-brown hair was swept up in a turquoise hat, a few strands escaping. Even in her duffel coat there was an air of summer about her, her skin tanned and freckles bridging her nose. Bella was toddling along by her side, wearing a red bobble hat and mittens.

'Two of my favourite people,' Anna said, smiling, lighting up.

'Mamma!' Bella called out. Anna brought her daughter up into her arms and hugged her tight, kissing her cool cheek. 'Hey Bella. Have you been good for your Auntie Imogen?'

Bella opened her clenched fist and showed her mother the pink and grey swirled shells clutched inside.

'We were doing a little beachcombing,' Imogen explained. She took a seat on a bar stool at the shop counter. 'Walked up to the pier and back, and found these down on the shore.'

'They're beautiful,' Anna said, admiring them. 'We'll put them up in the bathroom so you can look at them when you're splashing around.'

Bella looked at her and nodded as if she understood. 'Papà!' Bella shouted, before running off in the direction of the kitchen in search of Matteo.

'She's the only person I know who's got as much energy as you,' Anna said to her sister. 'Thanks for taking her out this morning.'

'No worries.' Imogen took a seat at the counter. 'Mum's going to pop by in a minute to take over. Mine's a waffle, with plenty of whipped cream, by the way.' There was a glint in her eye. 'Good childcare doesn't come cheap, you know, Anna.'

'I guess you have earned it.'

Anna went through to the kitchen, where Matteo was holding Bella up in the air, blowing a raspberry on her tummy. 'Could you manage a waffle with cream for Imogen?'

'Sure,' he said, putting his daughter down.

'Thanks.'

'Hey,' he said, as she turned to leave. He pulled her in

towards him gently, and kissed her. She took in the sweet cinnamon smell of him, and the freshly cooked crêpes, the two aromas merging.

'We should do this more often,' she said softly. She pulled away reluctantly.

'We should,' Matteo said. 'I miss it. If it wasn't for the customers—'

'Mamma!' Bella tugged at her legs.

'Bella ...' Anna said, scooping her daughter up into her arms.

'Anna!' Imogen's voice carried through from the café. 'Hurry up, I'm starving out here.'

'And a few other things,' Matteo said, laughing.

'We'll make time soon,' Anna said, touching Matteo's face affectionately.

When Anna came back over to where her sister was sitting, she saw that their mum, Jan, had joined them.

'Hi, Mum,' Anna said, giving her a hug. Jan kissed Bella and brought her up onto her hip.

'How's my favourite grandchild?' Jan asked.

'Good,' Anna said. 'She's had a great morning out with Imogen by the beach. Plenty of fresh air.'

Bella gurgled contentedly.

'I'll take her over to the guesthouse this afternoon,' Jan said. 'Your dad's up there in the garden at the moment and I know he's longing to see her.'

'Thanks, Mum,' Anna said. 'How's everything going over there?'

'Good, I think,' Jan said. 'A little slow, for my liking, but your uncle Martin has done so well with converting the bedrooms.'

In recent months, the whole family had had another project to focus on – Anna and Imogen's uncle Martin was busy converting Vivien's Victorian home into a seaside guesthouse, due to open in the early spring. Their dad and mum were helping out, although their dad still seemed a little hesitant about it all. While he'd been a tearaway in his youth, motorcycling through Asia and embarking on artistic projects, as he'd got older, and with the death of his parents, change had become more difficult for him.

'Has Dad been very involved?' Imogen asked.

'Not really,' Jan said. 'But you know how it is. He'll get there.'

When Vivien died, they'd all been deeply affected. Tom had always been close to his mother, seeing her regularly, and talking to her whenever he could – and it was he who felt her sudden loss most keenly. He'd needed the space to mourn her in peace, but, instead, he was being pressured to make difficult decisions about her estate. Martin's ex-wife Françoise, a headstrong woman with little time for the inconvenience of emotions, had put them all through additional stress that summer. She'd insisted that Martin sell the family home in Elderberry Avenue in Hove swiftly, driving a wedge between Martin and Tom – and then she'd done everything in her power to undermine Anna and Imogen's takeover of the ice cream shop. She had had her own designs on Vivien's legacy, and her attempts to grasp more of the inheritance for her and Martin had caused Tom to internalise his grief.

Increasingly estranged from his brother, and being forced into making decisions he disagreed with, Imogen and Anna's father had sunk into depression. Jan, accustomed to his being her rock, struggled to adjust to the new situation, and felt unable to support him. Imogen had discovered him at his lowest ebb, locked in his garden studio, having broken some of his treasured sculptures in a moment of deeply felt frustration and grief. She'd spoken to him through the locked door, and in time, they saw the glimmers of a fragile recovery.

Small things had helped – they'd scattered Vivien's ashes in the sea, so they all had a place to think of her now. Each of them found time to spend a moment alone in quiet contemplation by the stretch of sea that Vivien had chosen as her final resting place. By the end of the summer, as Finn and Imogen had left for Thailand, Tom and Jan had found their way back together, with a different balance to their relationship. With her daughters' guidance, Jan had started to understand that she was capable of being there for her husband, and she'd been instrumental in getting Tom onto the right treatment. When Martin realised the full extent of his wife's destructive behaviour, he took the decision to break up with her, get divorced and come home to England. He had wanted to live in Elderberry Avenue, but not alone; the idea for the guesthouse then came about.

Now, with Tom stronger in himself, the family's hope was that the ice cream shop and the guesthouse would provide a lasting legacy that he could look to whenever he missed his mother. Already, Tom and Martin had regained the friendship as brothers that they'd once had, before things went wrong.

Matteo brought Imogen over her waffle, and kissed Jan hello. 'Tea?' he asked her.

'Thanks, but no. I won't stay long,' Jan said.

'Great, I've been dreaming about one of these,' Imogen said, taking a forkful of the dessert.

'Really?' Anna said. 'You were out in Zanzibar and you were thinking about waffles?'

'OK, not the whole time.' Her sister laughed. She'd got back from the work trip two days earlier, and her mind was still partly there, in the heat and vivid colour. 'God, it was beautiful out there. The plants, the animals . . . Incredible. I was up at dawn getting as many shots as I could.'

'Up at dawn? You?' Jan said, incredulous.

'Yes, I was, Mum – *actually*.' Imogen rolled her eyes good-naturedly. Her mother still had the power to wind her up like no one else around, but in general things between them had eased a lot since Imogen settled back in Brighton. But even with Tom's backing of his younger daughter's career, Jan had her reservations about it.

Imogen went on. 'I got most of the shots the travel company wanted in the first couple of days, so I was able to use the rest of the time to build up my portfolio.'

'What's next, then?' Jan asked.

'Do you remember I mentioned the Brazilian project, the woman who spent years studying a colony of pink dolphins and is now publishing a book about it?'

'Oh, yes,' Anna said. 'That sounded wonderful.'

'Well, of course it does. Who doesn't like an exotic holiday?' Jan said. 'But really—'

'Come on, Mum.' Anna nudged her.

Imogen studiously ignored her mother's comment. 'Well, I spoke with Sally, the author, and she seems to think it's almost certain that I'll get to go on the final research trip with her – we're just waiting on the final details,' Imogen said. 'I'm going to swing by Lauren's studio now and develop some of the Zanzibar photos in her darkroom. I'm meeting with Sally again in a couple of weeks and I want to be able to show her some prints.'

'The way things are going you'll need your own darkroom soon,' Anna said.

'Hopefully. Money's still a bit erratic for that.'

'Well, if you would listen—' Jan started.

'Mum, didn't you say you needed to be getting back to the guesthouse?' Imogen said.

'Grandpa!' Bella called out gleefully.

'Oh, right, yes,' Jan said, checking the time. 'I did tell Tom I wouldn't be long. I'll see you ladies later.' She kissed them both goodbye. 'I'll drop her back at six,' she told Anna.

When Jan and Bella had left the café, Imogen resumed her story.

'God, she's never going to believe I've got a proper job, is she?' she said to Anna, laughing. 'Anyway, as I was saying . . . Lauren's been great about letting me use the stuff at her studio.'

'Listen, before you disappear off again, to Lauren's, or wherever else is next on your agenda, how do you and Finn fancy coming around for dinner on Sunday night?' Anna asked.

'So we can whisper over glasses of wine in your front room, trying not to wake Bella up?' Imogen said, raising an eyebrow. 'On Valentine's Day?'

Anna bit her lip. 'Ha! Oops! I completely forgot . . . Well, I totally understand if you two have something more romantic to do.'

'Of course we don't,' Imogen said. 'It'd be fun to hang out with you. Seven thirty?'

'Perfect. It's a date,' Anna said.

Matteo passed Anna, carrying a plate, smiling hello to Imogen and pointing out of the window at a crowd of tourists approaching the shop. 'It looks like it's about to get busy,' he said.

'He's right,' she said to her sister. 'I'd better get back to work.'

'And there you were, worrying about a quiet winter season.'

'I know. It's been the opposite, thankfully,' Anna said. 'Our only issue is keeping up.' Anna took a second to retie her chestnut hair in a ponytail. 'Does that look OK?'

Imogen smiled. 'Yes. Just one thing.' She reached up and wiped a finger by Anna's mouth. 'Chocolate sauce.'

'Ha! Thanks. No idea how long I had that there.' Anna laughed. 'New recipe. I was quality-control testing with Matteo this morning.'

'At times like this, I almost miss working here,' Imogen said.

Chapter 2

In the dim red light of Lauren's darkroom, Imogen stood back to look at her freshly developed photos from Zanzibar. For now, she had to imagine the colours – she could still recall the lushest greens and brightest citrus tones – but, from what she could see, they had turned out really well.

Getting away had re-energised her, as it always did, bringing inspiration and igniting her adventurous spirit. And now, back in England, the flowers and animals she'd seen were coming to life again.

She rarely missed Finn when she went away, or when she did it was only fleetingly – her trips were so short, and she kept herself so busy that she barely had time to. But, when she'd come back to find him waiting for her in the arrivals hall at Gatwick, her heart had lifted. Kissing him, chatting on the way home in the car, and catching up on what they had both been up to, she'd felt a piece of her slip back into place. Her phone buzzed with a new message.

'*Surf at sunset? x*'.

His message made her smile. She tapped back a reply.

'*See you at 4.30 down at the arches x*'.

Imogen went out into the studio, skirting quietly past the shoot Lauren was doing of a young couple with their Pekinese dog.

It was great, Imogen thought, that Lauren, a schoolfriend she'd recently reconnected with, had her own studio now, and that she got so much session work – even more so that she enjoyed it. Just the thought of days spent cooped up indoors snapping photos of newborns and pets made Imogen feel stifled. All of those staged scenes and uncooperative children and canines – rather Lauren than her. After struggling at school, and a long search for work after college, Imogen was finally getting the kind of work she was most passionate about.

That afternoon, after she left Lauren's studio in the north laines, Imogen walked down to the arches for the second time that day. This time she passed Vivien's and carried on walking, past the souvenir shop run by their grandmother's friend Evie, and on to Finn's surf school. Inside, Finn was closing up with his friend and business partner Andy.

'Hey, Andy,' Imogen called out.

'The traveller returns,' Andy said, brightly.

Imogen kissed Finn hello.

'He's missed you loads, you know,' Andy teased.

'Ahh,' she said, turning to her boyfriend. 'Is that true?'

'Don't believe a word of it,' Finn said.

'He was unbearable, moping around the place,' Andy said.

'So, you all set?' Finn asked, throwing his friend a stern look.

'Ready.' Imogen nodded.

She looked at the boxes of surf equipment that were filling up the room Finn and Andy used for tuition, before they took the students out. 'You're kind of outgrowing this place, aren't you?'

'That's what we were just talking about,' Andy said. 'We've had a lot of demand from students to sell boards and equipment, but we just haven't got the space for it here.'

'Victims of your own success,' she said warmly.

Imogen and Finn left, and headed over to his van.

'Maybe you should think about expanding,' Imogen said, looking back at the shop. Finn had set the surf school up a decade before, when he was in his mid-twenties and long before he'd met Imogen, and in the past couple of years business had really picked up. The surf school was located a couple of doors away from Vivien's Heavenly Ice Cream Shop, in one of the arches on the seafront in Hove, a stretch of shops and cafés with a warm, friendly atmosphere. The shop owners – Anna and Matteo, Finn, Evie, who ran the souvenir shop, and an assortment of others – regularly met up and helped each other out. They would bring each other hot drinks and snacks and stop by to chat. In the summer the place really came to life, with parties on the bandstand, barbecues and fundraising fairs for local charities – the community spirit that Vivien and Evie had invested so much in over the years was still going strong.

'If we did expand, where would we go, though?' Finn said. 'I wouldn't want to move, but everyone here at the arches has settled in for good.'

'There must be somewhere,' Imogen said, mulling it over.

They got into the van, and Finn drove down the main coastal road out of town. As the hazy winter sun lowered in the sky, they headed towards their regular beach, a secluded cove a half-hour outside town.

She looked out of the window at the sandy cove they were approaching. 'We're going to be the only ones out there today. Perfect.'

Finn parked and she leaped out of the passenger-side door. Together they got their surfboards down from the roof of the van, then slipped on their wetsuits.

'Race you,' Imogen called out, already running with her board. Finn caught up with her as they hit the waves and brought her down into the water. She emerged from the surf spluttering and laughing. 'Get out there, then, and let's see what you can do.'

Finn paddled far out into the sea, but Imogen stayed closer to the shore, and stopped and waited for the right wave to come. She wasn't tempted to compete – Finn had been surfing since he was a kid and she had only been doing it for a couple of years, since she'd met him. She was content that she was no longer learning from him – he'd taught her the basics but after that she'd taught herself, responding to the ocean's ebbs and flows, guided by nature, the ocean something she knew well from diving. Going deep underwater, diving and taking photos of the sea life and coral, had once been her only way of experiencing the sea – and down there she was the one taking the lead, showing Finn the way.

She dipped her head underwater until her face, neck and hair were totally immersed, the freshness of the water waking her senses. Finn was just a dot in the distance. She took in a lungful of sea air and caught a wave, popping up to her feet swiftly and skilfully. She rode into shore, barely feeling the cold air as she was caught up in the buzz of it. Knowing Finn was out there, somewhere, thinking of her, made her feel she was capable of anything.

She'd met him back when she was running Vivien's, and after a summer of working alongside each other in the arches – at points harmoniously, others less so – they had found their way together at a party there. Imogen hadn't been looking for a relationship – she'd been burned by the way things had turned out with her ex, Luca – but being with Finn had just happened. When they first kissed, on a quiet spot on the beach, she'd felt a rush of excitement, but she'd also felt torn. She hadn't wanted to stay back in Brighton when there was so much of the world still to explore. When the time came for them to make a decision, she'd persuaded him to come back to Thailand with her, giving him a career break, and her opportunity to put her photography project together.

The time in New York, where a friend, who'd become her agent, had arranged an exhibition for her, had changed Imogen's life. It was in those humid summer days in the city that her dream of becoming a professional photographer had finally become reality – and the offers for her work had come in. After the years that she'd struggled at school, her visual memory and different way of seeing the world holding her back, those same things were now taking her further than she'd ever dreamed possible.

When they had got back home to Brighton, and moved into Finn's house together, she'd worked hard to keep up with the contacts she'd made. She'd decided to part ways with her agent and go it alone. Things seemed to be working out, with plenty of initial requests for new projects, most of them abroad. That was the way she wanted it. As much as she liked Brighton, when she was away from home good things happened to her. It had always been that way.

When Finn came up onto the shore, his usually warm skin tone was pale, his lips turning blue. She kissed him in an attempt to warm them. Both of them were shivering.

'Pub?' Imogen said. 'I think we need to warm up.'

'Great idea.'

Half an hour later, Imogen and Finn walked into the Rose, their local pub, lively with chatter from the locals as the weekly quiz started up. Finn and Imogen greeted the bartender and a few of their neighbours, then took a seat in a cosy booth with wooden seats and original frosted-glass panelling, away from the noise.

The feeling was slowly returning to Imogen's chilled hands and feet.

'It was great out there today,' she said. 'I love it when there's no one else out there but us.'

'It was so peaceful today. And being with you beats saving a group of beginners from drowning, that's for sure,' he said. 'It's good to have you back.' He put his arms around her and brought her towards him for a kiss. She kissed him back.

'Oh, I meant to ask you,' Imogen said. 'OK if we go round to Anna and Matteo's for dinner this Sunday night?'

'Sure,' he said. He paused. 'Hang on, isn't that Valentine's?'

'Yes, but . . . I mean it's just like any other day really, right?' Imogen said.

'I guess,' he said. 'If you're fine with it, I'm fine with it. It'll be good to see her and Matteo.'

'Great. Because I kind of already said yes.'

He laughed. 'Right. Any other arrangements you want to let me know about?'

'Nope. Although hopefully there will be soon. I'm meeting with that author, Sally, about the Amazon trip next week.'

'The pink-dolphin lady?'

'Yes. Two years studying them – it's amazing how much she knows, and she's been working on this book the whole time. She's been looking for the right photographer to go with her out to the Amazon on her final research trip.'

'Didn't she take photos of her own out there?'

'The publishers weren't sure about the quality of them, and by the sounds of things, they're going in big on the book. They want it to be their lead title for next year, so she seemed confident that there'd be a budget to send me out there.'

'Sounds great,' Finn said. 'For how long?'

'I don't know – weeks, months maybe?' Imogen said, picturing it. 'She'll be able to tell me more when we meet.'

'Right, so you're going to be sunning yourself in South America while I'm braving the wintry English Channel with beginner surfers in wetsuits.'

'I'll be back soon to tell you all about it,' Imogen said brightly, landing a kiss on Finn's mouth. 'And I'll make sure I send a postcard.'

That Sunday night, Imogen and Finn were at Anna and Matteo's for dinner, with warming, home-cooked Italian food and good red wine on the table between them.

'Great pasta, Anna,' Imogen said, twirling more of the tagliatelle around her fork.

'Thank you,' Anna said. 'I'm getting the hang of the pasta machine Matteo got me for my birthday. It's a bit fiddly but I think it's worth it.'

'Look at you, making everything from scratch,' Imogen said, laughing. 'Will you just stop? I can still barely cook an egg.'

'Oh, come off it! You're a good cook these days,' Anna said.

'Is she?' Finn said, with a mischievous smile.

'Finn does most of the cooking at ours,' Imogen admitted.

'And you . . .?' Anna asked.

'I provide the entertainment,' Imogen said.

'Pretty much what happened back at home when we were growing up, then,' Anna said, laughing.

'You seen Mum and Dad lately?' Imogen asked.

'Yes, we dropped in to see them at Elderberry Avenue last night.'

'How are things going over there?'

'Good, I think,' Anna said. 'It's still a bit chaotic in there, with the decorating, but they're making progress. Martin's plan is to open it at the end of March, so they've got just over a month to get things sorted.'

The house in Elderberry Avenue had always been a place where people felt welcome. Vivien had a habit of taking in friends, old and new, and letting them stay for a while. She had been generous by nature and, after the death of her husband, had valued the company.

'Has Dad been round much?' Imogen asked.

'I'm not sure how much Dad is really helping, to be honest,' Anna replied. 'He's making sculptures for the front garden, and helping make a bit of furniture, but I think there's a lot of daydreaming going on.'

'That's Dad for you,' Imogen said. 'It can't be easy for him – seeing Granny V's house change. I hope it's not setting him back, being around so many of Granny's things, watching as his old family home turns into something different.'

'I was wondering the same,' Anna said, her brow creased with concern. 'Mum said there are some rooms he hasn't even been in yet.'

'It'll be good, in the long term. For us all to have the guesthouse, for Dad to see the place move on. There's no going back to how things were, after all. I mean we all have memories, don't we?'

39

'Do you remember the slumber parties we'd have upstairs? Granny would pretend not to hear us.'

'But, when we opened the door at midnight, she'd have left us snacks there, so we could have a feast.' Imogen smiled at the memory.

'Dad and Martin must both have a million memories like that,' Anna said. 'They grew up there – as kids, as teenagers. Dad bought his first motorbike when he was living there. But the only way to keep those memories alive is to keep the place alive, full of people, love, laughter.'

'Hopefully, Dad'll get used to things in time,' Imogen said. 'But, if he still seems resistant, I'll talk to him. Has Mum said anything?'

'She's been giving him a gentle nudge towards having a proper look round, but she doesn't want to force the issue. In any case, she's been busy arranging the launch,' Anna said, 'sending out press releases and getting local publicity.'

'So much for being retired,' Imogen said. 'I knew she wouldn't be sitting still for long.'

'My mother's the same,' Matteo said. 'Happiest when she's busy.'

'Your family should all come and stay again,' said Imogen. 'Once the guesthouse is open there'll be much more room, they won't be squashed into the spare room at Mum and Dad's cottage.'

'Good point,' Matteo said. 'The Elderberry Guesthouse –

it has a nice ring to it. As English as fish and chips. I'm sure Mum, Dad and Caro would love it.'

Anna flashed her sister a look, and Imogen instantly regretted what she'd said. The previous Christmas – which Matteo's family had joined them for – hadn't been a tremendous success. A week had felt long to them all. Elisa, Matteo's mum, a confident and forthright woman, had taken charge, and made more than one comment about Anna and Matteo still not being married. She'd also swamped her grandchild with gifts, even though Bella, at only a year old, was only really interested in the wrapping paper. On the day that Elisa, Giacomo and Carolina left, they'd all breathed a sigh of relief. Elisa meant well – but the truth was that Anna often struggled to get on with her.

Conscious of her sister's unease, Imogen quickly backpedalled. 'I mean in the future, next year or whatever. The place isn't even open yet, after all.'

A small cry came from Bella's room, then all fell quiet again.

Anna went out into the corridor to listen out.

'Anna, leave her. She's asleep,' Matteo said. 'Don't worry.'

'You're right. Nothing now. I thought she'd woken up. You know how she loves a party.'

'She's a Mediterranean girl at heart,' Matteo said, with affection. 'She'd stay up till midnight if we let her.'

'Your mother says you were the same,' Anna added, recalling the stories that Elisa had told her over Christmas.

'I was. Carolina and I would be running through the square on festival nights, playing games with the other children and hiding underneath the dinner tables. No one minded us staying up late.'

'We won't be trying that one out with Bella,' Anna said, shaking her head. 'She'd be impossible the next day.'

'I like the sound of it,' Imogen said, Matteo's description capturing her imagination. 'It sounds like a wonderful way to grow up. All that freedom. Hanging out with kids of different ages. Better than how it was in our house, in bed at seven whether you were tired or not. You were all right, Anna – burying your head in a book or whatever – but I remember going out of my mind with boredom on the days when I wasn't sleepy. I think the Mediterranean way of life sounds much more child-friendly.'

'You see, Anna,' Matteo said, nudging his wife gently. 'There's a lot to be said for the Italian way of things. The occasional late night isn't going to make any difference to Bella.'

Imogen clocked her sister's expression and sensed that she might have touched a nerve.

'I didn't mean for Bella, necessarily,' Imogen said. 'I'm just speaking generally.'

'I know,' Anna said. 'I do wonder if she's more of an Italian at heart. But this is where she's growing up.'

A look passed between Anna and Matteo, and Finn, sensing the tension, jumped in to change the subject.

'How is everything going at Vivien's?' he asked.

'Really well,' Anna said. 'The winter menu's gone down well – though I think we're both looking forward to spring, and being able to bring back the sorbets.'

'I remember that first summer,' Finn said. 'I was in there all the time looking for an excuse to chat to her …' He looked over at Imogen.

'So it wasn't just our ice creams you were interested in?' Anna raised an eyebrow.

Finn shook his head and laughed. 'Nope.'

'I didn't think she'd ever meet a man who could tempt her to stick around here,' Anna said.

'Well, it looks like I did,' Imogen said, briskly. 'Anna, didn't you say you had a new recipe you wanted to try out on us?'

'Yes!' Anna said, brightening. 'Of course. I almost forgot. You are in for a treat. Come on, Matteo, let's get the desserts ready.'

Anna and Matteo came back into the dining room a few minutes later with steaming hot mugs.

Imogen caught a scent of the drinks, carrying on the air. 'Cocoa?'

'Yes, but more than that.' Anna put the mugs down on the table. 'I hope you two are up for being our guinea pigs.'

'Always,' Finn said.

'Hot ice cream,' Matteo pronounced. 'Our winter ice cream revolution. For you, on Valentine's Day.'

'Homemade cocoa,' Anna said, 'with a scoop of praline ice cream, a scoop of dark chocolate, and a sprinkling of finely chopped hazelnuts on top.'

'Give me that,' Imogen said, clamouring for it. 'Sounds amazing.'

She passed Finn's mug over to him.

They both took a sip. 'Oh, this is good,' Finn said. 'Really good.'

'You have to put this straight on the menu,' Imogen said. 'No question.'

'I can't get enough of what you guys make,' Finn said to Matteo. 'But a lifetime of ice cream – you never get tired of it?'

'I never could,' Matteo said. 'But you have to mix things up from time to time, of course. Running Vivien's gives us space to experiment.'

'I'm not sure what Granny would think if she saw the place now,' Imogen said. 'All those granitas and sundaes. She'd kind of settled into selling 99s and Milk Maids, hadn't she?'

'Vivien's passion was for people, not so much for food or finances,' Anna explained to Matteo. 'By the end she was running the ice cream shop pretty much as a community centre, caring for anyone who dropped in. I think her love for the business itself went out of her a little when Granddad passed away.'

'It must have been hard for her, keeping their shop going after he died. They really loved each other, didn't they?' Matteo said.

'So much,' Anna said. 'They did everything together, in the shop and out of it. They would even finish each other's sentences.'

'I think the only time they were apart was that trip she and Evie had to Italy,' Imogen said. 'They relied on each other. She was devastated when he died.'

'I don't think she ever got over losing him. Not really,' Anna said.

Chapter 3

The following Thursday, Anna was in Vivien's, preparing some white-chocolate-and-hazelnut ice cream for their Sundae of the Week. The bell rang to announce a new customer, and she looked up to see Evie, her candyfloss-pink hair pinned up loosely, and a blue denim jacket on. Anna smiled – it always comforted her to see her grandma's best friend – and, with her souvenir shop just two doors away, she was a frequent visitor to Vivien's.

'Hey, Evie,' Anna said. 'Good swim this morning?'

'Very invigorating, thank you,' she said, taking a seat up at the counter. 'Best thing about this time of year is that I seem to have the whole sea to myself.'

Anna laughed. 'You're the only one mad enough to go out there, that's why.'

'Vivien would have been out there, too, of course, if she

were still here. There was no holding your grandma back from her morning swim.'

'I think she passed that love of wintry waters on to Imogen. Not to me, that's for sure.'

'She rescued a boy out there once. Did she ever tell you that?'

'I didn't know that, no – what happened?' That was the thing with Vivien: there had been so many layers to her. Anna was used to hearing snippets and stories from people, lighting up dark corners that she and Imogen had never known about.

'A young boy, he was, about five – out walking the dog with his parents. When the dog dived into the water, he followed, and the tide dragged him out. His mum and dad couldn't get far out quickly enough, but Vivien was already out there. Got hold of him and brought him back into shore. The dog came trotting up soon after, totally oblivious to all the trouble it had caused.'

'That's amazing,' Anna said, feeling proud.

'Made the local paper, that one. I've got a cutting somewhere. I'll dig it out for you.'

'Please do. Maybe we could get it framed for the guesthouse – Dad would like that. In the meantime, what can I get you to warm you up, Evie?'

'Do you have any of those pastries left?'

Anna called back into the kitchen. 'Matteo, are there any more cannoli out there for Evie?'

'Yes. I've got a batch here fresh from the oven,' he called back.

'Fantastic,' Evie said.

'Would you like an espresso? I know you're normally more of a tea drinker, but, really, you need coffee with them.'

'Yes, please,' Evie said. 'Although you'll have to deal with me talking a mile to the minute.' She laughed warmly.

'So how are things with the shop?' Anna said, pressing down the coffee grains and setting up the machine for Evie's drink.

'Fine,' she said quickly. Anna noticed then that the usual brightness in her eyes was absent today, and she looked older, more like the late sixties she really was, rather than the younger woman she so often appeared to be.

Anna saw right away that she wasn't being completely honest. She raised a questioning eyebrow.

'Oh, you know how it is, running your own business,' Evie said. 'There's always something to worry about, isn't there? It's been giving me grey hairs lately.' She touched her hair, dyed a pale pink for as long as Anna could remember.

'Really?' Anna said, looking at her hair and smiling.

'Well, let's see what you think when I can't afford the hair-dressers' bills any more.'

'Are things really that bad?' Anna asked, concerned.

'Business has been slow for a long time. Winter's always a challenge – you know that as well as me, in a town like this.

But normally I've earned enough in the summer months to tide everything over. This year, I have to admit I'm only just scraping by.'

'Do you think changes to stock would make any difference?'

'I've tried, Anna. I've tried almost everything, but profits keep dropping.'

'I'm sorry to hear that.'

'Thanks. But perhaps it's a sign.' Evie's normally bright blue eyes were weary, and there was a heaviness in her words. 'I'm not one to give things up easily, but maybe it's time for me to move on. Sell the place and do something new.'

'Are you sure?' Anna said.

It saddened Anna to see Evie look so defeated. When she and Imogen had been working hard to make Vivien's a success, Evie had been with the sisters every single step, counselling and supporting them. And now her business was struggling. It didn't seem right. More than that: if Vivien had been alive, she would have been doing everything in her power to make sure that Evie was OK, and Anna felt that same responsibility and loyalty towards her grandmother's best friend.

'Some days I'm sure,' she said. 'Others less so. It's a difficult decision, after so many years. Selling souvenirs is all I've ever really done, other than travelling, that is.'

'Here,' Anna said, passing Evie her coffee together with the warm cream pastry Matteo had brought over. 'I'm sorry. It doesn't solve things, but ...'

Evie bit into her cannoli and gave an appreciative nod. 'It certainly helps.'

Anna smiled.

'These pastries take me back to that trip I took with Vivien – to Sorrento, the Amalfi coast. Thirty-odd years ago it was now. We sat in pavement cafés all afternoon – the sea sparkling in front of us and nothing to do but while away the sunshine hours with a paperback.'

'It must have been lovely,' Anna said, feeling a pang of nostalgia for the carefree days she'd had in Florence before Bella was born.

'You'd like it out there,' Evie said.

'Maybe one day,' Anna said.

'It was special to your grandmother, that place.' She paused and seemed to cast her mind back to that time. 'We laughed so much, back then.'

That afternoon, Anna's mum Jan came into the ice cream shop with Bella. They all kissed hello, Jan's cheeks cold from the fresh air.

'Thought I'd pop in and say hi.'

'Hey, Jan,' Matteo called out from the kitchen.

'Your dad and Uncle Martin are busy with DIY at the

guesthouse, so Bella and I are on our way to the park. Would you like to join us?'

'Matteo, do you mind if I go out for a while?' Anna asked him.

'Of course, no problem.'

Anna bundled up a couple of the unsold pastries. 'Some fuel.'

They walked along the pebbled beach in the crisp winter sunshine, and she passed her mother one of the pastries.

'How's it all going up there?' Anna said.

'Good, I think. Well, there's still a lot to do, but you know how the McAvoys are with pulling things together at the last minute. It's our forte.'

Anna laughed. 'Yes. There's nothing like a deadline. I hear Finn's almost done with the website design, though.'

'Oh, he's a wonder,' Jan said. 'I've had a look at an early version and it really brings the place to life. *I'd* want to stay there. And you know how picky I am about these things.'

Anna laughed. 'How's Dad doing?'

'Head in the sand a bit, I think. I've told him it's time he has a proper look round the guesthouse. There's only a month till it opens, after all. Your sister said she'd come on Saturday afternoon, give a bit of moral support, just in case it's needed. Are you free?'

'Yes,' Anna said. 'I think so. I'll be there.'

'Your sister really has struck gold with Finn. He's so good

for her. I'm just so happy that she's starting to grow up a bit, choose the things and the people that are good for her, at long last. Do you remember when she was out in Thailand the first time? Came back talking about some beach bum or other. American he was, I think.'

'Luca,' Anna said. She'd never met him, but had seen photos of him – dark and good-looking, with tanned skin. Imogen had come home from the trip full of mixed emotions – brought back by Vivien's death and the funeral, kept at home by her concern about her father's health. There was so much that was unhappy in their lives at that time, and yet somehow Imogen had still had the slightest buzz of holiday around her. She had always seemed to come alive when she was far from home. It was only when she and Luca broke up permanently – when Imogen heard that he was seeing a friend of hers – that she'd come properly back down to earth.

'I nearly lost hope then,' Jan said. 'I mean your dad's always had an adventurous spirit, and he's travelled plenty in his time, of course. But he didn't miss his chance of something good, something long-term, when he met me. From what Imogen's told me, which I'll admit isn't much – you know how she is – I don't think she would have found that with any of the men she went out with before Finn.'

'She was only twenty-three back then,' Anna said. 'I don't think she was ready herself.'

'I was settled with your dad by then.'

'Imogen's very different from you. You know that, Mum. I don't know if she'd be much readier to settle down now, to be honest. Twenty-six is still very young, these days.'

'All this travel she's intent on doing – I'm not sure I'll ever really understand it. I'm just glad we've always had you, Anna – knowing that there's at least one of our daughters we can rely on to stay close by. Because it means a lot, that – you'll understand, when Bella grows up, how much it matters.'

'Travelling makes Imogen happy, Mum.'

'For now, perhaps,' Jan said.

'Just like your work did,' Anna replied.

'Yes,' Jan said, glancing down.

'Do you miss it?' Anna asked softly.

Jan looked up and their eyes met. 'It sounds silly, doesn't it? But I suppose I do. I had these ideas of what being retired would be like: relaxing days in the garden, going out for strolls with your father, baking some wonderful creation or other. But instead, aside from the bits of publicity for the guesthouse, I feel like I've slowed down. Your father has his own things to be getting on with, and the truth is, Anna, if it weren't for Bella I think I'd be at rather a loose end.'

Jan squeezed her granddaughter's hand.

'Granny!' Bella called out. 'Mwah.' She blew a kiss. Her grandmother sent her one back.

'Well, we have an awful lot to look forward to this summer, don't we?' Jan said to her granddaughter. 'Sleepovers at

Grandma and Granddad's house, our picnic up in the bluebell woods ...' Jan turned to look at Anna. 'It'll be the first time Bella's really seen our annual get-together, won't it?'

'Yes, it'll be lovely,' Anna said.

Each year the McAvoys invited the whole family to join an outing up to the woods near Jan and Tom's house in Lewes, East Sussex, at the time of year that the bluebells were out in bloom. Some of Anna's favourite childhood memories were of that time, and she wanted Bella to share those.

'Bella has a way of giving us all focus, don't you think?' Jan said.

Anna saw in her mum's eyes how much it mattered to her – having her family close, being able to be the grandmother she wanted to be. After years of Imogen's living abroad, the McAvoys were all back together again, and all of them treasured that.

That evening, Matteo and Anna settled down to dinner at their kitchen table, Bella asleep in her bedroom.

'This is good,' Anna said, pointing to the pasta bake he'd made.

'Thanks.' His dark eyes were cast down.

'You OK?' she enquired gently, putting a hand on his arm. 'You seem miles away tonight.'

'Me? I'm fine,' he said, shaking his head. 'It's ... it's nothing, really.'

'Come on.'

'It's just something today got me thinking, I suppose.'

'Yes?'

'It's not worth talking about,' he said, dismissing it.

'Is this something to do with that older guy you were talking to in the shop today?'

'Yes. Sort of.'

'Who was he?'

'He's from Siena originally, but he's been running a fish-and-chip shop in Hove for years,' he said. 'Heard about the cannoli and came to try one. I gave him a few free samples of the ice cream and you should have seen him. So happy. He was in another world.'

'That's lovely,' Anna said. Seeing customers light up at the taste of one of their ice creams was what made her feel so passionately about what they did.

'We got caught up talking about Siena and the food back there. He said how much he missed the place.'

'What brought him here?'

'He fell in love. Thirty years later he's still here. He always meant to go back, but he said the years just passed.'

The tone in his voice unsettled Anna. 'You've been thinking about home a lot recently, haven't you?' Anna said. She felt a tug at her heart as she asked the question. She knew she was opening up a conversation – perhaps the only conversation – that could drive a wedge between them.

Matteo nodded, not saying a word.

In his silence, Anna saw that his feelings ran deep. In their early days he'd joked about what he was missing in Italy – reciting his favourite meals from Florence's restaurants wistfully, his nostalgia a playful, amusing thing. This was different.

'You can be honest with me, you know that,' Anna said.

'I miss so many things,' Matteo said. 'Being able to talk in my own language, for a start – I still get in a muddle with English sometimes, even when I'm talking with you. Then there's just that sense of connection. I feel it here sometimes, but others . . .'

'You want us to go there,' Anna said, the realisation hitting her with a jolt.

He shook his head. 'You and Bella are what matter most to me, and when I came here I made you a promise: that we would live here, where you have your family, the shop. I won't break that commitment to you, Anna. I wouldn't ask you to leave this.'

'But how can we stay, when I know that, deep down, you're not happy?' Anna asked, her voice cracking.

'I am,' he said. 'I'm so happy, Anna.' He paused and she could see he was holding something back.

'But . . .?'

'The truth? I feel torn.' In his eyes was a deep sadness. 'I don't want to be that man, Anna.'

Chapter 4

On the Friday evening, Finn and Imogen were in the living room at their beach house, relaxing on the L-shaped sofa. The sea, unsettled and stormy, was visible through the floor-to-ceiling windows, but the large white rug, scatter cushions and prints of Imogen's photos from Thailand softened the room's minimalist look.

Finn was showing Imogen the website he'd put together for the Elderberry Guesthouse. He passed her his tablet so she could see it clearly. 'I've kept the home page simple, but you can click on each of the doors here to take a look at the guestrooms. See – here, in the *Roman Holiday*-themed room ...'

He clicked on the white door and started the virtual tour of the room that Tom and Martin had filled with prints and Italian-inspired memorabilia from Vivien's favourite Audrey Hepburn film.

'Then, here, the Prohibition bar, and you can see how it leads through to the *Great Gatsby* room . . .' On screen, he led Imogen through what had once been her grandmother's kitchen and lounge.

'It looks great,' Imogen said proudly, giving him a squeeze. 'Thanks for putting it together. Dad and Martin are going to absolutely love it.' She couldn't wait to show it off to her family. 'I'm going round there tomorrow. Dad's going to have his first proper look round the whole place, so I told Mum I'd come and be there when he does. Anna said she'd join us, too. There's only a month till it opens, so I think Mum's told him quite firmly that he needs to get used to how things are, and voice any objections now, while there's still time to change things. I think Martin's getting a bit nervous that he's going to hate it.'

'I'm sure he won't,' Finn said. 'It looks great, and your dad is a reasonable man. But, in any case, that's nice – that you'll both be there.'

'One thing I am certain of is that Granny would've have loved it,' Imogen said with confidence. 'You remember what she was like – always welcoming in waifs and strays, inviting friends in. She wouldn't have wanted to see the house empty.'

Imogen recalled the times they'd spent together at the house when she and Anna were little – playing in the garden and chasing each other up and down the stairs. As she and

Anna had grown up, their relationship with their grandmother had changed, and they talked with her more. Imogen had always loved their chats. Her grandmother had always been full of wisdom and positivity, urging her to follow her dreams no matter what. Imogen bit her lip to stop herself crying. Two years after her grandmother's death, the sadness still caught her out from time to time.

'I guess with this trip to the Amazon I might not be here to see the launch,' she said. 'I'm sad about that.'

The next day, Imogen stopped by at her uncle's guesthouse. 'Hi, everyone,' she said. Her dad was standing in the hallway, looking a little uncomfortable. He seemed uncertain of his own footing in the house that had once been his home, now that it was being transformed into something else. Imogen went and kissed him hello.

'Anna here yet?' Imogen asked.

Her mother shook her head. 'She said she was coming, but I'm not sure where she is. Her phone seems to be switched off.'

'Weird.' Imogen tried her, but got through to answerphone too. 'I expect she's on her way. In the meantime, look – I've framed some of my prints to decorate the hallway.' Imogen took them from her bag to show her parents and Martin. 'To brighten the place up.'

She held them up against the wall, to see how they'd look.

'And, well, I've put prices on them, too. Hope you don't mind.'

'I'm sure some of the holidaymakers will take a shine to them,' Tom said, softly.

Imogen laughed. 'Never one to miss an opportunity, Dad.'

Imogen watched as her father looked round at the home he'd grown up in. His eyes came to rest on the places his mother's trinkets and furniture had been, and a sadness seemed to settle into his features.

'Let's go for a walk round,' Imogen suggested. She led him up the stairs, round the guestrooms, and then back down.

When they returned, Martin looked on nervously as his brother took in the changes. Imogen glanced over at him. They were all conscious that Tom, who had been so devastated at the loss of his mother, might find it difficult to accept that the house was now entering a new era.

He turned round to them after what had felt like an endless wait. 'I think it looks good,' he said.

Tom soberly shook his brother's hand, before hugging him too. 'You've done a wonderful job, Martin. I think Mum would like it, don't you?'

'Well, I must say that's a relief,' Martin said, breathing out. 'Now all we need to worry about is getting the guests in.'

'You'll be fine,' Imogen said calmly.

Jan nodded. 'We've had lots of local interest.'

'It's exactly what we need round here,' Imogen said, 'an

affordable home from home – classy, not touristy. The launch party next month's going to be great for building a buzz, too.'

'Oh, absolutely,' Jan said.

Tom left the room quietly, and Martin and Jan looked at each other, uncertainly. Imogen followed her father out into the front garden.

He was placing his sculptures of birds around the pond. He turned and saw her there, watching.

'What do you think?' he asked her, pointing at the arrangement.

'They look great, Dad.'

'I want to get this bit right. The garden. The first thing that guests see. It would've mattered to Mum.'

'Is it strange for you, all this?' she asked.

He nodded. 'I know it's for the best – but it still feels a little odd, the idea of people paying to stay here. That's the truth of it.'

Imogen stepped closer to her dad and they hugged. 'I just have to deal with things one step at a time,' he said. 'It'll be OK.'

'Of course. It's what she would have wanted, you know – people in here, enjoying her house.'

'I know,' he said. 'You're right.' He looked at her proudly. 'You're becoming quite wise in your old age, Imogen.'

She nudged him playfully. 'Less of that, eh, Dad? I'm only twenty-six.'

'Here, there's something else I want to show you,' Tom said, going over to his bag. He took out a circular ceramic plate, with the words ELDERBERRY GUESTHOUSE on it in pale green. 'I fired it over the weekend.'

'That's beautiful,' Imogen said.

'Help me put it up?' he asked.

She looped her arm through his. 'Of course, Dad.'

Chapter 5

Anna was walking on the pebbly beach in Hove on Saturday afternoon, wooden rowing boats on the shore beside her. Up to her right were the bright tones of beach huts, and, beyond that, a backdrop of elegant Regency hotels. Brighton and Hove's landscape was deeply familiar to her, and she knew the places to go when she wanted to find calm. She had left the ice cream shop that morning, telling Matteo she was going to pick up some more milk – but the truth was she needed some time to think. What Matteo had said, about missing Italy, had really unsettled her.

Almost always, walking this stretch of beach cleared her mind, but today the fog remained. All she could think of was Matteo saying those words: '*I don't want to be that man, Anna.*' Until that moment, she'd always thought she made him happy – it was what he always told her – but in that conversation she'd seen an echoing sadness in him. It wasn't possible for her to get rid of that feeling for him – and, worse, she'd realised that, by wanting to stay in England, she was the person causing it.

But leaving? Leaving her parents, and Imogen, the business, their home, whether for a whole summer, or – and at this her stomach flipped over – for ever? It seemed too much to contemplate, particularly now that they had Bella. He was asking too much of her. And yet, now that he'd said it, she couldn't see how it could ever be undone. She would always wonder now what discontent might be there underneath. What might surface after a year, five years, when Bella was grown. It was like a crack in the fabric of their home. She could try to ignore it, avoid looking in that corner of the room. But then one day – when she did – it might have grown so much she would no longer be able to fix it.

A couple and a child were walking towards her on the beach, and, as they neared, she realised it was her ex-boyfriend Jon with Mia and their son Alfie. Her emotions whirled as she saw the little boy – much taller now at five years old, but, in yellow wellingtons and a red coat, he still looked a tiny bit like the toddler she'd known and loved so much.

'Anna!' Alfie called out. He ran up to her with his arms outstretched, and her heart swelled with love. She wanted desperately to sweep him up into her arms, just as she would have done with Bella – but she caught herself. Things were different now. They had been different ever since Anna had discovered Jon's infidelity, tracked back the trail of lies to his ex-wife, Mia. Furious, she'd broken off their engagement.

Anna looked to Mia, and her reluctant nod confirmed that it was OK for Anna to hug her son. While she had been with Jon, living with him in her flat, Alfie had stayed at the weekends, and for a while she had felt almost like a parent to him – but after the break-up that connection had disappeared. When Jon and Mia had reconciled – breaking Anna's trust, and, she'd thought at the time, her heart – it wasn't just Jon who left her life abruptly: it was his son, too.

She felt a surge of affection as she hugged Alfie. He had grown up and his mouse-brown hair was longer, but the essence of him was the same, his gurgling laughter, the familiar smell of his shampoo. Anna let go, and stood up to her full height again. Her hand remained on Alfie's hair, gently stroking it, until a glare from Mia reminded her to step back.

'Hello, Anna,' Jon said, coolly. Anna nodded in greeting. The three of them stood there for a while, locked in an awkward silence. Usually, the seafront felt like an extension of home to Anna. On her strolls she'd bump into friendly, familiar faces, other workers under the arches, old schoolfriends, friends of her parents or Vivien. But seeing Jon and Mia brought her up sharply. Anywhere you have history, you are likely to find traces of darker times, issues that resist resolution, emotions and people you'd rather forget. For a moment, looking into Jon's eyes, she was taken back to that time, when she'd seen their future together, wondered if maybe they'd have their own child, a brother or sister for Alfie. She recalled the rawness and pain of discovering how he'd lied to her, how everything she'd believed and invested in had been a pretence, nothing more.

Alfie looked from his parents to Anna, then finally spoke, breaking the silence: 'I haven't seen you for *ages*, Anna.' He lingered over the 'ages', drawing it out. 'Where is Bella?'

The last time they'd seen each other, Bella had been a newborn, and Anna had been carrying her in a sling. Alfie had delighted in the way she was curled up there, like a pea in a pod.

'She's at nursery today,' Anna explained. 'She's a much bigger girl now. She can walk now. She can even say a couple of words.'

'Cool,' Alfie said. He kicked a stone with his welly. 'I liked her.'

'How are things, Anna?' Mia asked, her smile forced. 'I hear the shop's doing well.'

Mia had never set foot inside the ice cream shop, and probably never would. The two women skirted around one another. When Jon and Anna had first broken up, Anna had seen Alfie from time to time, but those visits had become less frequent – Anna could only assume that Mia had had something to do with that. She could understand it. At least Mia and Jon were still together, and Alfie had his family – it had all been for something, that pain.

'The shop's doing well, thanks,' Anna replied.

The conversation ran painfully dry, and Jon glanced around awkwardly.

'Listen, I'd better get going,' Anna said. 'It's quite busy in there this morning and we'll be needing some milk soon. It was good to see you, though.' She bent to Alfie's level. As he looked at her, his eyes wide, Anna felt a tug at her heart. She would do anything to spend an hour with him, to play together as they'd used to.

She pictured Bella's room in their flat. One time, not that long ago, it had belonged to Alfie. She and Jon had decorated it just for him. She had thought he would be a part of her life for ever. It still hurt, to know for sure that he wouldn't be. She hugged him goodbye, and bit her lip to stop herself from crying.

When Anna got back to the ice cream shop, she felt dazed. Seeing Jon and Alfie again had brought memories, both welcome and unwelcome, flooding back. Matteo was busy in the kitchen, and Anna realised part of her was avoiding talking to him. When she and Imogen had first taken over Vivien's, she had thought Jon and Alfie were everything she wanted. She had been wrong, and, since she and Matteo had got together, she'd never once looked back – but it felt like a slight betrayal to be revisiting those thoughts.

She saw Imogen's face at the door of the shop, and her spirits lifted instantly. She walked out from behind the chrome-and-pistachio counter and greeted her sister with a warm hug.

'Come and sit down,' Anna said, leading Imogen in the direction of the counter and bar stools.

'I will, but first, what's up?' Imogen asked. 'I was expecting to see you at the guesthouse last night.'

'Oh ... God, I forgot about that,' Anna said, putting a hand to her forehead. A pang of guilt shot through her. She'd been so caught up in her own thoughts that it had completely slipped her mind. 'I'm sorry. How was it. Was Dad OK?'

'Yes, it went well,' Imogen said. 'Dad had a bit of a wobble, but that wasn't a surprise to anyone, really. He seems much better now.'

'Oh, good,' Anna said, relieved. 'And how's it all coming together for the launch?'

'It looks great. Finn's finished the website. Have you seen it?' She got her phone out to show her sister, but Anna seemed distracted.

'You OK, Anna?' Imogen said, putting her phone away. 'You seem miles away today. Is something on your mind?'

'Oh, I'm all right. I just saw Alfie and it shook me up a bit.' She bit her lip, the tears threatening to return.

Imogen touched her sister's arm. 'You must miss him.'

'God, I do. I really do. And at times like this part of me wonders if it wouldn't be easier if we weren't still living in the same place.'

'Exes should automatically leave town. I think that's a good policy, in general,' Imogen said.

'You've done a great job of leaving yours scattered across the globe,' Anna said.

'Yes. All carefully planned,' Imogen agreed. 'Although Finn and I still ended up going to Thailand, where I met Luca. Thankfully he was long gone by then.'

'Are you two still in touch?'

'No.' Imogen shook her head. 'Easier that way, like you say.'

Anna paused for a moment, and went quiet.

'Listen, is this really all about Jon and Alfie?' Imogen asked. 'I mean, that doesn't explain you missing the other night. Is something else going on?'

Anna glanced behind her, into the kitchen. 'Actually there is something else. Matteo and I were talking the other night, we had a . . . a differing of opinion.'

'An argument?' Imogen said, her eyes widening. 'But you guys never argue.'

'No, not an argument. We don't really argue. But it was upsetting.' Anna's voice caught as she spoke. 'Imogen, I think this is big. He wants to go back to Italy.'

'Really?' Imogen asked, putting a hand out to touch her sister's shoulder. Anna nodded. 'That's a bit of a turnaround, isn't it?'

'Yes. He always said he'd be happy to live here – that

provided we went back to visit from time to time it would be fine. But with Bella our whole lives have changed, been turned upside down and back round again. So I guess I shouldn't be surprised that he feels differently now to how he did back then.'

'Well, it might not be such a bad idea,' Imogen said.

'That's what I'm starting to wonder. I mean, initially I was dead against it, and then, well, this morning reminded me, there's a lot of history here. Some of it wonderful and some of it difficult. Maybe making a change might do us some good. I mean, if Evie's considering it – at her age, then ...'

'Evie?' Imogen said, surprised.

'Oh, yes. Sorry, I thought I'd mentioned it to you already. The shop's not doing very well. I think it's only a matter of time before she sells it.'

'I didn't realise that. Poor Evie,' Imogen said, quiet for a moment as the news sank in. 'But back to you ... I mean, I don't want to see you go anywhere, believe me. That's the last thing I want. But I remember when you got back from Italy last time, after the course when you met Matteo. You seemed so energised and happy.'

'I suppose I was,' Anna agreed, her mind drifting back.

'You loved it over there. Why shouldn't you go back?'

'I don't know. It's just ... There are a couple of reasons I'm not sure about it.'

'Starting with Matteo's family ... and ending with Matteo's family?' Imogen asked.

'They are good people. And I'll always be grateful to his mum for raising him the way she did. But we're different. His mother is really full on. I don't think it would work, us living right by them.'

'Do you have to, though? Is he set on Siena?'

'No,' Anna said. 'Actually, I suppose he never said that.'

'Italy's a big enough country. Why not suggest somewhere else? It'd still be far easier for his family to visit, but you'd get to have your own space.'

'That's an idea.' Anna thought about it. 'I'll talk to him about it.'

'Good luck, Anna,' Imogen said. 'I'm sure it'll all work out.'

That evening, when Bella was in bed, Anna turned to Matteo. What she and Imogen had talked about earlier that day had been running through her mind, and it had made her realise that the main sticking point, really, was his family – and the thought of losing their independence – not the move itself.

'I've been thinking about what you said, about Italy,' Anna said. His eyes lit up. 'Thinking, that's all,' she added, trying to manage his expectations. 'If we were to go there – and that's still a big if – it wouldn't be for ever, would it?'

'Any time there – a couple of months, longer – it would be wonderful,' Matteo said. 'I'm not expecting you to move. It wouldn't be fair after what I promised you.'

'Could we try somewhere new?'

'Other than Siena?' he said.

'Yes. It's not that I don't like it – it's a beautiful place. But we have our own family now, and if we were to run a business of our own I think it might be nice to ...' She paused, stumbling over the words.

'Not to do it in the shadow of my family, you mean?' She was anxious that she'd offended him. 'I don't see why not,' he said.

'I was wondering about the coast. We both love being by the sea – and Bella would like it.'

'Yes. I guess she would. Whereabouts, though?'

'The Amalfi coast?' Anna said. 'Sorrento, maybe?' She recalled what Evie had said about the place, how happy she and Vivien had once been there. 'I know it's a long way from Siena, but your family could still visit easily enough. It would be our place. Our new start.'

He mulled it over. 'It's a beautiful place.'

'You'd consider it?'

'Yes. Of course.'

'So shall we start researching where to go – with an open mind?'

'Absolutely,' he said, his smile widening.

Chapter 6

Finn and Imogen were at the Rose, their usual Sunday lunch spot when they were both in town. The weather outside was dull and grey, but inside it was cosy, and they were relaxing with glasses of wine and roast beef with Yorkshire puddings.

'How was Anna when you saw her?' Finn asked.

'OK,' Imogen said. She paused, recalling the conversation she'd had with her sister. 'Fine. Well, confused. Matteo seems to want to go back to Italy – and I have a feeling I might have just persuaded Anna to do it.'

'What?' Finn said, surprised. 'Move the whole family out there?'

'Yes. I mean nothing's decided. She was quite hesitant – but I think I might have talked her into at least considering it seriously.'

It had seemed like a great idea when she'd been talking to Anna, but now, a day later, the reality had started to sink in.

What would she do without Anna here in Brighton with her? Anna was as much part of her life as . . . taking photos, breathing . . . chocolate cake. Bella, too. If they left, it would leave a massive hole in Imogen's life – and she couldn't even bring herself to think about what it would do to their parents.

'I want her and Matteo to be happy, and I think they probably would be – if the setup was right. But the truth is I don't really want her to leave,' Imogen said. It was upsetting her now even thinking of it as a genuine possibility.

Finn covered her hand with his, and their eyes met. She felt instantly reassured, by his touch, the steadiness of his gaze. Finn had a way of making her feel grounded, complete.

'I'd miss them too. But I guess I can understand where Matteo's coming from. He must want Bella to see some of the country that he grew up in. I imagine if it were me, and we had a kid—'

'Well, yes,' Imogen said, eager to change the subject.

'How likely d'you think it is that they'll go?'

'I'm not sure. There's no plan yet.'

'They'll make the right decision for them. For what it's worth, I think it's great that you're supporting her. And, if she does go, I'm sure you'll be able to work something out – with the business, I mean.'

'Yes,' Imogen agreed, her heart heavy as she said it. 'God knows what we're going to do about that.'

'Anna knows you're going to Brazil, right?'

'Yes. And, even if I weren't, she knows that my days of running that place are firmly behind me.'

'Talking of plans,' Finn said, 'I've given some thought to what we were talking about – expanding the business.'

'Oh, yes?' Imogen replied.

'It really does feel like time to grow. As well as the surf lessons, I'd like a space for video screenings, so that we can film the students when they're surfing and they can see how they look out there. That way we can work on fine-tuning their skills. Andy and I have been talking about a shop, too, selling surfboards, bikinis, wetsuits . . .'

'Sounds good.'

'I actually went out to see a couple of places today.' He pulled some brochures out of his bag. 'There's a new build down the coast, about half an hour away. It wouldn't be cheap to lease, but it would give us a lot of room.'

Imogen cast her eye over the photos of the commercial seafront units, shiny glass and steel contrasting with the colourful beach huts and Georgian houses nearby.

'What do you think?' Finn asked tentatively.

'Honestly?'

'Of course,' he said. 'That's why I'm asking. You know I value your opinion on this stuff.'

'I think they're horrible,' Imogen said, wrinkling her nose. 'Sorry. Cold and characterless. Not like the surf school at all.'

'I'm with you,' he said. 'Damn. I was kind of hoping you'd disagree.'

'There must be other places out there,' Imogen said.

'Yes. I'm sure there are, and Andy and I will keep looking. It's just going to be hard – leaving the arches. It's where we started, and neither of us really want to move.'

'There are compromises, and compromises,' Imogen said, closing the brochures and passing them back to Finn. 'And this would definitely be going too far.' Imogen's mind drifted back to a recent conversation with her sister.

'What are you thinking?' Finn asked.

'That maybe you should have a talk with Evie about all this,' Imogen said, her mind whirring.

'Evie? Why?'

'You might be able to help each other out. I've only just thought of it. Anna mentioned that Evie's been having financial issues at the shop and was considering selling up. Maybe you could offer her a deal.'

'You see, this is just one of the many reasons I love you, Imo. You're full of good ideas – and always tell it like it is.'

'That's what I'm here for.'

He kissed her.

Even as she enjoyed the kiss, the moment of being close to Finn, she felt a stab of guilt, because the truth was that, even then, part of her wasn't there at all. She was already day-dreaming about going away, about bright sunlight, and adventure, and the colours of life she'd not yet seen – and she just hoped that it didn't show.

The next day, Imogen made a couple of phone calls, to Anna and Evie, and that afternoon they all met, together with Finn, at Vivien's Heavenly Ice Cream Shop.

Once Anna had brought over the drinks, Imogen got straight to the point.

'OK,' she said. 'Evie, Finn' – she pointed to them both – 'you work next door to each other and yet there's something really important that I don't think you've been talking about. And so I thought it was worth us all getting together.'

Evie looked at Imogen quizzically, but Anna caught her eye, urging patience. 'Hear her out. I think this might be useful to you.'

'Finn wants to expand his business – but not just anywhere. Right?'

'Yes,' Finn said, gently. Imogen could tell that he didn't want to make Evie feel uncomfortable. 'I mean, ideally, Andy and I want to stay here at the arches. But it's just a question of . . .' He trailed off.

'Well, I have the feeling Anna's already mentioned this to you, or I suspect we wouldn't all be here now,' Evie said. 'But I've come to the conclusion it's time to make a new start, cut my losses. The souvenir shop's been good to me over the years, but times have changed, and I need to move on with them.'

'Would you consider selling to Finn?' Imogen asked. 'To create a surf shop attached to the current surf school?'

'Yes,' Evie said, with certainty. 'I think I would. One of the things that's been holding me back is the idea of selling to strangers, not knowing what the place would be used for after I've moved on. Not that I'd want to control that, but, you know, having an idea would be nice.'

'Well,' Finn said, 'I'm pleased to hear that. Obviously, this is only the start – we'll have a lot of facts and figures to put together before we agree to anything. But I'm really happy that you'll consider it.'

Finn's face had lit up, and Imogen took his hand under the table, squeezing it. Anna looked over at Evie. 'You OK, Evie? This must be quite emotional for you.'

Evie paused, as if she were mulling it over. 'You know what. I thought it would be. I really did. But now that it might be really happening . . .'

They all waited to see what she would say, and Imogen desperately hoped for confirmation that they weren't pushing Evie into anything.

'I just feel relieved,' Evie said. 'And, actually, a little bit excited.'

That afternoon, Imogen met with Sally at her house over on the other side of town, near Preston Park. They'd planned the meeting to go over the final details for the trip before fixing their travel dates for Brazil. On the walk over, Imogen thought about what Finn had said. It seemed as if they were putting roots down in Brighton, more and more. It wasn't as if she wanted to live anywhere else, but, at the same time, it made her feel uneasy. She was still young. There was so much that might change. And maybe she wanted some of that change.

When Sally opened the door to Imogen, it was clear something was wrong. Her eyes were red, and she looked exhausted.

'Come in,' Sally said. 'But I'm afraid I've got bad news for you. The publishers have cancelled the trip.'

'What?' Imogen said in disbelief. 'They haven't.'

'They have. Budget restrictions. That's it – no final research, and no new images.'

The words sank in, but the news still didn't feel real to Imogen. 'But ... Why?'

'They had a worse year than expected,' Sally explained, 'and have decided to run my story as narrative-led, using the pictures that I took when I was out there.'

'There's nothing for *any* more photos?' Imogen said, her spirit sinking.

'Nothing,' Sally confirmed. 'I'm so sorry. I've let you down, and I feel like I'm letting the project down, too. The photos I have don't do the place or the animals justice at all.'

'It's not your fault,' Imogen said, still numb and dazed from the news. 'It's just one of those things, I suppose.'

'I shouldn't have made it seem so certain.'

'Don't worry,' Imogen said. She'd have no work for the next month, she realised glumly. And the closest she was going to get to a rainforest that year would be watching nature documentaries on iPlayer.

'I wish there was something I could do,' Sally said.

'I'll be fine.' Imogen waved away her concern. Inside, though, she felt crushed.

'Something else'll come up,' Sally said.

'Of course it will,' Imogen said. 'I'm sure it will.'

Chapter 7

On the following Saturday evening, Anna and Matteo bathed Bella, read her some stories together, and then Anna tucked her into bed with her soft rabbit, pulling the string on a musical toy to help her drift off to sleep. Anna pulled her bedroom door closed softly behind her.

She crept into the kitchen, poured herself and Matteo a glass of red wine, then passed one to him. 'And . . . relax,' she said, smiling.

Matteo gave her a hug. 'I love Bella. In all her craziness. But this time,' he said, 'it's special.'

Anna smiled. 'Definitely.'

'Come over here,' Matteo said, beckoning Anna over to the sofa. 'There's something I've been wanting to show you.'

He picked up his tablet and opened a page. 'Since we talked, I've been looking at a couple of places for rent on the Amalfi coast.'

Anna leaned closer to him on the sofa, full of anticipation and also slightly nervous. This Italy plan was moving on already – from a chat to something more concrete.

'So this one really stood out,' Matteo said, his eyes bright with enthusiasm.

Anna looked over the details in the 'For Rent' advert. It was an established gelateria in one of Sorrento's most popular squares, housed in a handsome stone building with an apartment above.

'I like the look of it,' Anna said.

'The owners are retiring – so they're looking for someone to rent the place for six months. After that – well, it would be up to us, but I wonder if there might be an option to buy it. Look at the photos, Anna. It could be really special, I think.'

She looked over the images of the interior – black-and-white marble floor and glass cabinets full of gelato. 'Actually, it is a bit gorgeous, isn't it?' Anna said. 'A little old-fashioned, perhaps, but we could work with that.'

'I'm sure we could do a few things with the décor, and, of course, if we ended up buying it, we'd have free rein on that.'

'I think I can picture us there,' Anna said. She imagined them running the place, and her own positive feelings surprised her.

'Let's call them,' Matteo said decisively. 'Make it happen.'

'Hang on a minute,' Anna said. 'We don't want to rush into this. All we've seen is a couple of photos.'

'OK. Sorry. Maybe I am getting a bit carried away.'

'I like that you're excited – it's just, it all feels like a bit of a leap in the dark right now,' Anna said. 'A bit more information would go a long way. I wish we were a little closer by, so that we could go and see it for ourselves.'

Matteo seemed to be mulling it over. 'Why don't we ask Carolina to go and have a look?'

Anna thought about it for a moment. She trusted Carolina's opinion completely – the two women had similar taste, and Carolina was smart with good business sense. They'd clicked from the moment they'd first met, and Anna often felt that, if Carolina lived nearer, the two of them would have been good friends.

'I'd love it if she could go and view the place. But it's a long way for her to travel, isn't it?' Anna said.

'She loves a road trip. And she was saying the other day that she could do with a break from Siena. Filippo's been away for work a lot lately and she says the house feels too big with just her in it.'

'OK, great. It would certainly give us more of an idea.'

'I'll talk to her now,' Matteo said, getting to his feet.

It was all starting to feel more real – a genuine possibility that she and Matteo might be giving up their lives in Brighton.

'Are you all right?' Matteo asked.

'Sort of,' Anna said. 'But sort of not. I mean, what about

this place?' she asked, gesturing to the flat. 'I saved up for years for it. And now what? We rent it to strangers?'

'I'm sure we could find someone who'd look after it. A friend of a friend maybe.'

Anna recalled how she'd felt in the days leading up to the opening of the ice cream shop – the meetings in banks, the nagging doubts that she might be making a huge mistake. It had been a really stressful time in her life. Was she really willing to enter into that uncertainty all over again so soon, and now, when they had their young daughter to think about?

'Shall I still call her?' Matteo asked.

This was her chance, Anna thought. She could still back out.

Then she thought again about Vivien's. OK, so setting up the business hadn't been easy, but without a doubt it had been one of the best decisions she'd ever made.

'Call her,' Anna said, excitement building. 'Let's find out if this shop is the one.'

Carolina's face – her tanned skin and large brown eyes – filled the screen of Matteo's tablet and she spoke animatedly. 'I've just had a very quick look and a chat to the current owners,' she said. Behind her was a sun-drenched square, with pretty stone buildings. 'But look at this place.' She panned round with her tablet's camera so that they could see the town. 'I think you are going to love it.'

There was something contagious about Carolina's enthusiasm. Anna had warmed to her sister-in-law from their first meeting, in her family's gelateria in Siena. Back then she'd been working as a graphic designer, busy but never hesitating to linger over a coffee or ice cream with friends and family. She had come over to England at Christmas with her parents, Elisa and Giacomo, but had stayed fairly quiet during the visit. Carolina's husband Filippo had been busy with the business and hadn't been able to make it.

'So the owners are getting ready to retire. It seems like it would be a fantastic opportunity for you to put your own mark on the place.'

'Great,' Matteo said, the excitement in his voice echoing his sister's.

'It's only a short walk from the coast, and it's a proper old-fashioned gelateria, well loved in the town. And the Amalfi coast ... Well, I had the most fantastic drive down here. Matteo, you already know it – but Anna, you'll need to take my word for it. It's totally spectacular.'

Anna pictured the place, Bella playing in the sunshine on the picturesque Amalfi coast, rather than stuck indoors on one of the many rainy days like this one.

'Anyway, follow me,' Carolina said. Holding her tablet up, she showed them the front of the shop, with a pretty balcony with tall wooden shutters above it. 'Look up there – the apartment comes with the shop, and it's two bedrooms, so there'd be plenty of room for all of you. There's this outside area.'

She panned round to show a few tables and chairs in the square, and then revealed a fountain in the middle, with children playing around it. 'And inside . . .' She pushed open the glass door, and Anna could hear her talking to the owners in Italian, explaining what she was doing. 'You've got all of this space out the front, and then a good kitchen . . .'

Anna took in the traditional décor – some stylish but a lot of it tired, and she felt a wave of excitement about doing it up.

Carolina showed the tables, full of people enjoying their weekend ice creams. 'You'll have the existing customer base, with room to build on that – and this is winter, of course. Your plan is to come out for the summer, isn't it?'

Matteo and Anna looked at each other, and he waited for her answer.

'Yes,' Anna said, nodding. 'That's right.'

'Just the summer?' Carolina asked.

'Well, maybe longer,' Anna said.

'Really?' Matteo said hopefully.

'We'll need to stay long enough to make the investment worthwhile, won't we?' Anna said. The thought still unnerved her, but it excited her too.

Chapter 8

Imogen sipped from a bottle of Sol, her gaze drifting out to the seagulls that were swooping down on to the pebbles, hoping to find a discarded chip wrapper. She and Finn were sitting at a bar down by the arches, after he'd closed the surf school.

'How did it go today?' Finn asked her.

She looked back at him, feeling bad that she'd drifted off. 'It was OK. Lauren's offered to give me some assistant work on some of her shoots, weddings, kids' photography sessions. It'll help pay the bills.'

'That's good,' he said. He noticed the look on her face. 'Isn't it?'

'Yes.' She shrugged. 'I guess. I mean work is work. But I just thought . . .' She tried to fight back the feelings of disappointment. 'It's assistant work. It feels like a bit of a backwards step, to be honest. I thought I'd be out in Brazil now, putting together photos for the book, and instead I'm going to be here, helping Lauren take photos of people's weddings and babies.'

'It won't be for ever,' Finn said. 'And at least it's photography.'

'I know. I'm being impatient,' she said. 'I just thought, after New York, you know, all of those photos getting sold. I thought I was going to get somewhere.'

'You *are* somewhere,' Finn said. 'You're just not quite where you want to be yet, that's all. Anything worth having takes time.'

'I thought I'd already put in that time, back when we first got together – and now I feel like I'm treading water,' she said. She felt frustrated. She was stuck here on the south coast while there was a whole world to explore.

'Look, I know it's not the Amazon,' Finn said, 'but how would you like a break away this weekend, a change of scene?'

'I don't know. I should probably be saving … I don't know what work's coming in for the next few months.'

'Don't worry about that,' Finn said. 'I've got some savings. It would be good to spend some time together, just the two of us. It feels like ages since we did that.'

'OK,' Imogen said, brightening at the thought. 'Let's do it.'

'This weekend?'

'Do you really have to ask?' She laughed. 'I haven't got any plans for the rest of the year.'

That Saturday night Imogen and Finn were out in the New Forest, in a cosy log cabin, by an open fire. There were no other houses for miles around, and the evening was still and quiet. That day they'd gone horse riding together, the rest of the world disappearing for a while as they galloped through the trees. The owner of the cabin, a kind man in his mid-forties, had come and helped them saddle up, then left them to it. They'd come home to a fully packed fridge and cooked up chicken with roast vegetables, dining by the fireside and drinking wine before retiring to the sofa, where they were now sitting.

'What a perfect day,' Imogen said, leaning back into the sofa, content and tired. 'That was just what I needed.'

'It was great, wasn't it?' Finn said.

'Thank you for arranging it,' she said. She curled in closer to Finn, and kissed him. He stroked her hair back gently.

'I love you,' he said. 'And I thought you looked like you could do with some cheering up.'

'You were right.'

'It's just a bump in the road,' he reassured her.

'I know. I'm sure it won't be long till I get something new. Lauren's got me signed up to help with a wedding next week, and I've already heard about a couple of leads that sound promising – one thing in Nepal. With any luck, I'll be away again in no time.'

'Do you need to be in quite such a hurry?' Finn asked, with a half-smile.

'Of course not,' she said, flippantly. 'Don't take it that way.'

'It's hard not to, sometimes.'

'Oh, come on,' she teased him, light-heartedly.

'I'm serious,' he said, his tone changing. 'Would it be all bad, having a bit of time over the summer together? You've been working back-to-back projects for almost a year now.'

'You know how it is,' Imogen said. 'If inspiration hits – or I get a good commission – I can't miss it.'

'I do – and I completely respect that you're passionate about what you do. It's one of the things I love most about you. But, at the same time, I wonder if this might also be an opportunity for you to take your foot off the gas for a bit. Maybe this is selfish of me – but sometimes I wouldn't mind seeing just a bit more of you.'

His expression was calm but serious, and she realised that it wasn't the time for off-the-cuff replies any more.

'OK. I guess I see what you mean,' she said. 'And I'd like to see you more. If I had the choice …'

'But don't you?' he asked, gently. 'Don't you have that choice, right now?'

'Why are you saying all this? You just want me to stay here in England, taking safe little photos, living a safe little life …'

'Of course I don't,' Finn said, shaking his head. 'That's not what I mean at all. I just happen to be in love with you, Imogen. And I'd like it if we got to see each other more.'

'When you talk like this' – her heart raced – 'it all makes me feel tied down.'

'When I say that I'd like to spend a bit of time with you now and then, in between your travels?'

'Yes,' she said, hotly. 'It makes me feel trapped.'

'God, Imogen! Do you know what you sound like?' She glanced down at the floor. 'You're not the only one in this relationship. I'm not trying to stop you doing anything you want. I just want us to think about the future, how we could try and find a bit more balance. Is that really such a bad thing?'

Chapter 9

Since Anna had seen the shop in Italy, it seemed as if one thing after another was starting to fall into place. She and Matteo had put down a deposit on it that week, with a six-month commitment starting in May. A friend of Anna's from her old marketing job had been in touch looking for a place to rent in Brighton and was interested in her flat. Anna felt much better about the idea, knowing that their home wouldn't be lived in by strangers, but by someone she knew and trusted. The only issue that remained was whom to entrust the ice cream shop to.

Anna was typing ideas into her iPad when Matteo joined her for their morning coffee.

'So, how does this sound?' she asked. '"A splash of English Eccentricity on the Italian shores. Come and taste our delicious port-and-Stilton sorbet, and mojito ice lollies!"'

As Anna had noted down some ideas for the sorbet menu

that morning she'd felt a buzz of excitement at what lay ahead for them. Anna thought of the traditional Italian granita – the closest equivalent to the English sorbet, fresh and light with crunchy ice, weighed down deliciously with the fresh fruit flavours it carried. They would be producing those, of course – and Matteo was an expert at making them – but she also wanted to make the light, almost fluffy lemon sorbets of her youth, the tangerine sorbet her grandmother used to make her and Imogen, hidden away inside a real tangerine, appearing when you lifted the cut lid.

A whole summer out in Italy. And it now seemed as if that might just be the start.

'You look excited,' Matteo said, happily.

'I am. Now that it's taking shape, I really am. I know some of it'll be challenging, but how amazing to have a new start, and, with the business here doing well, we can afford to take some chances and experiment with the Italian shop. It's always paid off for us here, after all.'

'Carolina is so happy that we're going through with this. She says the shop's pretty much ready to go, so there'll just be a bit of admin to arrange when we arrive, but we can open up within the fortnight.'

'Brilliant!' Anna said. 'I know Bella doesn't really know what's going on, and where she's going – but I can't help thinking she's excited about it too, don't you think?'

He came closer to Anna and touched her glossy dark hair

gently, then kissed her on the top of her head. 'Thank you,' he said, 'for agreeing to do this. I know it wasn't an easy decision.'

'It wasn't. But I'm starting to feel surer that it's the right one.'

Hepburn leaped up onto the sofa, and nuzzled against Anna's lap.

'The guilt,' Anna said. 'What will we do with Hepburn?'

'Do you think your uncle would take him in at the guest-house? It was his home once, after all,' Matteo said.

'Maybe. I'll ask him. Or, failing that, my parents . . .'

Anna thought of her mum and dad. She still hadn't mentioned a word of the Italy plan to them. Even thinking of it made her feel guilty.

She had found herself unconsciously avoiding them, so that nothing would slip out in conversation – telling herself that it wasn't final yet. And it *hadn't* been certain. But now it was. With the preparations for the guesthouse opening, her parents had become closer and happier than ever. And now Anna felt deep down that she was about to shatter all of that.

Chapter 10

The midmorning light was perfect, Imogen thought – not too bright, just enough to bring out the colour of each leaf and flower, the shades of grey and green within a wave, the delicate patterns on a bird's wing.

Or St. Tropez-toned shoulders and the multiple layers of a synthetic wedding dress, studded with diamante.

'Could we have all of the bride's side now?' Imogen said, ushering a crowd of bridesmaids and flower girls, along with elderly relatives, over to where Lauren was standing.

Lauren was setting up her camera to take the photos, out on the pier, and Imogen's main role was shepherding the party into position.

'Beautiful, yes. So, if we could just have the flower girls here at the front, please.'

The bride let out a yelp of pain. The pageboy, a toddler, had somehow crept under her skirt unnoticed, and now the bride was looking in fury at her sister-in-law. 'He bit me,' she said, sternly. 'Could you try and keep him under control, please?'

The groom kept quiet, shifting awkwardly.

'He never bites,' the sister-in-law said firmly. 'It must have been someone else.'

'Who, exactly?' the bride said, stepping out of the photograph formation. 'Look at the size of the bite marks.' She lifted up her skirt, to reveal a reddened patch of her calf.

'OK, enough,' Imogen said, over the din. 'Pageboy on the edge of the shot, please, Bride back in the centre, and let's get on with the photos, please.'

Imogen felt like a stage manager, running the show. Because that was all a wedding was really, wasn't it?

When Imogen got back home that night, her spirits were low. Her face ached from keeping a smile on her face all day, and now she was struggling to summon one up for real. She kept telling herself she was lucky to have any work at all, but it didn't help. She knew it was mean-spirited, but she just hadn't been able to find it within herself to feel joy on the bride and groom's special day.

'How did it go?' Finn asked, when she got home.

'It went well,' Imogen lied.

'Come on, I can see right through you,' Finn said.

'The wedding was a bit intense, I guess. A lot of fuss ...'

Finn was listening, but she stopped herself. She didn't want to start moaning about her day to him. 'But enough about that. How were things at the surf school today?' she asked.

'Good – we had a group cancellation, not ideal, but actually it gave Andy and me a chance to chat through the business plan for the shop. We're meeting with the bank this week about loans. I'm starting to think this is something we could really do.'

We? He was right, of course. They were a team. But deep down it nagged at her – the new shop was Finn's project. As far as her career was concerned, it was taking a total nosedive.

The next day, Imogen met her mum for tea in the south lanes. She spotted Jan right away, a splash of her trademark turquoise by the window of the busy café, a book in hand. The moment she noticed her daughter approach, she put her paperback down and looked up at her eagerly.

'Imogen, sweetheart!' she said, getting to her feet and giving her daughter a hug.

'Hi, Mum,' Imogen said, her voice calm and level. She pulled out a chair. 'What are you reading?'

'One of my naughty books,' she said, showing Imogen the cover, which had a pair of handcuffs on it. 'Elaine from the hairdresser's recommended this one to me. It's about a woman who—'

'Oh, you mustn't spoil it for me,' Imogen said, hurriedly. 'Keep it a surprise. Is that for Bella?' she asked, looking at a gift bag next to her mother's coat.

'Yes, just a little thing.'

'You know that Anna's put an embargo on more pink, don't you?' Imogen said. '"Normal, not princessy",' she told me.'

Jan took a look at Imogen's outfit – boyfriend-cut jeans and an orange T-shirt, her tousled hair pulled up into an untidy topknot.

'Well, normal is a little different from when I was young,' Jan said. 'But don't worry: it's only a pair of leggings. I'm sure she'll approve.'

'Cool.'

'Anything you'd like to tell me?' she said.

Jan looked at her daughter expectantly.

'Like what?'

'Nothing,' Jan said.

'Why are you looking at me like that?' Imogen asked, bringing one hand up to her cheek. 'Have I got something on my face?'

'No, you're fine,' her mum said, with a knowing smile. 'Was it a good weekend?'

'It was great, thanks.' And it had been, most of it. Right up to the point she and Finn had argued. Even after that, the next morning they'd slowly got back to normal, not talking any more about their relationship, just going out into the forest and taking in their surroundings. 'Beautiful out there – horses, a stream, so peaceful.'

'That's nice,' Jan said. She raised an eyebrow as if she was waiting for Imogen to say something.

'What?'

'Oh, nothing,' Jan said, her cheeks colouring a little. 'Forget I said anything.'

'What is it?' Imogen asked, growing irritated. 'You obviously meant something.'

'Here's your tea,' the waitress said, putting down a red teapot. She glanced at the two women and, sensing from the atmosphere that she'd interrupted something, stepped back. 'Flapjacks coming right up,' she said.

'It's nothing, really,' Jan said. 'I must've got the wrong end of the stick.'

'Just say it.'

'Oh, don't, Imogen. You know I'm terrible with secrets. And I don't want to ruin the surprise.'

'What surprise?' Imogen said.

Jan's cheeks turned a deeper pink. 'Finn came over to ours last week.'

'To speak to you?'

'To your father.'

'To Dad?' Imogen said.

'Yes.' She nodded. 'They could have been talking about

anything . . . But I suppose I did wonder . . . Silly me, jumping to conclusions. But with Granny Vivien's ring at our house, and the traditional way of doing these things, I just assumed . . .'

'Don't assume,' Imogen said, her skin burning hot. 'You don't know a thing about my relationship.'

Imogen cycled quickly through Brighton's narrow lanes, the fresh breeze on her arms and face a welcome distraction. She couldn't stop thinking about what her mum had said. Finn had gone to see her dad, and they'd talked together. She'd never known Finn to go on his own to the cottage.

Imogen locked her bike down by the arches on the seafront. She had a meeting with Lauren coming up, but she needed to be on her own for a few minutes. She walked down the beach away from Hove, the ice cream shop and Finn's surf business getting further and further away from her. She should feel elated right now.

She loved Finn, didn't she? So why did the thought of his proposing feel like a stone in her stomach?

Chapter 11

Imogen had intended to cycle straight home that evening, after her meeting, but instead she'd found herself down on the seafront again, this time at the ice cream shop. She propped up her bike and went in. Her sister was bent over wiping down the tables, her dark hair pinned up on top of her head and an emerald-green shirt dress on with T-bar shoes.

'If it weren't for the apron and the Marigold gloves you could almost be a film star,' Imogen said.

Anna laughed. 'Really?' Her cheeks glowed. 'That's as close as I get to a compliment these days, so I'll take it.'

'Please tell me you're in the mood for noodles,' Imogen demanded.

'Always,' Anna said. But then her brow furrowed. 'I don't know, though. We've got the till to do, and Bella to pick up from nursery, the—'

Matteo put his head out of the kitchen. 'Imogen, take her out,' he called out. 'She needs a break.'

'Thanks, Matteo,' Imogen called back.

Anna turned to her husband. 'Are you sure?'

'Of course! Go on, get out of here. I can close up and get Bella.'

Anna undid her apron and pulled off the gloves. 'OK, then. Let's go.'

The sisters walked together past the fish-and-chip shops and amusement arcades on the seafront. The city was still rel-atively quiet and they had both learned to appreciate the lull of late winter, the calm before the Easter holiday storm. Normally Imogen might take the lead in a conversation, and Anna would follow, but that evening both of them were quiet, and they made their way to the small Japanese restau-rant barely saying a word.

They ordered bottles of beer, and their usual noodle dishes, and then looked at each other over the table. Imogen took in the fine lines around her sister's pretty eyes, and the slouch in her shoulders. Anna seemed to be noticing her sister's less-than-bright appearance, too.

'Why do you look so miserable?' Imogen said.

'Why do *you* look so miserable?' Anna said. The tension broke as both of them collapsed into an easy laughter.

'Go on, I asked first,' Imogen said.

'Because I think we really might be going to Italy. And I

can't believe I'm really going to leave behind all of the good things that we have here. And I can't bring myself to tell Mum and Dad.'

Imogen touched her arm. 'Yes. Not an easy one.'

'With the guesthouse about to open, and how sensitive Dad's been recently, I don't want to land them with this. Not right now.'

'But you know you have to tell them sometime, right?'

'Yes – and I need to do it soon. Everything's been moving so quickly out in Italy – if things continue smoothly we should be out there by May.'

'That soon?'

'Yes. Mad, isn't it? One minute I was talking about it with you, it was all just a vague idea – and now it's really happening.'

'Why don't you tell them at the party?' Imogen suggested. 'When the guesthouse is actually open it should all be easier, right? Everyone will be relaxed, and you can tell everyone in one go rather than separately.'

'Yes,' Anna said, still looking nervous. 'That could work, I guess.'

'You're probably worrying about nothing, anyway,' Imogen said.

'Really?' Anna laughed. 'You really think that? Mum reacts badly enough when you go away. I'm the one she expects to stick around.'

'She'll get over it. She'll have to,' Imogen said.

'So, go on. What's eating you?'

'If I say it, it's going to sound ridiculous. And spoilt. I know that.'

'Both things I am used to hearing from you. So fire away.'

Imogen wrinkled her nose and made a face at her sister. 'I think Finn's planning on proposing to me.'

'Really?' Anna said, unable to keep the excitement from her voice.

'Yes,' Imogen said, the unshakeable nature of her feelings clear now. 'Only I don't feel excited about it. Not at all.'

'Right,' Anna said.

'I don't know if this is even just about Finn,' Imogen said. 'I don't really know what's going on. I just feel in a slump. The Amazon project falling through, nothing new in the pipeline ... I feel stuck here at the moment, just like I did that first summer when we set up the shop. And me and Finn – well, I love him. I really do. That's not in question. But all I can think is that getting married would tie me down even more. Does that sound horrible?'

'It sounds like the truth,' Anna said.

'It is. Maybe I'm overreacting. I may've got the wrong end of the stick anyway. It was just something that Mum said that made it seem like he might be planning on asking.'

'Well, it wouldn't surprise me,' Anna said. 'I mean, he clearly adores you, anyone can see that, and he's always said he wants to have a family, hasn't he?'

'Yes!' Imogen said, her emotion welling up. 'That's it. You see? I feel like everything's racing ahead, far more quickly than I'm ready for, Anna. Marriage, a family, this expansion he's planning for the business, things that would keep us here for the long term. Of course I want to support him, and I definitely want to stay with him. But I want it to be relaxed like it used to be. Spending time with each other because we enjoyed spending time with each other, the simple pleasure of that, taking a day at a time.'

'I know what you mean,' Anna said. 'But I think there comes a point in any relationship when that needs to change. Don't you?'

'Maybe. But now? I'm only twenty-six,' Imogen reminded her sister. 'I never thought the age gap would matter. It's only a few years, but now ... I'm starting to wonder. I feel like we're in different places right now.'

'You should talk to him,' Anna suggested.

'I know,' Imogen said. 'But seriously – how can I talk to him about something that hasn't even happened?'

Chapter 12

The next morning, Imogen and Finn were sitting in their house by the window, a breakfast of croissants and eggs on the table between them. Imogen had woken up to the smell of fresh coffee, and for a moment everything seemed perfect. Then she'd remembered the conversation with Anna, the feelings of unease she'd had over the past couple of days that were refusing to shift. As she looked at Finn now, dressed in a grey T-shirt and his favourite jeans, his sandy hair falling in one eye, she tried to push those thoughts aside. She was lucky. She just needed to get her head straight, that was all.

'I've got some really good news,' Finn said. 'Evie and I sat down with the figures yesterday, and I've made her a formal offer. She's accepted it.'

'That's fantastic,' Imogen said, smiling. She was genuinely happy for him. But then – then there was also the feeling of being on a rollercoaster that she couldn't get off.

'Yes. And she seems keen to get going with it, now that it's certain.'

'So, once it's all finalised, what would happen next?' Imogen asked.

'We'd have to do a lot of the work ourselves. Probably a bit crazy doing it in high season, but Andy and I are both keen to get on with it, and it seems like Evie wants to get going with the sale sooner rather than later. She seems happy about the idea of the place staying in the family, so to speak.'

'That's nice.'

'And you'll be off again soon, I'm sure, so I might as well be busy.'

'Maybe.' She shrugged. The heavy sensation in the pit of her stomach wouldn't shift, and she was starting to think that maybe this was how it felt to be a failure.

'I've got the assistant work for Lauren, but that's about it at the moment,' Imogen said. 'I might help Uncle Martin out at the guesthouse, in the short term. I'd rather be busy. I'm going to see if he could use someone on reception, perhaps with a bit of online marketing, that kind of thing. There's so much potential, and a few hours here and there isn't going to stop me taking on a good project.'

Imogen tried not to think about what she'd be doing now if things had worked out differently – that only led to a deepening of the disappointment that had weighed on her ever since Sally told her the news. There was still time for her to fulfil her dreams of taking photos out in the Amazon. They were just going to have to go on hold for a little while, that was all.

On the way over to Lauren's studio, Imogen dropped by at the ice-cream shop to pick up Hepburn.

'Thanks a lot, Imogen,' Anna said. 'I couldn't face leaving him in the flat today. He's started whining when we go out, and it's driving the neighbours mad. But bringing him here probably wasn't the best idea, when it's so busy. He's been under our feet all day.'

Imogen bent down to pick him up and brought him up close to her to cuddle him. He licked her face. 'It's fine, I've been wanting a bit of quality time with him, anyway. And I haven't got much to do at the studio today.'

'Great. I appreciate it,' Anna said.

'So, have you heard anything from Evie lately?' Imogen asked.

'Yes! Anna said. 'She just popped in. Told us about selling the shop to Finn. What great news.'

'Isn't it?' Imogen said. 'He's over the moon about it.'

'She seems so relieved to know she'll be dealing with someone she knows.'

'So I was thinking about it on the way over here,' Imogen said. 'Evie's hardly going to want to sit still and retire, is she? She's not really the type.'

'You don't think so?' Anna asked. 'What would she do?'

'We could ask her to run Vivien's,' Imogen said.

Anna paused, letting the idea take shape in her mind. 'I suppose it could work. It's worth asking.'

'I could talk her through the recipes, and keep an eye on things while you're abroad. She's always been good in the kitchen.'

'I love the idea,' Anna said. 'Once the lunchtime rush is over, I'll go and ask her.'

'Great,' Imogen said, lighting up.

'God!' Anna paused and then bit her lip.

'What is it?' Imogen asked.

'If she says yes . . .' Anna said, her voice faint.

'What?'

'We would be all set.'

'But you want to be, don't you?' Imogen said.

'Yes, I do,' Anna said. 'That is . . . I definitely think I do.'

Imogen arrived at Lauren's studio with Hepburn after a long walk on the beach. Her friend caught her at the doorway, looking stressed and frantic, her cheeks flushed.

'Imogen,' Lauren said, her expression panicked. 'You've got to help me.'

'Have I?' Imogen said, bringing Hepburn up into her arms and stroking his head.

'Yes.'

Imogen raised an eyebrow.

'I mean please,' Lauren said. 'I've double-booked myself. I've got a wedding up by Seaford and I've messed up – I completely forgot about baby Jacob coming in.'

Imogen peered past her friend and into the room, where a young couple were jiggling their baby on their laps. 'Could you cover this session – as a favour to me?'

Imogen hesitated. 'I've never—'

'Come on – we both know you could do this standing on your head,' Lauren said. 'I've got to go. I've explained the situation to them. Equipment's all there. Thanks a million.'

Lauren hugged her quickly and went out of the door.

Jacob's parents cooed over him.

Imogen introduced herself and tried to put them at ease, even though she felt far from it herself.

'How about you hold him between you? Yes, just like that,' Imogen said.

The baby's parents looked full of pride as they cradled his small body between them.

Actually, he was kind of cute. She got a few shots of him smiling and laughing.

'What about this toy?' Imogen suggested, passing them a fluffy bear. She'd collected together a few props that she thought might help things to move smoothly. Baby Jacob frowned and then started to cry.

Imogen looked around for something else to use, and then Hepburn, the dachshund, dashed in through the gap in the door. The baby's face lit up immediately as he spied the black-and-tan sausage dog. With one hand Imogen beckoned for Hepburn to come and lie by her feet, keeping his distance from the baby, and with the other she took photos of the boy and his parents, who were by now all in fits of giggles.

Later, over tea, she showed the couple a few of her favourites on the screen of her laptop. 'I haven't edited these yet obviously, but I think there are some great shots here.'

'They're perfect,' said Jacob's mum. 'Just what we were looking for. We didn't want anything formal, just pictures of us as we are at home.'

'Great. Well, I'll edit them and get the disc ready for you then.'

'Thanks, Imogen,' they said, glowing.

Imogen went home via Elderberry Avenue. The day at the studio hadn't been so bad, she thought. It would do, as a stopgap. Until something better came along. After Jacob and his parents left, she'd phoned around old contacts, letting them know she was available for work, and a few had promised to keep an eye out for assignments. At least there was one positive thing about her still being in Brighton: she'd get to see the guesthouse open.

She knocked at the door and her uncle Martin answered. 'Hello, Imogen,' he said, brightly. 'You're a sight for sore eyes.'

'Oh, yes?' she said.

'Yes. The party's tomorrow night and I seem to have a hundred and one things still to do – picking up all of the drinks, delivery, the final pieces of furniture, getting the rooms cleaned up ... It feels endless. Could you give me a hand?'

'Of course,' she said. 'That's why I'm here.'

Which was true. At least it was half of the reason. The other half, if Imogen was completely honest, was that she was avoiding going home to Finn. She was so happy that things were progressing well with his plans for the business, and yet, after the day taking photos she just couldn't really bring herself to care about, she felt less inclined than ever to consider settling in Brighton for good. And, at the moment, every time she looked at him, that was what she thought about.

Martin tugged at the little that was left of his hair. 'We'll have forty guests coming, and then the extras from the press that your mum's organised.'

'Let's get things set up. Don't worry, it'll be great,' Imogen reassured him.

'I hope so – and, anyway, I suppose I'd better get used to all this organisation: it's going to be my working life from now on, after all.'

'Advance bookings still coming through?'

'Oh, yes,' he said. 'Since we got the website up they've been coming through at a rate of knots. It's not that I can't cope with it, Imogen. I can – it's just ... Well, Françoise, you remember, she was such a dominant personality.'

Imogen recalled her uncle's ex-wife, and the way she would frequently speak over and for him, undermining his decisions or making decisions for the two of them without consulting him.

'And now you're doing everything on your own,' Imogen said.

'Yes. Which is a good thing – I mean I'm enjoying it, and I'm happier than ever now that your dad seems more on board with it all. But I don't know ... It can feel a little lonely sometimes. The responsibility of it, I suppose.'

'You've got all of us on your side,' Imogen said, giving him a hug. 'This place is part of our family, and we'll be there for you every step.'

At around seven in the evening, Imogen realised that the job was too big for her and Martin to manage alone. She called in backup – their dad Tom went with Martin to pick up some of the furniture they still needed and Finn drove Anna and Imogen to the drinks wholesalers.

On the journey over, Anna, in the passenger seat, couldn't stop herself from smiling.

'OK, I can't hold it in any longer,' Anna said, happily. 'I

asked Evie, about running the ice cream shop. And she said yes. She wants to do it.' Her grin got even wider.

'That's amazing,' Imogen said. 'I knew it!'

'She seemed really pleased with the idea, didn't take any persuading at all.'

'That's fantastic,' Finn said. 'So I get to keep her as my neighbour after all. Hopefully, she won't mind all the noise while we rebuild her old shop. Andy and I were going over the plans with his dad today and I think it's going to be quite a big job.'

Finn's eyes were bright – he looked more excited about the project than he had done about anything in months.

'I can't wait to get started on it. We've been running the business in the same way for years, and this is a chance for us to push ahead, make the surf school a real destination for people wanting to learn to surf.'

'A new start for everyone,' Anna said. 'I have a feeling it's going to be a really great year for us all.'

Imogen glanced out of the window at the traffic going by.

'You OK, Imo?' Finn asked, catching sight of her in the rear-view mirror and turning to look at her.

'Oh, yes, I'm fine,' she said. She tried to force a smile, but inside all she felt was heaviness. With all the positive things happening around her, she couldn't figure out why, or where it was coming from. Only that when she looked ahead, into her future, she wasn't quite sure what she could see any more.

114

Chapter 13

ELDERBERRY GUESTHOUSE OPENS ITS DOORS

by Sam Graham

Brighton and Hove today sees the opening of a brand-new guesthouse.

Once home to one of the city's best-loved residents, Vivien McAvoy – who many will remember as the proprietor of the now-famous ice cream shop under the arches – the Elderberry Guesthouse has now been given a new lease of life by her sons, Martin and Tom.

Under their guardianship, the premises, on Elderberry Avenue, have been transformed into a boutique guesthouse, with rooms inspired by classic movies. The proprietors say the hotel is already drawing plenty of attention with advance bookings from the UK and abroad . . .

Evie and Anna walked down Elderberry Avenue on the cool spring evening, with Matteo and Bella following close behind. Evie squeezed Anna's hand in anticipation as they neared what had once been Vivien's home. Anna, Imogen, Finn, Martin and Tom had worked until midnight getting everything ready, putting the final touches to the guesthouse and setting up for the party. But, when she'd come home, she'd been buzzing, and had woken Matteo up so that she could fill him in on everything they'd been doing. In good-natured sleepiness, Matteo had listened, smiling and nodding in all the right places, until Anna had finally calmed down enough to fall asleep. Her excitement had been mixed with nerves – because tonight meant more than just the guesthouse opening. She'd vowed to herself that at the party, she'd tell her family she and Matteo were leaving, and that they weren't exactly sure when they would be coming back.

'I've been so looking forward to this,' Evie said. 'I haven't seen anything he's done, so it'll all be a surprise. I intended to pop in, see how Martin was getting on, but, well, as you know, there's been quite a lot going on lately, hasn't there?'

'Are you feeling OK about it all?' Anna asked.

'Yes.' She nodded.

'It's a lot of change.'

'I know. And it's the end of an era, so of course I have some mixed feelings about that. But it's also a new start for me, Anna – and I need that. This idea you've had – about me taking over the ice cream shop – well, it's just given me a surge of energy. I thought by closing my shop I'd be moving further away from Vivien, all my memories of her. Instead, I'm getting even closer. It's an honour, really. I can't wait to get started.'

'I'm so happy – and of course Imogen is too,' Anna said. 'I can't think of anyone more perfect for the job.'

'It's going to be a steep learning curve, though,' Evie said, laughing. 'I've never made an ice cream in my life.'

'If Imogen can learn it,' Anna whispered to Evie conspiratorially, 'you'll have no problems. Believe me.'

'And you, Matteo and Bella – off to Sorrento. You must be counting the days.'

'I am.' Anna said. 'But it doesn't feel real yet. I think it will after tonight. Once I've told everybody.'

'Of course,' Evie said, sympathetically. 'But after that, well, you won't look back. I'm certain of it. It's one of the most beautiful places in the world, the Amalfi coast. Intoxicating.'

'Have you ever been tempted to go back there?' Anna asked.

'Oh, I did, once,' Evie answered. 'Just once.' Her eyes

glazed over slightly as she said it. 'Look, here we are,' she said, pointing at the house.

'The Elderberry Guesthouse,' Anna said.

'What a lovely sign.'

Anna looked at the ceramic sign with the guesthouse name on it, recognised her father's handiwork right away and felt a wave of pride.

'I think it's time to join the party,' she said, pushing the front door open.

Anna and Evie stepped inside. What had once been Vivien's hallway and study had been transformed into an elegant reception area, filled with lively guests drinking wine. The living room had been decluttered, and new, mid-century furniture brought in, but the shelves remained full of Vivien's books and her favourite armchair − upholstered in green velvet − was still over by the bay window, where it had always been. Anna pictured how Vivien had looked sitting in that chair, Hepburn in her lap as the two of them had talked over tea and Anna's homemade cake. It felt for a moment as if she were there at the party with all of them.

Anna looked around at the new framed photos on the walls, some of Imogen's prints, and then old photos of their family and friends: Vivien in a full-skirted 1950s dress in front of her shop; standing hand in hand with Evie on the pier, both holding umbrellas; and her treasured black-and-white wedding photo, with Stanley, outside Brighton Town Hall, in the late 1950s.

In the living room were stills from Vivien's favourite films – *Roman Holiday*, *Breakfast at Tiffany's*, *Casablanca*.

'Oh, look at this, Evie,' Anna said. She pointed at a large map of Sorrento and Capri.

'Hello, you two,' Imogen called out. She was carrying trays of canapés through for the guests congregating in the living room. 'Oh, yes, I found that one folded up in the bureau drawer – nice, isn't it?'

'Lovely,' Evie said. Something passed across her face, and her gaze lingered on the map for a while.

Anna looked through to the living room, where Martin and Tom were chatting to friends and neighbours, showing off the converted house with pride after the months of work they'd put in. Matteo and Evie went over to congratulate them. Anna held back for a moment, standing with Bella and Imogen and taking in the new surroundings. 'It looks so beautiful,' she said.

'It does,' Imogen said. 'Uncle Martin's worked wonders with it.'

'Is Mum here?' Anna asked.

Imogen pointed through the crowd at where Jan was standing, talking to someone she recognised as a journalist on a local newspaper. When she caught Anna's eye and saw Bella, she excused herself politely and came over.

'Hello!' she said, greeting Anna and then giving her granddaughter a heartfelt kiss. Bella beamed, and hugged Jan back tight.

'OK if I give her a tour?' Jan asked.

'Go ahead,' Anna said.

Jan led Bella away, holding her tiny hand, and they walked together round the guesthouse. Bella seemed delighted with all the new things in the house that she could look at.

'Now, here's where your great-grandmother used to do her reading,' she said, chatting to Bella, 'in this big chair – see, here's a picture of her.' She took a framed photo down from the mantelpiece and showed it to her.

'Granny Vee!' Bella said pointing.

Imogen nudged her sister. 'How cute is that!'

A lump came to Anna's throat. In just a few weeks, she would be breaking up the family, taking Bella hundreds of miles away from her grandparents and from Imogen and Finn.

'You're going to tell them tonight, aren't you?' Imogen asked.

'Yes,' Anna said, worried that her tears might spill over. 'I'll tell them.'

After the canapés had been eaten, guesthouse rooms explored and most of the wine drunk, Martin climbed a couple of steps and knocked against his wine glass with a silver spoon, drawing the attention of the room. A hush gradually fell over the lively party.

'I'm proud to declare the Elderberry Guesthouse officially open!' His face glowed with pride. 'Thank you all so much for coming tonight.'

A cheer went up from the crowd.

'Many of you knew our mother well, and, if you did, you'll know that the doors of this house were always open to people who needed a helping hand. That's why setting up the guesthouse seemed right.'

He looked around the room, and his eyes rested on his brother. 'Tom, come up here. You've been part of all this too.' Tom edged his way shyly through the crowd, but, once up on the stairs beside his brother, he looked every bit as proud. 'Here's to Mum,' Martin said, raising his glass again. 'To Vivien!' Jan called out. Glasses clinked around the room.

'The guesthouse is ready to receive its first guests, and we couldn't have got here without such a fantastic team. This was a real family affair. So, thank you to Jan, for the publicity, Finn for the website, Imogen for helping out with just about everything – and for the welcome news that you're not leaving us just yet! – and to Anna, Matteo and Bella for the refreshments as we worked, and for the entertainment.'

Imogen drew close to Finn, and to her sister and mother, and they smiled as Martin spoke. Finn put his arm around her, kissing the top of her head. He was a part of the family now, and everyone adored him, just as she did. Whatever mixed feelings she had about committing, she owed it to everyone else to work past them.

After a couple more toasts, Martin stood down and the guests returned to their conversations, refreshing their glasses from what was left at the bar.

Anna whispered to Matteo that it was time, then called her dad and mum over. The area of the living room near to Vivien's chair was quieter now, and her whole family surrounded them, together with Evie. Anna took a deep breath and readied herself.

'Have you got an announcement to make?' Tom asked, jovially. 'And I thought we were done with those for the evening.'

Matteo took Anna's hand, and she drew strength from his touch. She was grateful to have him by her side.

'You're not . . .' Jan said, putting a hand to her mouth.

'No, Mum,' Anna said, shaking her head. 'I'm afraid we haven't got plans for any more children just yet.'

Bella was clambering on some furniture nearby, and Imogen brought her over. Imogen caught her sister's eye, nodding for her to continue, and silently offering moral support.

'But we have got something to tell you all,' Anna said. 'I'm sorry I haven't mentioned anything before. Things have been moving fast.' She paused. 'Me, Matteo and Bella have been very happy the last two years, living here, close to all of you, and running Vivien's. But the time's come for us to try something new.'

Jan looked at her husband, concerned, and he put his arm around her.

'We're going away – to Italy. We're not sure how long for yet – definitely for the summer, but perhaps longer. We've put down a deposit on a wonderful gelateria on the Amalfi coast. We want Bella to see Matteo's home for a while.'

Anna saw the sadness in her parents' eyes and had to fight back her tears as she waited for them to respond.

'Well, I think it's a great idea,' Imogen said, trying to break the tension. She nudged Finn.

'Absolutely,' Finn said. 'Congratulations.'

Jan's eyes started to fill with tears. 'But you can't . . .' she said. Evie offered her a handkerchief and she took it gratefully.

'It hasn't been an easy decision for us to make, and we are going to miss you all so much. We very much hope you'll come out and visit.'

'Just you try and stop us,' Imogen said.

Jan came over to her elder daughter and gave her a hug. 'I'm sorry. It's just a shock, that's all.'

Anna hugged her back. 'I should have said something. We just wanted to make sure everything was certain.'

Anna turned to her dad and Martin. 'Vivien's is going to

be in very safe hands,' she explained to them. 'Evie's agreed to take over the running of it, and we're delighted about that. So, Finn may be taking over her shop, but the arches won't be losing her just yet.'

Evie gave a bow, lightening the atmosphere for a moment.

Anna looked to her dad, hoping desperately that he wouldn't be as upset as her mum was. His expression was kind, and he managed a smile.

'We understand, love,' Tom said, coming over, putting an arm around her shoulders. 'A chance for Bella to see some of her father's country, and spend time with her other grand-parents. You know we'll miss her – we'll miss you all. But we can still be in touch, and we're not going anywhere. We'll always be here for you.'

Anna and Matteo hugged her parents, and Anna felt a wave of relief wash over her. Imogen and Finn joined them. Anna let loose all the tears she'd been bottling up, and Jan laughed to see that her daughter was crying even more than she was. Eventually, the group separated.

'OK,' Anna said, 'Well, there is one more thing.'

'Yes?' Tom asked, anxiously.

'Does anyone have room for a well-behaved dachshund?' Anna asked hopefully. She looked in Martin's direction.

'I thought you might ask that,' Martin said, laughing. 'Of course. It feels right that Hepburn should come back home for a while.'

Part Two

Chapter 14

When they arrived in Sorrento, on a Wednesday in mid-May, Anna and Matteo walked out into the sunlit square, Bella toddling beside them. Elegant shuttered apartments and cobblestones surrounded them, and as Anna breathed in she could smell the sweet aromas coming from the bakery. A wave of contentment and relief came over her, along with something else – a curious sensation of *déjà vu*.

'Here we are,' Matteo said, smiling at her. He pointed over at the ice cream shop and the apartment above it. 'That's it.'

A flock of birds rose from the fountain in the centre of the square and Bella squealed in delight. They flew up and over the pretty stone building that would soon be their home.

Anna smiled. 'It's strange – I almost feel like I've been here before.'

'Well, Carolina did show us around on the webcam,' Matteo said. 'And there are a lot of films set here—'

'It's more than that,' Anna said, watching her daughter run out across the square. 'I really feel like I know it.'

'Do you get a sense of her here?' Matteo asked, gently.

'Yes,' Anna said, tears springing to her eyes. She brushed them away. 'Happy tears,' she explained. 'I don't know if it's the stories Granny told us, coming back to me. Being here, somewhere that I know she was happy, it makes me feel closer to her.'

Matteo took her hand and squeezed it gently.

'And now we'll be making our own memories here,' Anna said.

Anna and Matteo went up into the apartment and out onto the balcony. From up there they could see the bright blue sea, sparkling under the hot Italian sun. Anna could just picture it: romantic meals out on the balcony on a balmy summer's evening, the bustle of the evening promenade playing out below them.

Bella ran into one of the bedrooms and slammed her chubby hands down on the bed delightedly. Anna looked at Matteo's face and saw the same expression of happiness, excitement at being back in his home country. Even though Sorrento was a new place for both of them, he had relaxed instantly when they arrived, conversing easily and laughing with everyone from the passport officials and taxi driver to the woman at the lettings office where they picked up their keys.

After a quick look round the flat, Anna was impatient to

see the shop premises. The three of them made their way downstairs to the shuttered shop. They stepped inside with trepidation and put on the lights.

Anna let out a sigh of relief as she took in their surroundings. The previous owner had made it cosy and welcoming with a pretty mural of hilltops and sea on the wall, and glass cabinets, a little dusty but in otherwise good condition.

'It's far bigger than it looked on the webcam,' Matteo said. 'It looks good.'

'Yes – it looks a whole lot better than Vivien's did at the start. There's lots of potential here.'

Excitement at the prospect bubbled up inside Anna.

'I can't wait to get started,' she said.

The next morning, Anna poured out some cereal for Bella, and Matteo made coffee with the silver stove-top coffee maker. It was 6 a.m. and the town was almost silent. When Anna had daydreamed about the move to Italy she'd imagined waking gently from a luxurious sleep, turning towards Matteo on their crisp white sheets and kissing him, the only sound from outside the waves on the shore. Somehow she'd edited out the early starts that Bella had brought to their household, and that now it would be necessary to get the shop up and running.

'So you're meeting with a supplier this morning,' Matteo said. 'You're sure you're OK to do that on your own?'

'Of course I am,' Anna said.

They took their breakfast out onto the balcony. Even first thing in the morning the air had an enveloping warmth, freshened by the sea breeze. From the balcony there was a good view of the square below – the cobblestones, the bakery opposite, the only place open at that early hour, selling bread and sweet buns. Beside it was a restaurant with a red awning – Luigi's. A flock of pigeons rose into the morning sky.

'I think I could get to like this place,' Anna said.

'You're not missing the rain?'

'Not one bit. Listen, before we get started on the shop, I just want to give Mum and Dad a ring, let them know how things are going.'

She picked up her phone and dialled through.

'Hey, Mum,' Anna said. She could hear her mother squealing excitedly in the background for her dad to come and join in the phone call.

'Hang on, love, just putting you on speakerphone,' she said. 'So you got there OK?'

'Yes, we're here and getting settled. Bella's having a great time. She keeps bringing out her bucket and spade and asking when we can get to the beach.'

'We miss you all already,' Jan said.

'Us too. But it's so great to finally be here.'

'You'll be going out to explore, will you?' Tom asked. 'Your granny always talked about the colourful houses, said they stretched all the way up the slopes. Well, that and the tiramisu.'

'We'll be doing a tour of the local desserts. That's our top priority.'

'Once we've opened the shop,' Matteo called out, from his seat beside Bella.

'Yes, yes,' Anna said, laughing. 'Matteo's insisting there's something more important than pudding, but obviously I'll put him straight on that.'

'Can you put Bella on the line?' Tom asked.

Anna passed her daughter the phone, and she gabbled into it excitedly.

Matteo came to stand beside Anna. She held his hand and squeezed it. Her family didn't feel that far away, after all.

Later that day, Matteo took Bella for a walk around the square while Anna started getting the shop ready. She raised the shutters and cleaned the slightly grimy windows with a bucket of soapy water. At least this was something she could manage on her own. She'd spent the morning trying to arrange an order with their supplier, her broken Italian meeting with his broken English, until the two of them had ended up thoroughly confused. Frustrated and disappointed, she'd had to call Matteo and get him to return from the supermarket to translate. It pained her to have to rely on him when she was used to placing orders herself in the UK. She was distracted from her task by a friendly male voice.

'*Benvenuta!*' it intoned loudly. Anna turned at the sound,

and saw a grey-haired man in a smart suit approaching the shop. 'Welcome,' the man said. 'My name is Luigi.'

'Anna,' she said, holding up her soapy hands apologetically.

He laughed. 'I am your new neighbour here in the square.' She was relieved to hear his English, a little stilted but far better than she would manage in Italian.

'Of course, the restaurant. I see!' Anna said, recalling the crowds of lively customers she'd seen the previous evening. 'I saw how busy it was last night.'

'Forty years I have been running it, and it's like that every night. I am getting old now but I think they'll have to carry me out of there.' He laughed.

'You and your family come from England?'

'I do. Matteo's from Siena, and we met in Florence. Our daughter is a bit of both.'

'Well, it is always a pleasure to see young people starting here in the square. They were a good couple, the people who used to run this gelateria, and people here were fond of them. But I think what they really wanted was to retire. Now it's your time.'

'Thanks. We have a week to get everything in order, but then we'll be open next Saturday. Will you come?'

'Of course,' he said enthusiastically. 'I would not miss it.'

'Great,' Anna said. 'We'll see you then.'

*

After lunch, Anna turned her attention to testing out the new menu that she and Matteo had just finalised. She tasted the strawberry sorbet on a small silver spoon – it was light and sweet, bursting with flavour. Absolutely delicious. It had been simple to make. She'd adapted a basic recipe, but there was something about the fruit here in Italy: it was tasty and rich from days soaking up the sun. She and Matteo had spent over an hour at the local fruit market that morning, picking up the ripest fruit and fresh mint to experiment with as they finalised their menu.

Matteo put his head round the door of the kitchen. 'Ooh, that looks good,' he said. 'Do you need a second opinion?'

'Of course,' Anna laughed. 'I've been testing this one pretty extensively actually. What do you think?'

He took a spoonful. 'It's good. But I think it needs a little something else. Texture. Could you put more chunks of fruit into it?'

Anna mulled it over. Perhaps it *was* a little too smooth. 'I'll try that. I'm also thinking it's all a bit healthy at the moment, not nearly indulgent enough – so I'm going to make up some more chocolate-dipped waffle cones to serve it in.'

'Perfect.'

'How are things going out there?'

'OK, the furniture we bought looks great outside. We've got room for four tables, and then people can always sit on the edge of the fountain when those are full. Seems like kids like playing around there.'

Anna peeked out into the restaurant. The pictures she and Matteo had brought over were up on the walls, and it was starting to feel as if it was really their place. 'I'm excited, Matteo. It feels good, doesn't it? Being here.'

'Vivien's will always be special – the first place we worked together. But that place was yours and Imogen's, and my family's shop is my family's. This one, this is all ours.'

'Let's take some time out this Sunday,' Anna said. 'Everything's shut then, anyway. We could go out as a family. Rent a car and drive down the coast.'

'I'd like that,' Matteo said. He wrapped an arm around her shoulders. She curled in towards him and kissed him gently on the mouth.

That Sunday they loaded up the car and Matteo drove out onto the coastal road. Bella chattered contentedly to herself in her car seat, oblivious to the hairpin bends.

Anna was starting to relax, looking out of the window and taking in the scenery. The Amalfi coast was every bit as spectacular as she'd hoped – villages and towns scattered over the hillsides, the houses stacked vertically in a way that made Anna feel dizzy. The sea was bright blue, glittering with the reflected sunlight. Vintage convertibles sped past them, and boats bobbed up and down on the water towards Capri. As much as Anna loved Britain's south coast, and felt a certain loyalty towards it – be it Brighton's characterful pebbles or the rugged cliffs and rock pools of Cornwall – this part of Italy was certainly more glamorous. The landscapes sent a tingle of excitement running over her skin.

They passed Positano, less a town than a cliff with houses on. Anna looked out at it, captivated. 'Can we stop here?' she said.

'Later,' Matteo said. 'There's somewhere else I think you'll like that I want to go to first.'

'OK,' Anna said. They continued west down the coast, and then parked. Having put Bella into a carrier, Matteo and Anna walked tentatively down a rocky path, ending up in a hidden cove. A couple of local families were there, sunbathing and dipping in and out of the water, but it still felt quiet, a haven away from the buzz of Sorrento.

With the sun high in the sky, Anna, Matteo and Bella sat by the water's edge, the tips of their toes touching the surf as each fresh wave came in. Bella gurgled and laughed as the waves tickled her. Anna put a hand gently on her daughter's wet hair and swept it back off her neck. They stayed there for most of the morning, collecting stones in Bella's new red bucket, and watching as the local children included her in their games.

That evening, Anna and Matteo were in the living room of their apartment. With Bella napping, and a pot full of freshly made tea between them, Anna was taking the opportunity to have another look at the marketing plan for the shop.

Matteo put down the book he'd been reading and laid his head on the sofa. He smiled at Anna. 'I'm just closing my eyes – for a minute or two,' he said, his voice almost a purr in its snooziness.

'Matteo!' she reprimanded him gently. He had curled up on his side and didn't look as if he'd be moving any time soon. 'OK, well, if you're going to sleep, can I use the iPad? I want to run some of these ideas I've had past Imogen.'

'Mmm-hmmm,' he said, pointing vaguely in the direction of the coffee table without lifting his eyelids.

She picked it up and typed out an email.

Hey Imogen,

So here we are! And you would love it. You MUST come and visit us all this time.

I've had some ideas for local marketing and would love your input . . .

She paused as an instant message popped up in the corner of the screen. She didn't recognise the username.

Matteo!

She froze for a moment and went to shut the messenger and return to her email.

Ciao Matteo!

136

Two new messages popped up in Italian and – with one eye on her sleeping boyfriend – she cast a glance at them, making sense of what she could. They had no secrets, she told herself – and he'd known she'd be on the iPad, after all. The language was simple and she was pretty sure she could understand it:

I've called you twice, why are you not answering?

Anna reread it, confused. She told herself not to jump to conclusions. It seemed quite direct, but it could be anything. Business, an old friend anxious to get in touch again.

Then,

I can't wait to talk to you.

Then another. Anna was less sure of the meaning and – feeling a little guilty as she did it – copied it over into Google translate:

Where are you? Does she have you doing the laundry or something? Changing nappies?

Anna flinched, surprised at the tone. She reread it. The messages were definitely about her.

Who was saying this? Fury rose in her.

You should tell her that's a mother's job.

She clicked on the message so she could see the avatar more clearly.

A woman with red-brown curly hair, and warm tanned skin.

Elisa. Her mother-in-law.

Chapter 15

In the reception area of the Elderberry Guesthouse, Martin was staring at his laptop a little blankly as he checked in some new guests. One of them repeated her name. 'Ah, yes. Here we are – Rodriguez. The Gatsby Suite.' He handed over the keys. 'I'll show you up.'

From the harried look in his eyes it was clear that Martin was finding the first day of business a little challenging, and Imogen stepped in.

'Let me, Uncle Martin,' she said, leading the guests upstairs confidently. 'The Gatsby Suite is a wonderful choice. How long are you staying in Brighton for?'

'We is here for …' The man glanced at his wife. '*Como se dice diez dias?*' he asked her.

'Ten days,' his wife said shyly. 'For visit friends.'

'Wonderful,' Imogen enthused. 'Well, you have come to the right place. My uncle cooks a fantastic English breakfast.'

She helped them take their bags into the newly decorated room, and they commented appreciatively at the tiny touches to the themed suite – the pretty antique mirrors and the long-stemmed cigarette holder on the dressing room table.

'If you need anything at all while you're here just let us know.'

'Thank you,' they chorused.

Back down in the reception area of the Elderberry Guesthouse, she glanced around for a sign of Martin. She couldn't see him in his usual spot over by the files, or in the kitchen.

She looked out into the garden, and saw that he was sitting on the terrace, talking with a woman with long, dark-red hair.

'Hey, Martin,' Imogen called out. 'They're all settled upstairs now.'

'That's great. Thanks, Imogen.'

The woman with Martin looked around, and her eyes, a bright green, settled on Imogen. She was strikingly attractive, with high cheekbones. She must have been a little younger than Martin, somewhere in her mid-forties. 'This is Clarissa. She's just arrived. Clarissa, this is Imogen, my niece. Vivien's granddaughter.'

'Hi,' Clarissa said, getting to her feet, her pale-blue dress swirling around her. 'It's nice to meet you, Imogen.'

There was a sadness in Clarissa's eyes, which Imogen was seeing only now that they were up close.

'Welcome,' Imogen said. 'Did you know Vivien?'

Clarissa shook her head. 'Not well. But I remember her. My mother used to bring me down to her shop when I was little – back when it was Sunset 99s. We'd stop by for a 99 Flake when we were in Brighton.'

'Were they friends, she and your mum?' Imogen asked.

'I think so. Something like that,' Clarissa said.

'That's nice. We miss Vivien so much. How did they know each other?'

Clarissa shook her head, and Imogen thought for a moment that she might cry. Martin looked over at his niece, clearly concerned about the same thing.

'I don't know, or at least not the details of it,' Clarissa said. 'That's why I came. I'm just so sorry I'm too late.'

At lunchtime, Imogen headed out to the beach and towards the Hove seafront and the shops under the arches. What had once been Evie's souvenir shop was now empty with the exception of piles of rubble and clouds of plaster dust. Things had moved quickly. Andy's father, a local builder, had stepped in to project-manage the conversion, and had advised them on how to avoid the need for planning permission. With Finn and Andy both working late into the evenings, the three of them had made a solid start in just a few days.

Finn was sweeping up, while Andy kept the surf school next door running.

'Hey,' Imogen said, giving Finn a hug.

'You probably shouldn't have . . .' he said, apologetically.

She looked down at her dark-blue top, now patched with white dust, and brushed at it. 'Oh, see what you mean.'

The room was bigger than it had seemed when the shop was full of sea-life inflatables and gaudy postcards, and knocking the wall down had made it and the surf school into a seamless space. 'You guys were certainly busy last night.'

'We did a lot. We're making progress, although we did find a couple of structural issues we hadn't predicted.'

'Can Andy's dad help with those?'

'Yes. He didn't seem overly concerned,' Finn said. 'We'll get there. But I'll be working late most nights this week. That's OK with you, isn't it?'

Imogen nodded. She could hardly complain when she was so often the one taking a long-haul flight away from him. 'That's fine.'

'How are things at the guesthouse?'

'Good,' she said. 'A new guest arrived this morning. A woman called Clarissa.'

'Settling in OK?'

'I think so, yes. She'd come to see Granny V, but then – well, she arrived and Martin had to explain that she'd had a wasted journey.'

'That's sad.'

'Yes. It is. But she was adamant that she wanted to stay

anyway. That she'd decided on the trip to Brighton and she'd make the most of it.'

'Well, that's good. And I'm sure she'll have a good time. Martin's worked so hard on the place.'

'Yes,' Imogen said, trying to forget the way that Clarissa had looked: the emptiness, the yearning sadness in her eyes. 'I'm sure you're right.'

Imogen headed over to the ice cream shop. It had been good to see Finn, even if just for a short while. With one thing and another, she might as well have been abroad somewhere. With the long hours he was working converting the shop building, they sometimes got to catch up only last thing at night before bed. Sometimes Imogen wondered if she should ask him about it – her mum's suggestion that he might propose. But then it seemed easier to carry on, as if none of it had happened.

Evie was busy cleaning tables when Imogen arrived. The post-lunch lull was the perfect time for Imogen to run through things with her and they covered most of it quite quickly. Mid-afternoon, a young couple came in.

'Why don't you serve those customers, and if you have any last questions I'll be here?' Imogen said to her.

Evie looked over at the young couple coming in through the door. They walked excitedly over to the glass counter, the woman admiring the array of ice creams in front of them.

'Hello, Evie,' the man said. 'How come you're working here?'

'I've had a career change, Ben,' she said proudly. 'It's never too late.'

'Nice one. Well, it's great to see you – I was sorry to see your shop shut.'

'Thank you,' Evie said graciously. 'Times change. What can I get you?'

'Can we have two of your Super Sundaes, please?' the woman asked.

'Coming right up,' Evie said confidently. 'Take a seat and I'll bring them over to you.'

Imogen whispered to her. 'You remember how to make those, right?'

Evie tilted her head slightly, remembering. 'One scoop of praline and one of mocha, with white chocolate sauce and hazelnut sprinkles – that right?'

'Spot on,' Imogen said. She leaned back on the counter as Evie prepared the ice creams.

That week Imogen had been getting up early to prepare the ice creams to Anna's recipes, coaching Evie as she went, but watching Evie now – her candyfloss-pink hair swept up into a bun and her gingham apron on, deftly putting the sundaes together – she had a feeling that she'd be able to take a backseat with the ice cream shop from now on. Evie seemed to pick up the recipes effortlessly – and she also had the

143

advantage of knowing most of the locals, none of whom minded waiting a few extra minutes while she double-checked Anna's recipe book.

Over the course of the morning, Evie perfected the heart-shaped swirl on a flat white, and Vivien's trademark drizzle of chocolate sauce on the sundaes, with a perfectly placed hand-made wafer.

'I don't think you're going to need my help much around here after all, do you?' Imogen said.

'Let's see. It's good to know that you'll be on the end of the phone, but I think I'm getting the hang of it now.'

'Incredibly well,' Imogen replied. 'You're a natural.'

'I'm ready to give new things a go, that's all. I'll never be too old for that.'

Anna had been right to trust her gut instinct, Imogen thought to herself. Everything was working out just fine.

Chapter 16

'Dear Mum, Dad and Imogen,' Anna wrote. 'I know it's a long way ... but we couldn't resist inviting you to the launch of our shop.

She put the card inside a silver envelope and wrote her parents' address on it. She slipped the invitation inside:

Anna, Matteo and Bella
invite you to the opening of:

The Little Ice Cream Shop
in the Square

Saturday 5th June, from midday.
Free cones until 3 p.m.
Come and enjoy some Italian gelato
with a splash of English elegance!

'Come and taste some of this one,' Anna said to Matteo. 'I think I've struck gold. And just in time for our launch tomorrow.'

Matteo took a spoonful of the peach granita Anna had just made, and nodded in appreciation. 'Not bad.'

Anna smiled with pride. Matteo was more than just the man in her life: he was also one of the best food critics around, and he didn't hesitate to let her know when one of her creations needed more work.

'Those peaches from the market are something else,' Anna said.

'I told you.'

Anna put the tray in the glass counter.

'I wonder what everyone's going to make of our flavours,' she said.

'Well – not long till we find out.'

'That'll be Carolina,' Matteo said later that day, hearing the knock at the front door and dashing over to the window. 'Hello!' he called down to his sister.

'Lina!' Bella exclaimed, catching hold of what was happening. 'Lina!'

'Let's go and see your auntie,' Anna said, scooping her daughter up into her arms.

Matteo opened the door and Carolina's face lit up when she saw her brother and his family. '*Bellissima!*' she cried, darting over and taking Bella into her arms. 'You've grown so much.' She covered her niece in kisses.

She enveloped her brother in a loving hug.

'So – I had a look though the window of the shop, very *chi-chi*,' Carolina said, appreciatively. 'You've done a really nice job.'

'Thank you. Your hair, Caro – I love it,' Anna said, taking in Carolina's new bob.

Carolina touched her hair. 'That's kind of you. Yes, I've had it long for years – I felt like a change.'

'It suits you,' Anna said.

'I needed something to cheer myself up to be honest. These past few months . . . well . . .' Her voice tailed off.

'Everything all right?' Anna asked.

'Yes, it's fine. Maybe later.' She forced a smile. 'Right now I want to be happy and play with little Bella,' she said, tickling her. Bella emitted a peal of easy laughter.

'OK, sure,' Anna said, gently.

A fresh coastal breeze drifted in through the doorway, reminding Anna that she was far from home. 'Shall we go out into the square?' she said.

Matteo and his sister led the way and they sat on the edge of the fountain while Bella played nearby.

'This coast is spectacular, isn't it?' Carolina said. 'What do you think, Anna? Worth the trip?'

Anna shook her head. 'Absolutely. Every view is like a postcard.'

'I love it out here,' Carolina said. There was a distance in her gaze, though, as if her mind were elsewhere. 'The people, they're so much more relaxed than where we're from. You'll have to come down to the summer house, you get a fantastic view over the sea, and out to the villages, those pretty colourful houses.'

'Sounds beautiful. We will. Where's Filippo today?' Anna asked.

Carolina shook her head and her eyes took on a sheen of tears. 'That's a long story.'

Her brother put his arm around her shoulders, and hugged her. 'What's he done?'

'Another time.' There was pain in her eyes. 'Tell me about the shop. When are you opening?'

'This Saturday,' Anna said.

'A few things still to organise,' Matteo said. 'But we're nearly there, aren't we, Anna?'

'Yes. Almost. You'll come to the opening, won't you?'

'Of course! I wouldn't miss it for the world,' Carolina said.

'Thanks for finding this place for us,' Anna said.

'My pleasure.'

'I think it's going to be a good summer,' Matteo said. He held his sister close. 'We'll make it a good summer.'

On Saturday, Anna and Matteo stood behind the counter of the ice-cream shop, watching the crowd of eager customers build. They'd spent the week putting up posters around town, announcing the opening, and talking to as many locals and tourists as they could. Anna had wondered if they might encounter resistance to the change – she knew that the old gelateria had been popular – but it turned out people were really curious and ready for a new place. A queue snaked out into the square. At the front of it was Luigi, the owner of the restaurant opposite.

'What would you recommend?' he asked.

'You know what I love – this mojito ice lolly,' Anna said, mischievously. 'It hasn't got *that* much alcohol in it.'

'A lol-ly?' Luigi said, stumbling with the word. 'I do not know what that is – but mojitos I am certainly familiar with. I'd like one of those, please.'

He tasted it and raised an eyebrow appreciatively. 'I like it.'

A young woman came to the counter and rattled off her order in Italian. Anna struggled to catch hold of her meaning.

Luigi translated for her. 'She would like the fruits of the forest, two scoops.'

'Thanks,' she said quietly to Luigi, serving up the ice cream and passing it to her new customer.

'If you're going to be staying here for a while, I think there is someone you might like to meet. Maria!' he called out to a woman seated in the corner.

The woman joined them, and greeted Anna. Anna recognised her from the grocery shop, had seen her picking up eggs and milk in the morning, chatting to the staff with an easy familiarity. She was in her late forties or early fifties, with dark hair that had gone grey in strands around her face, lending a certain grace to her features.

'Maria is the best Italian teacher you'll find around here, and her rates are very reasonable,' he said.

'He's flattering me,' she said. 'But it's true that I do give classes. I live in the house over the square, the one with the blue door. Just give me a knock if you're interested.'

'I will,' Anna said, smiling. It would do her good to immerse herself a little more in the language, and it had never really worked out having Matteo teach her. 'That would be nice.'

That afternoon, Anna and Matteo served up old favourites and new flavours to one person after another, sending a steady stream of satisfied customers out into the square. Carolina had helped them put out wooden furniture painted pistachio, pale pink and a pastel blue in the square, and was serving the tables. People crowded around the fountain, perching on the edge, dipping their little plastic spoons into friends' sorbets and ice creams for a taste.

Matteo whispered in Anna's ear, 'I don't want to speak too soon ...'

'But it seems to be going quite well, doesn't it?' she

finished for him. 'So much for the slow start and adjustment period we were expecting. It looks like we've managed to hit the ground running here.'

At the end of their first week of trading, Anna lowered the shutters on the shop with a deep sense of pride. She and Matteo had slipped naturally into the same way of working together that they'd honed in Vivien's, and the number of repeat customers to the shop was building. Faces were becoming familiar to her, and that helped her to feel at home – and, what was more, they seemed to be particularly enjoying the more experimental recipes that she and Matteo had brought to the menu.

'It's all going well, isn't it?' she said to Matteo.

He nodded and gave her a hug. 'It's great.'

'I'm glad we came,' she said.

'Yes, and I can't wait to show it off to Mamma,' he said, proudly.

'When is she coming to visit, again?' Anna asked. She had a flash of the message she'd seen on Matteo's iPad, but forced herself to put it aside. She didn't want to cause friction by raising it.

'Next week.'

'Great,' Anna said. It would be fine, she told herself. It was only for a few days.

Chapter 17

While the guesthouse was quiet, Imogen sorted through some old files on Vivien's shelves. In one, she found some photos of Vivien and Evie – from the early days of starting their two shops, back in the 1960s. Then there was one of the two of them, arm in arm, with what must have been the island of Capri in the background. Tucked in behind it was a map of the Amalfi coast, similar to the one she'd framed, but this one had crosses marked on it in pen – places she and Evie had visited together, presumably. Vivien had never forgotten that holiday, Imogen thought. A few days in the sun had stayed with her till the end. Imogen tacked the photo up by the reception desk.

'Imogen, have you got a moment?'

She looked up at her uncle Martin, standing by the desk, glancing around uncomfortably.

'Sure, what is it?'

'It's . . .' He lowered his voice to a whisper. 'It's Clarissa.'

'Oh, yes?' Imogen said. 'I noticed she was still here. What's up?'

'I thought she'd just be staying a couple of days. She said at first that she had things to get back to. She's got her home in London, and she mentioned a job . . .'

'But so long as she's paying, that's not a bad thing, surely?'

'No, of course not. She's paying on time, and she's very welcome. It just seemed surprising.'

'Well, people change their minds. It's nice that she likes this place enough to want to stay. I can't really see the problem.'

'It's not a problem as such. Just seems strange – she rarely goes out, Imogen. She's been in the room, or wandering around the guesthouse, almost the whole time she's been here.'

'Right.'

'And it's the nighttimes.'

'What happens then?'

'I've had a couple of comments from other guests. Not complaints, exactly – everyone seems to like her – but people have noticed that she walks around a lot during the night. I even found her in the kitchen the other day, at about three a.m. She seemed dazed.'

'That does sound a bit odd. How does she seem, in herself?'

'That's the thing. The reason I'm concerned, really. She

seems very low, and sad. I've tried to ask her how she is, once or twice, and it's like she looks right through me.'

Imogen reached a sympathetic hand out to her uncle. 'Let me have a word with her.'

Imogen knocked at the door of the Gatsby Suite gently, and waited for a reply, not really knowing quite what to expect.

Clarissa opened the door wearing a floor-length silk kimono, her auburn hair tied up loosely. She had a natural elegance that seemed to transcend age, but that same melancholy air hung over her. 'Hello, Imogen,' she said, politely. 'How nice to have a visitor. Come in.'

Imogen stepped inside the room. Clarissa motioned for her to sit down, and she took a seat by the window. 'I'm sorry to bother you. But I just wanted to check everything was OK.'

Her cheeks coloured. 'Your uncle said something ... about the other night.'

'He didn't send me ...' Imogen said.

Clarissa bit her lip. 'You don't need to explain. He must think I'm awfully strange. I'm so embarrassed that he saw me walking around the other night. I shouldn't have gone into those rooms.'

'He's just concerned, that's all.'

'I'm not surprised. He must be wondering why I'm still here, and, for that matter, why I'm still staying in a B&B,

barely going out, when I could be living in a house of my own.'

'I suppose so,' Imogen said. 'A bit.'

'I have a house, up in London, like I told Martin. But I don't want to be there now. My stepfather died a month ago, you see, and he was all I had.'

'I'm so sorry to hear that.'

Clarissa looked down, her eyes filling with tears. 'I knew it was coming. Mum died when I was young, so he and his parents were the ones who brought me up.'

'It must be a lot to get used to.'

'It is. And it's not just losing him. The thing is, he told me a few things before he died. And I suppose they're just starting to sink in.'

'And being here helps?'

'Yes. It does.' Spots of pink came to Clarissa's cheeks. 'It's calm here. And I suppose it feels a little like home.'

Imogen walked back down the guesthouse stairs, wondering how to explain the situation to Martin. He looked up at her eagerly from his spot behind the reception desk.

'How did it go?' he asked, getting to his feet.

'OK, I think,' Imogen said.

'Should I do something, say something?' Martin said, anxious.

'Just keep doing what you're doing,' Imogen said. 'She's

just lost her stepfather, and it sounds like she doesn't have much in the way of family. I don't really understand why, but she says just being here is helping her.'

'Right,' Martin said. 'Well, I know what Mum would do if she were still alive.'

'Let her stay, and bring her tea, until she's strong again. That's what she always did for people, isn't it?'

At lunchtime, Imogen went out into the front garden of the guesthouse and called Finn. He picked up, banging and construction noises in the background.

'Hey there,' she said, sitting down on the wall, ready for chat.

'Hi, Imo.'

'How's it going over there?'

'What was that?' Finn shouted back, over the noise.

'*I said how's it . . .*' She glanced back through the window, where her uncle Martin was walking around the living room. 'Don't worry, it's not important.'

'I'm outside now, bit quieter,' Finn said. 'Everything OK at the guesthouse?'

'Yes,' she said. And it was true – everything was going smoothly. It was only her email inbox – stubbornly empty after the emails to photography contacts that she'd sent out – that was nagging at her. 'You?'

'Really well, thanks. As you can probably hear.'

'Listen, I was thinking. Do you fancy going out for dinner tonight?' Imogen said. 'Try out that new dim sum place in town?'

'Imo ... I'd love to. But, if we're going to stay on schedule, Andy and I really need to use every minute we have. We're going to be working late tonight.'

'OK, sure,' Imogen said. 'No worries. I've got plenty to be getting on with, anyway.'

'Everything all right with you, though?'

'Yes. Fine.'

She wished he'd say something. Ask her again. So that the white lie wouldn't be left hanging between them like that.

In the end it was someone calling out to Finn from the building site that broke the silence.

'I'd better go,' he said.

'Right – sure,' Imogen said. 'Well, I'll see you at home, then.'

'See you, then.'

She hung up, feeling empty – the opposite of how she usually felt after talking to Finn. Phone conversations, she thought to herself. They were never the best way to talk. She was much more of a face-to-face person. Next time she saw him it would be fine.

Imogen went back into the guesthouse. In the living room, Clarissa was sitting by the bay window in a patch of sunlight, looking through a book. She wore a thick cream cardigan over her top and jeans, and her legs were curled up under her.

'What's that you're reading?' Imogen asked, gently.

'One from the shelf. *A Room with a View*. It's good so far. Your grandmother had a lot of books.'

'She did. Although, to be honest, she had a habit of starting them and then leaving them halfway, caught up in cooking, or chatting to a neighbour over the fence. She loved books and films, but real life was what really got her.'

Clarissa smiled, and, for the first time since she'd arrived, she looked almost relaxed.

'She'd always give us ice creams for free,' Clarissa said. 'Me and Mum. Did she ever talk to you about my mum? Emma she was called. Wilkinson.'

Imogen thought back, but the name wasn't familiar. 'She might have mentioned something. My memory isn't great.'

Her eyes grew more distant then.

'I'll leave you in peace,' Imogen said.

Clarissa nodded. 'See you later.'

Imogen headed back to the reception desk. She sorted through some of the junkshop frames she'd picked up for the guesthouse, and found one to fit the photo of Evie and Vivien. She put it up beside the large map.

She went back to the things she'd found in the old files, pulled out the smaller map and found a frame for that. As she turned it over to put it in, she noticed a name scribbled in pen on the back: 'Sr L. Esposito – Piazza Tasso, 30.'

She turned the map back over, but there was no further note there, nothing apart from a cross that she could see the name linked to. She thought of the postcard Anna had sent her, with her new address. Searching across the street plan, she saw that the two addresses were only a few hundred yards from each other.

She put the frame away, folded the map back up and put it away in the bureau drawer. Her grandmother had always been open with them, but Imogen was starting to suspect that there were some things she had held back from saying. She had made her choices, though – and to pry, now, didn't seem right.

Chapter 18

Matteo took over the running of the ice cream shop in the early afternoon, and Anna went over to Maria's house across the square. She knocked on the door, with a slight feeling of trepidation. She'd warmed instantly to Maria when Luigi introduced them at the shop, but she felt nervous about speaking Italian – her understanding was quite good but the words she wanted to say so often escaped her. But she steeled herself – she knew that she needed to improve her language skills, and this seemed like a good opportunity.

'Signora Anna,' Maria said brightly, as she answered the door. 'Come in.'

'Thank you,' Anna said awkwardly, in English.

'*Italiano*,' Maria said, firmly.

Anna felt suitably reprimanded. There wasn't much point coming for an Italian lesson if you were going to talk in English, was there? And she needed to learn quickly.

Maria led her inside to the living room, asking simple questions and smiling in appreciation at Anna's effort as she haltingly replied in Italian with the aid of her phrasebook.

'My mother-in-law is coming tomorrow. She speaks good English, but I want to be able to talk to her in Italian.'

'Good, well, I can help you with that.'

Anna put her phrasebook down on the coffee table between them.

'You won't need that,' Maria said. 'I'm going to teach you the Italian you'll really need to know.'

They spent the hour going round the kitchen, Anna learning the names of fruits and vegetables, the equipment she used every day to make sorbet, the things in the fridge. It was vocabulary she heard Matteo use all the time, but his early attempts to teach Anna had fallen flat – she felt embarrassed in front of him, unable at this stage to master the pronunciation and aware that she sounded like a hapless tourist. With Maria it was different: she felt relaxed about making mistakes.

At the end of the class, they arranged to meet again. 'I think you're going to learn very quickly,' Maria said, confidently.

'I hope so,' Anna said, the Italian phrase tripping off her tongue. With those words, she felt as if she had in her hands the seeds of a new life.

*

Anna had come back to the ice cream shop that afternoon full of confidence and enthusiasm, and had even practised some Italian with Matteo over dinner in their apartment. She felt ready to make a new start with Elisa, on a more equal footing, and, when her mother-in-law came into the ice cream shop the next day, she readied herself to use some of the new phrases she'd learned.

'Bella, my love!' Elisa was cradling her granddaughter in her arms and coming into the shop, her son by her side. 'Welcome to Italy!'

She covered Bella's chubby arms and legs with kisses as she walked. 'Thank you for bringing this precious thing to Italy,' she said to Matteo.

Anna smiled politely, and formed the sentence she wanted to say in Italian.

'It's good to see you, Elisa. Can I get you a coffee? You must be tired after the journey.'

'Ah, she speaks Italian,' Elisa said. 'Or at least she's trying,' she said to Matteo. 'Yes, a coffee, please,' she said to Anna.

Anna got the stove-top coffee maker from the side.

'A strong one,' she added. 'I want to hear everything, but of course we have plenty of time for that,' Elisa said to her son.

'Is it just the weekend you're staying?' Anna asked.

'Just the weekend?' Elisa said, laughing. 'Of course not.'

Anna looked at Matteo for clarification.

'Mamma, I haven't told Anna yet . . .' Matteo started. Anna just caught the meaning of the Italian.

'That's OK, then I can be the one to share the *marvellous* news!' Elisa said, switching to English.

Anna felt increasingly uneasy.

'Mamma will be staying with Carolina . . .' Matteo said.

'I'll be here for the whole summer!' Elisa exclaimed. 'Isn't it wonderful?'

Anna felt the breath go out of her. *What?* She glared at Matteo as discreetly as she could. He shrugged his shoulders and mouthed, 'I'm sorry.'

'Matteo's father is going to run the business on his own for a while. And Filippo's been so generous, paying for the summer house, and even giving us some spending money. I really couldn't be luckier with my son-in-law, could I, Matteo? He'd doing so well at the moment. Did Carolina tell you? One of the richest men in the region. We're so proud of him.'

Anna struggled to take it all in. Why would Matteo have kept this from her?

'I need to use the toilet,' Elisa said. 'Is it . . .?'

'Just through there.' Matteo pointed to the back of the shop.

'It's great to be here,' Elisa said, clapping her hands together. 'And I can see already, from the look of the shop, that you're going to need my expert help around here.'

*

163

As Anna and Matteo set the table for their dinner that night, Anna was stonily quiet.

'Come on, Anna, we have to talk about this,' Matteo insisted.

'I'm fine,' Anna said, but inside she was seething.

'Look, I'm sorry I didn't explain earlier,' he said. 'But don't you think it could be good? Mamma can help out with Bella, maybe help with some of the Italian queries when I'm not around.'

'We don't need help,' Anna said, her resolve to keep her feelings to herself snapping. 'And I'm learning Italian, so soon I won't be completely useless.'

'I didn't mean that—'

'Sorry,' Anna said, trying to steady her emotions. 'I didn't mean to snap. But, Matteo, I thought we said we were doing this on our own. I thought that was the whole reason we decided to come here, to Sorrento.'

'We still will be doing it alone,' Matteo said. 'OK, so Mamma might have the occasional bit of advice, but we don't have to take it.'

'Right,' Anna said. Maybe she was overreacting. Maybe she should just accept what was happening, learn to live with the new situation. Matteo was right, of course, that there were some benefits. 'It's different from what I was expecting, that's all,' Anna said. 'I thought she'd be coming to visit rather than staying for weeks, probably months. Why didn't you mention that her plans had changed?'

'I don't know,' Matteo said. 'I meant to. I was waiting for the right moment – and then, before I knew it, she was here.'

Anna looked at him sternly, but in a moment his soft brown eyes had made it almost impossible for her to continuing being annoyed with him.

'I couldn't say no. She just wants to spend time with Bella, and see what we're doing with the shop, that's all. She won't get in the way.'

Anna took a deep breath. Perhaps that really would be the case. But, somehow, she couldn't help but doubt it.

Chapter 19

At home, Imogen was sitting on the sofa in the living room with her laptop, typing notes into her online calendar.

Saturday 2 p.m. – Brighton Pavilion – The Rogersons' Wedding ceremony, followed by a reception in the gardens

Sunday 10 a.m. – Baby Joseph, studio shots –

The bookings for weddings, and baby portraits, were starting to build up in her work diary – Lauren had a surplus of projects, so had started passing Imogen the ones she couldn't fit in. It was a good opportunity to broaden her experience, yet Imogen was still struggling to feel enthusiastic about it.

Esposito ... The name drifted back into her mind. Why had that name and address been written on the map? It was

Vivien's handwriting, that was certain. Had she visited someone out there, out in Sorrento, where Anna was right now?

A Facebook notification distracted her, and she clicked to
open it. Luca. Now, there was someone she hadn't thought
about in a long while. Tanned, with dark hair – his Italian her-
itage coming through even though his accent was pure
American west coast. She hovered over 'Ignore' – two and a
half years had passed since she had been with Luca, an extended
holiday romance before she met Finn. It hadn't ended well –
Imogen's plans had changed after her grandmother's death, and,
while she understood Luca's hurt, he'd chosen to act it out by
getting together with a good friend of hers.

Something stopped her clearing the screen, though.
Enough time had passed, hadn't it? And she had enough
friends on the site that she'd barely shared any real life expe-
riences with – at least he had, for a while, been important to
her, and they'd had a connection once. Ignoring him seemed
petty. It wasn't as if they'd be chatting away or anything. She
clicked to accept.

Imogen took her bike and cycled down to the ice cream
shop. She needed some fresh air and company. She wasn't
used to time spent on her own at home, and she wasn't sure
she really liked it. That morning, the café was heaving with
customers. She looked on as Evie weaved expertly in and out
of the tables, delivering orders with grace and ease.

'Imogen, hi!' Evie called out, waving over.

'Hi,' Imogen said. 'I was just calling by to see how things were going. Have you been getting on OK?'

'Yes, brilliantly,' Evie said. 'Run off my feet as you can see.'

'Do you need help?' Imogen asked. She had a gap before she needed to get to the studio.

'Thanks for the offer,' Evie said confidently. 'But no. I have to admit I'm rather enjoying running the show here. It's what you and Anna pay me for, after all. And you have your wonderful photos to be getting on with.'

Well-meant as they were, Evie's words stung. Right now Imogen felt as if she might never take a photo again. Something had gone from her. The spark that drove her up and out to document the world around her in a way no one ever had before. To create beauty. She wondered if it would ever come back.

'Well, it's great to see how well you're doing,' Imogen said. 'Don't let me distract you.'

She walked her bike over to the surf shop, and Andy came over to the doorway to meet her, the work still in full flow.

'You've just missed Finn, I'm afraid,' Andy said. 'He's driven to the big hardware shop to stock up. Five minutes ago it must have been.'

'Oh, that's OK,' Imogen said, trying to hide her disappointment. 'I'll catch up with him later.'

'But listen, I'm glad you're here,' Andy said, 'because we

just found a small box of things that are yours. Well, your grandma's. I showed them to Evie – seeing as they were in her shop – and she said Vivien had left them for her, but she'd never looked at them. Said we could throw them – that there was nothing valuable. Sounds bad, but she was very upset, so I suppose perhaps it was that she didn't want to bring up the memories again. Anyway, it didn't seem right to chuck them out.'

'Thanks. Yes,' Imogen said, hurt and confused that Evie wouldn't have mentioned it. 'I'll take them.'

Andy went inside and returned with an A4-sized cardboard box, sealed with brown tape.

'Tell Finn I came by,' she said.

Imogen walked with her bike a little further down the beach, then got a drink and sat down on a bench. She looked at the box, then hesitated a moment. It didn't feel like it was hers to open.

In the end, curiosity overtook her, and she peeled back the brown tape. Inside, there was a letter, on pale-blue paper. She didn't recognise the handwriting.

Dear Vivien,

Thank you for writing to me. Of course I remember that summer. Ours was truly a big love, the strongest love I've ever known.

169

Imogen nearly choked. This wasn't a letter from her grand-father, that much was clear. And the date: 2010. It wasn't long before her grandmother had died. Every instinct in her told her to put the letter away, pretend she'd never found it. Undo what she'd done. But she'd gone too far already – she had to read on. Nausea gnawing at her stomach, she forced herself to read the rest of it.

I've never been happier than I was in those days we were together. That time made me the very best man I could be.

But what does passion and love mean, if you lose your family in the process? Back then I couldn't take that risk. I know what you are saying, that sometimes it's just the time that isn't right – maybe that's true. Back then I couldn't risk losing my family, but now that the children have grown up, well, things are different. It's hard for me to revisit those feelings – I shut the door long ago. I don't know why I'm saying all this to you now.

So, I'll be brave. I'm sending a photo of me, as I am now – old, a little tired, mainly happy. You asked me whether I would be willing to meet up again. I've given it a lot of thought.

Yes, yes I would.

She lifted the letter with a sense of urgency, and found a photo underneath. A man in his late fifties or early sixties, grey hair and a warm smile – wearing a smart shirt, against the backdrop of what looked like an olive grove.

There was no name, no sign-off. She flipped over the envelope and looked at the postmark that crisscrossed the Italian stamp: Sorrento.

Imogen tried to take in the words she'd just read, but her head was spinning. She couldn't make sense of it. Her grandmother and grandfather had been deeply in love. Even after Stanley died, Vivien had kept his memory alive. Had it really been a lie – all of it?

Imogen put the letter away, wishing she'd never opened it. Vivien had always told Imogen and Anna to be true to themselves. Now her words rang hollow.

Chapter 20

In Sorrento, the ice cream shop had been up and running for two weeks, and Anna was just starting to relax. She and Matteo had been pleasantly busy every day since the shop opened, juggling food preparation with serving tables, and they had a steady stream of friendly customers. She felt buoyed up, and, with so much to organise for the business, she'd found it easier than she'd expected to avoid crossing paths with Elisa. But that Monday morning, with Matteo in town getting supplies, and Bella and Carolina playing out in the square, she found herself alone in the shop with her mother-in-law.

Anna concentrated on the quince sorbet she was preparing.

'That's interesting, the way you're doing that,' Elisa said.

'We prepared the fruit last night, so it doesn't take as long,' Anna said, brightly.

'Personally, I prefer to do all the preparation in one go,' Elisa said. 'I'm sure everything stays fresher that way.'

Anna kept quiet and carried on getting the ice ready.

'I could show you,' Elisa said.

'Thanks for the offer,' Anna said, diplomatically. 'But I've kind of got used to doing it like this, and, to be honest, I'm happy with it.'

'It's not very ... Well, it's not very Italian, is it? When we talk about sorbets, we think of the granita, with chunks of ice in it. Your sorbets – the lemon, the tangerine – they're very smooth.' Elisa shook her head. 'I'm not saying they don't taste good, and admittedly the tourists seem to like them, but they are not traditional recipes, are they?'

'We're not a traditional shop,' Anna said, politely but firmly. 'Of course we respect the Italian way of making ice cream – and we have plenty of gelato on our menu, but we want to bring in a mix of new ideas too.'

'Your customers will soon tire of the novelty,' Elisa said, shaking her head. 'Take it from me. I have over ...'

Anna didn't need to hear the rest, she already knew it by heart: Elisa had over thirty years of experience in the ice cream business. She and her husband Giacomo knew Italian customers better than anyone else in the country.

'I know your grandmother had a shop, so perhaps you have a little of the history too, but it's *different*, what we do over here,' she said.

'I appreciate that,' Anna said. Her patience was starting to fray. 'Elisa, we have our own way of ...'

Matteo came back into the shop and Anna let what she was saying trail off.

'Hi,' she said, feeling a wave of relief.

'Darling!' Elisa exclaimed. 'Where have you been? I seem to be upsetting your wife again. She is always so very sensitive.'

'I was getting some supplies for the shop, Mamma. I told you that.' He put the bags up on the counter and started to unpack. 'And I'm sure Anna's fine. Right?'

He put his arm around Anna and looked at her.

She nodded, but looked pointedly at him to show her discontent.

'Actually, Matteo, I wonder if you and your Mum might need to pop back to the shops,' she said.

'What do you mean? I got everything . . .' he said, surveying the food he'd just bought.

'Oh there are *definitely* a few more things.' She widened her eyes and glanced at Elisa. 'Just a quick trip to the local shops. That's all.'

Matteo got the hint at last. 'Right. Yes. Mamma. Let's go and get some fresh air.'

Anna relished the relative calm of the shop, once Elisa and Matteo had left. Her cheeks still burned with the frustration of not being able to tell her mother-in-law exactly what she felt, but she took a couple of deep breaths to settle her nerves. Elisa was only trying to help, she told herself. She could handle it, keep her feelings in, so as not to upset her mother-in-law or Matteo. Provided she saw Elisa only in small doses, that seemed possible.

She set about serving the customers, German and English families and a trickle of local children. Around midday, Luigi came into the ice cream shop, smiling warmly.

'Good morning, Signora,' he said to Anna. 'How is everything today?'

'Good, thanks, Luigi. And you?'

'Excellent, actually,' he said. 'Today is a good day. Which is why I have come in for one of your ice creams, to celebrate. Pistachio and chocolate, please.'

'With pleasure,' she said, picking up the silver ice cream scoop. 'What is it that you're celebrating?'

'My daughter called me – she has just got a job in Naples,' he said. 'She is going to be a children's doctor there.'

'That's wonderful news,' Anna said. 'This one's on the house, in that case. You and your wife must be very proud.'

'Oh, no,' Luigi said, shaking his head. 'It's just me.'

'I'm sorry,' Anna's cheeks coloured. 'I assumed . . . Silly of me.'

'Don't worry. Their mother died a long time ago. I've raised my son and daughter for most of their lives.'

'You've never married again?'

He shook his head, and a weariness seemed to come over him. 'Life can be complicated, Anna.'

She passed him the ice cream cone. 'Of course.'

'And it moves so fast, doesn't it? But you and Matteo, with your beautiful daughter, you seem to have a good life. The *bella* Bella. Children are a gift, Anna. Once they are here they become the most important thing in your life.'

Anna smiled. 'Yes. Bella definitely insists that she's that.'

He paused. 'But I did not come in here to tell you my life story,' he said, the tone of his voice lighter. 'Where are your family today?'

'Oh, Matteo's with his mother,' she said. 'They've gone to the shops to get us some supplies.'

'Good, good. I only just heard – that your Matteo is a Bonomi. You are part of one of the most famous ice cream-making families in the country.'

'Yes, we're very lucky.'

'It must be helpful to have his parents' advice.'

'In a way,' Anna said, raising her eyebrows just a fraction. Luigi spotted her meaning at once.

'I see. A mixed blessing,' he laughed. 'That's families for you.'

Matteo came back to the shop later that afternoon. Anna kissed him, but she sensed he was holding back. When she pulled away he didn't meet her eyes, and seemed distracted.

'Everything been OK here?' he said, his voice flat and matter-of-fact.

176

'Good, thanks,' Anna said. 'Luigi popped in earlier, then we had a run of schoolchildren come in. Just now, we had a couple of Spanish backpackers, said they'd heard about our cappuccino lollies on a train coming here, that we're the talk of the interrailing crowd.'

'That's great.' He glanced away, his gaze unsettled.

'*I* thought so. A new stream of customers, potentially. Are you all right?'

'It's Mamma. We talked when we were out.'

'Oh, yes?'

'She's concerned about what we're doing here – she thinks we're pushing the boundaries a bit too much, too soon. People around here were used to a classic Italian gelateria, and what we're running here isn't that.'

'And we never wanted it to be,' Anna said, trying to remain calm. 'We've said that all along. Our plan is to do something new out here, take chances. And things have been going really well so far.'

'I know . . . but you know how it is.' Matteo gave a shrug of resignation. 'Mamma and Papà think we're going against the family traditions by diversifying.'

'And what? You agree with them?' Anna felt her cheeks grow hot.

'They might have a point. After all, what we've been doing for a couple of years, they've been doing for—'

'Over thirty,' Anna said shortly.

'There's no need to be like that,' Matteo said. 'She's on our side. They both are.'

'I'm sorry. But Matteo, it's our business. We don't need to get everything right all the time. The plan was always to do this our way.'

'And we will,' Matteo said, his voice soft. 'But perhaps with a couple of changes. That's all.'

The next day, while Matteo was outside looking after Bella, and the shop was quiet, Anna called Imogen. They spoke for a while about what had been happening in Sorrento. Anna told her about Elisa coming to live in the summer house with Carolina, and how she had started to interfere in things.

'Do you think I'm being oversensitive?' Anna asked. She felt too emotionally involved to judge the situation for herself any more.

'I don't think so, no. That kind of thing would drive me mad,' Imogen said. 'And, of course, it's the very reason you didn't go to Siena in the first place.'

'Yes,' Anna sighed. 'I'd really hoped we might avoid this happening. But perhaps I was being naïve – I should have realised she'd find some way to make herself part of our lives here. Although I don't think I could have predicted that she'd do this, come and live right around the corner.'

'Yes. Hmm. That's tough.'

'We came to Sorrento so that we could make a start with just the three of us,' Anna said, frustration coming into her voice. 'I know that Matteo's family have decades of experience with ice cream, but I want us to do this ourselves.'

'Of course you do. We made Vivien's a success – you don't need to lean on anyone else.'

Anna felt better just for letting it out, being able to talk openly with her sister, rather than bottling things up as she felt she had to with Matteo.

'I shouldn't be so negative,' she said. 'There are some really nice people here – and Carolina's great, I've always liked her – but there are things I'm starting to miss. Popping out for a coffee with you, feeling like I'm in my world for a bit. Do you know what I mean?'

'Yes, I do. I miss you loads.'

A lump rose to Anna's throat and she realised that she was feeling more homesick than she'd let herself admit.

'How are things back at home? What's the news?'

'Things are fine. The guesthouse is doing really well. I set up a new booking system for Martin, and it's a good job, as word-of-mouth recommendations have really started to spread.'

'Lots of weekenders?'

'Mainly, although there's one guest who's been around quite a while. Since it opened, actually.'

'Oh, yes?'

'It's a bit of a strange one. She's called Clarissa. She's a nice woman, says she met Granny back when the shop was Sunset 99s.'

'I'm sensing there's a "but" here.'

'I'm not sure what's going on with her. She's been asking me about Granny, and Martin, too. Just the occasional question, like she's trying to build up a picture of her, or something. I guess it's natural – in that house there are a few personal things, you might get curious ... But I'm starting to wonder if something else is going on. She's grieving still, I think, said her stepfather passed away.'

'Well, that'll probably be it, won't it? Maybe she thinks you've been through the same thing and she's trying to make a connection.'

'Maybe.' Imogen paused. 'Anyway, I don't want to be mean, she's perfectly nice.'

'How are things going at Vivien's? I got the latest set of accounts from you, thanks. It looks like things are OK.'

'They are. Evie's doing a sterling job of keeping things ticking over. The customers absolutely love her, and she insists that she's fine doing it on her own.'

'I'm glad. I'm so pleased we trusted our gut feeling on that. Granny would have loved it, wouldn't she, knowing that Evie was there, running the show.'

'Yes. And it's definitely softened the blow of losing the souvenir shop for her. She's seemed strangely relaxed about the fact that Finn, Andy and Andy's dad are smashing walls down over there.'

'They haven't wasted any time. Finn must be excited,' Anna said, half-wishing she could see what was going on at the arches for herself. She was used to knowing all the comings and goings in that little stretch of seafront, rather than hearing about them from someone else.

'He is. It's keeping him really busy – he's working late a lot.'

'Have you talked to him, about how you've been feeling?' Anna said. Imogen fell quiet. 'Sorry. It's your business.'

'No, it's fine. It's just he's been busy . . . and I've been . . . well. Actually I haven't been busy at all, not with work at least.'

'You haven't?' Anna said.

'No. Listen, how are you fixed for the start of July?'

'No plans. Other than the usual – juggling Bella and a load of ice cream cones, trying to fit in the occasional shower and conversation with Matteo. Why do you ask?'

'I'm wondering about a visit.'

Anna felt a rush of excitement at the prospect. 'Don't tease, Imogen. Do you really mean it?'

'Of course I do,' she said.

'How long for?'

'Ten days or so? Would that be OK?'

'The entire summer would be OK,' Anna said. 'We've got space for you and Finn to stay here at our apartment.'

'Oh ... it'd probably just be me,' Imogen said.

'How come?'

'Finn's been busy with the building work on the shop.'

'That's a shame.'

'I'll ask him, anyway,' Imogen said.

'Do you think Mum and Dad would want to come out, too? I've been meaning to ask them, just wanted to get everything set up here first.'

'I'm sure they'd love to, but Anna ...'

'I understand. They can come later on. They OK, though?'

'Yes, I think so. Mum's at a bit of a loose end still, but Dad seems fine. They come up to the guesthouse every now and then to check in on things.'

'Dad's getting used to the idea?'

'Oh yes, he's fine now.'

Anne paused. 'I'm *so* excited, Imogen. I really hope you can come. I'd love to show you around.'

From the Sorrento ice cream shop, Anna spied Matteo approaching across the square, with Elisa and Bella, and dashed out to tell him the good news she'd just heard.

'I've just been on the phone to Imogen, and she's coming out to visit,' Anna squealed. Then she turned to Bella and gave her a hug. 'Your auntie's coming!'

'That's great,' Matteo said, smiling broadly.

'Your sister's coming? That's wonderful,' Elisa said. 'Nice

182

girl, Imogen. A little ... how do you say? Well, like a boy. The way she dresses.'

'Mamma,' Matteo said, quietly.

'But perhaps that look is fashionable, in England,' Elisa said, correcting herself. 'Anyway, that's nice. She'll give you a little company.'

'I'm looking forward to it,' Anna said.

'Perhaps she'll be able to help you with some of the housework in the apartment,' Elisa said. 'It seems like you don't have much time to do that.'

'I don't think we'll be doing that while she's here, Elisa,' Anna said, keeping her voice calm and level and trying not to let Elisa's comments rile her.

'Well, you shouldn't let things slip for too long. Perhaps Carolina could help. The home that she and Filippo have in Siena ... well, it's like something off the television: every surface gleaming, the bed linen ironed ...'

Anna took a deep breath, to stop herself from talking back. It always seemed to be Carolina and Filippo this, or that – the money, the meals, the house. It was tiring to be compared with someone who seemed so perfect.

'Carolina's situation is a little different,' Matteo said, diplomatically. 'She and Filippo have a housekeeper, anyway.'

'Well, I never had one and—' Elisa started.

Keen to change the subject, Anna pointed to the plastic bags Elisa was holding. 'What did you get?'

'I couldn't resist buying my beautiful granddaughter some new things,' Elisa said, unpacking one.

Bella peered at the pink fabric excitedly and when her grandmother held it up, revealing the full extent of lace and frills, the little girl clapped her hands together in joy.

'See! I knew this little one would like it,' Elisa said, pleased with herself.

'It's a lovely thought,' Matteo said, diplomatically. 'Thank you, Mamma.'

'Yes, thank you, Elisa,' Anna added, as her daughter touched the frills, squealing with delight.

'Oh, that's just one dress. There's plenty more.' She delved into another bag and pulled out a pair of glittery pink shoes, with heels, and a makeup set.

Anna looked at Matteo, a little alarmed, and their eyes met. She waited for him to say something.

'I'm not sure, Elisa ... She's not even two yet. She's still very young for—'

'Shoes!' Bella exclaimed, grabbing at them with a look of unbridled delight.

Anna glanced over at Matteo for support, but he remained silent. Now they were living here there was no option of 'disappearing' the gifts to the back of Bella's wardrobe. Elisa would expect to see her wearing them. With her grand-mother's help, Bella opened the lipstick and Elisa dabbed a little on her mouth.

'It's really kind of you,' Anna said. 'Although I think it's best if she doesn't wear heels for a while. They are beautiful, but her feet are still growing and we need to be careful.'

'Oh, she'll be fine. We always put Carolina in shoes like this. And look, Bella loves them, doesn't she?' Elisa exclaimed. 'I think she prefers them to the other clothes she's wearing these days.'

Anna looked at the Osh Kosh blue-striped dungarees and red Clarks sandals she had dressed her daughter in that morning. 'She seems happy enough in them.' They were perfect for the things that Bella loved doing best: running, hugging dogs, playing in the mud. 'To be honest, I'm not sure she even notices what she's wearing.'

'They aren't very feminine, though, are they? Have you seen the other little girls around here?'

'I don't want her to look like everyone else.' The emotion rose in Anna's voice, and she was unable to keep her irritation hidden.

'Well, Matteo agrees with me. Don't you, Matti?'

'Mamma . . .'

'You see? He also thinks she's lucky to have a grandmother like me, to buy her such pretty things. Don't you think, Bella?'

Bella pulled pink garment after pink garment out of her grandmother's shopping bags, gurgling happily.

'Very lucky,' Anna said.

Chapter 21

After speaking to her sister, Imogen carried on walking along the seafront. It had felt strange, holding back from mentioning the letter and photo she'd found. It had seemed like a lie, to keep that from Anna, the person she was closest to in the world, and Vivien's other granddaughter. But what did Imogen really know? All that was certain was that the connection between Vivien and this man, this stranger, was so strong that she'd still been thinking about it years later, driven to get back in contact. She wanted to find out more before she risked upsetting anyone in her family over what might turn out to be nothing.

Imogen remembered her grandfather, Stanley – Vivien had doted on him. She had been crushed when he'd passed away in his fifties. Or perhaps Imogen and her family had got all of that wrong. Maybe all of the years she'd been with Stanley, and after his death, Vivien had really been yearning to be with somebody else.

Her grandparents' marriage – she'd always assumed it was perfect. They had all the best ingredients, kindness, love, staying power . . . And yet they still hadn't made it. Not in the way that everyone had believed they had, at least.

She looked out at the ocean where her grandmother's ashes had been scattered. Her final resting place wasn't a resting place at all, but one in a constant state of ebb and flow. Maybe her spirit was unsettled, too.

'Who was he?' Imogen asked, under her breath, looking out towards the waves.

Imogen had to find out. And something told her that going out to Italy was the only way to do it.

That evening, Imogen was woken by Finn as he let himself into the house, showered and then came through to their bedroom. She checked her phone and saw it was after midnight.

'You were out late,' Imogen said, pulling back the duvet.

'Yes. It'll be like this for a while, I'm afraid. We're getting there, though.' He got into bed beside her.

She propped herself up on one elbow and faced him. He kissed her gently.

'I spoke to Anna today.'

'Oh, yes. How are they doing?'

'OK, I think. We didn't talk for long, but it sounds like they're settling in. I bet they're going to have a great summer out there. And let's be honest, they're hardly missing much here, are they?'

Summer hadn't quite found the south coast yet, aside from the occasional sunny day, and the grey days had started to get Imogen down.

'It's usually the other way round, you know. You off in some glamorous location and us here in the drizzle. It's Anna's turn.'

'I know.'

'You want to go out there, don't you?'

She thought of how much she missed her sister – and then of the other reason she felt such a drive to go out to Italy: the letter that she'd found; the mystery around her grandmother that she felt compelled to get to the bottom of.

'Yes. I do. I really want to go.'

'Well, then you should,' Finn said. He seemed detached and quiet. The way he had seemed quite a lot, lately.

'Without you?'

He shrugged. 'I'd love to go, you know that. But with everything that's going on with the shop I really can't afford to take the time off. You're used to travelling on your own, aren't you?'

'Yes. Of course I am.' She hadn't expected to feel sad.

'More lamb, Imogen?' Jan said, offering the tray to her daughter.

'I'm fine, thanks, Mum.'

'Oh, come on, have some more. You've barely touched yours.'

That weekend, Finn and Imogen were at her parents' cottage in the town of Lewes, a short drive from Brighton. With jasmine around the front door, and her father's garden sculptures decorating the path, it was a place that would always feel like home to both Imogen and Anna. Which was comforting in some ways, Imogen thought to herself. But infuriating in others.

'It's true that you haven't eaten much, love,' Tom said, looking at the plate of half-eaten Sunday roast in front of her.

'I'm not that hungry today, that's all,' she said.

'Everything OK?' Tom asked her gently.

'Yes, absolutely fine,' Imogen said. 'We had a massive breakfast this morning, that's all.'

From the corner of her eye she could see Finn glancing in her direction, and it made her feel more conscious of the lie. The truth was that over the past few weeks her appetite had dropped. She couldn't put her finger on why, just that in the days since Anna had left, something had been out of kilter, and that feeling didn't seem to be resolving itself.

'I expect you'll be needing some fuel,' Tom said to Finn. 'I hear you've been working hard building the new shop.'

'Building – that's a nice way of putting it,' Finn said with a smile. 'We've trashed the place, really. Walls down, plaster dust everywhere. Evie's been very understanding – even dropping tea in to us while we work. I thought she might be upset, but she says in a way it's quite satisfying seeing the place change so completely. Anyway, by autumn we should have it all in good shape.'

'I'm sure you'll make a great success of it, just as you did with the surf school,' Tom said.

'It's something Andy and I have been talking about for a while, so we're really enjoying getting stuck in. It's costing quite a lot in the short term, but we're confident that it'll bring us a more solid income in the years to come.'

'That's good, isn't it?' Jan said. 'Don't you think, Imogen?'

'Yes, of course,' she said. 'It's going to be awesome when it's done.'

'A young couple like you need a bit of security when you're starting out, and your line of work, well, it's just not very reliable, is it, Imogen?'

Finn caught Imogen's eye over the table, seeming to sense her irritation.

'It's not, no, Mum,' she said.

'Small price to pay for doing what you love,' Tom said, smiling at his daughter. 'And, while it was a shame about that last project, I'm sure something even better will come through for you soon.'

'Thanks, Dad,' Imogen said. 'And it's not like Finn's paying my way. I've been doing studio work, weddings. I've even saved a bit.'

'Very sensible,' Jan said. 'I mean I'd still be happier if you weren't freelance – it really is terribly insecure: no pension, no sick days – but that does sound like better work. You should really think about an ISA. Tax-free savings can—'

'Actually I already know what I'm going to spend it on,' Imogen said bluntly. 'A flight out to Italy.'

'Oh,' Jan said. 'This all seems quite sudden. Have you spoken to Anna about it?'

'Yes, of course I have. She's excited,' she said.

'Sounds wonderful. Are you going, too?' Tom asked Finn.

'I wish I could. But with the building work I'm going to have my hands full here.'

'As well as seeing Anna, I think there might be some potential for photos – especially out on Capri. I've always wanted to go there.'

'How nice,' Tom said. His eyes misted over. 'Your grand-mother always said it was beautiful.'

Imogen thought of the letter she'd found, the complex web she seemed to have stepped into and hoped that – out in Italy – she'd be able to start unravelling.

'Well, as long as it's not just an excuse for a holiday, Imogen,' Jan said. 'Because you've had plenty of those.'

Imogen gave her mother a stern look.

'What?' Jan asked. 'Everyone has to settle down sometime. Even you. Now, anyone for dessert?'

Chapter 22

Anna crossed the square and went into Luigi's restaurant. At ten in the morning, the place was quiet, and her neighbour in the Sorrento square was occupied with cleaning the tables, singing to himself loudly and cheerily, operatic songs that Anna knew vaguely from ice cream adverts.

'The English Lady!' he exclaimed. 'You have come to brighten my day once again, *principessa.*'

Anna laughed. 'I got some good news yesterday, Luigi. My sister's booked her flights to come out here to visit.'

Anna had received the confirmation in an excited text message from Imogen late in the evening.

'Fantastic! If she is anything like you, meeting her will be a delight,' Luigi said.

'Imogen's nothing like me,' Anna said, smiling. 'But all the better for it. You'll like her.'

'I'm sure I will. And it will be nice for you to have some-one from home here with you, I imagine.'

Anna nodded. Loneliness had crept up on her, so stealthily she almost hadn't noticed it, and the thought of Imogen's visit had lifted her spirits.

'Bring her here for a meal,' Luigi said. 'I will get you the best table in the house.'

'Thank you. I will.'

'And today – I could flatter myself that you came just for my conversation, but I know that you are a busy woman.'

'Actually, Luigi, you're right. I did come to ask a favour. We're all out of ice cream bowls, if you can believe it. Do you have any spare?'

'Of course, of course,' he said, motioning for her to come behind the counter. 'The shop is getting busier than you expected?'

'I thought it would take a while for us to get established,' Anna said. 'But we've had queues into the square today.'

'That is good news,' Luigi said, loading a tray with bowls for her. 'And you've earned it. The tourists? Well, they're not too choosy. But the locals will not come for just any ice cream, you know.'

'Yes, it's a compliment. How's your daughter getting on in her new job, by the way?'

'Very well, thank you. Long hours but she really enjoys the work and she studied a long time to get there. As it happens, we're all waiting for a phone call at the moment. Her brother, my son – he works the land not far from here – he and his wife are getting ready to welcome a baby to their family.'

'That's great,' Anna said.

'Any day now, I'll be a grandfather.'

'Wonderful. Let me know when you hear.'

She saw something new in him, that excitement in his eyes. She thought of her own father and the way he had cradled Bella in his arms when she was a newborn. It wasn't just her and Matteo's lives that had changed that day.

Later that afternoon, Anna prepared tea and cake, and Carolina came and sat with her and Matteo out on the balcony. With Elisa out with Bella that afternoon, Matteo had suggested they invite his sister round.

'How is Filippo's trip going?' Matteo asked. 'Mamma keeps saying how well his business is going.'

'Business is terrific,' Carolina replied.

'But?' Matteo said. So he'd detected the coldness in her voice, too, Anna thought.

'It's going so great that I don't think he'll be coming down here at all this summer.'

'That's a shame,' Anna said.

'Is it?' Carolina said, with a shrug. Anna noticed that there were dark shadows under her eyes.

'Are you OK?' Anna asked gently.

'Not really.' She shook her head. 'I don't know what I ever saw in that man, really.'

Anna froze for a moment, shocked. 'Are things really that bad?' she asked. Matteo looked equally concerned.

'Worse,' she said. 'I think our marriage is over.'

'What's happened?' Matteo asked.

'There were problems before Christmas, and then he said he couldn't come to England to stay with you,' Carolina said, her English clear and precise. 'But I thought we could work through them – I thought our marriage vows meant something.'

'Is there someone else?' Anna asked, tentatively.

'Yes.' Carolina's eyes filled with tears.

Matteo shook his head and Anna saw that he was trying hard to keep his fury under control.

'You're sure?' Anna asked.

'Yes. I knew something was wrong. I looked through his credit-card bills and saw that he'd been staying in hotels and having expensive meals out when he had told me he was away on business.'

'Did he admit to it?' Matteo said.

'No, of course not. That would have made life far too easy.' She shook her head. 'He told me I was being paranoid, that I was wrong to have been looking through his things.'

'That's terrible,' Anna said.

She shrugged. 'It's hard. You doubt yourself. I've lost sight of who's right and who's wrong. Maybe I did something to push him away.'

'Nothing you did would mean you deserve to be cheated on,' Matteo said. 'You're going to divorce him, right?'

Anna gave Matteo a stern look, hoping that he'd understand and go in a little bit more softly.

Carolina looked up, tears in her eyes.

'You're too good for him, Caro.' Matteo said.

'I just need time to think clearly,' she said. 'That's all.'

Chapter 23

In the early hours of a warm July morning, Imogen checked over the contents of her suitcase: summer trousers, three bikinis, flip-flops and a sunhat on top of some other clothes. Then she got her camera bag ready. Everything that she'd need for a trip to the Amalfi coast.

She couldn't wait to see Anna, and feel the sun on her face again. It was the right time for a trip away. Over the past few weeks, Evie had proved herself to be a complete natural at Vivien's; and, at the guesthouse, Martin had found his feet. So Imogen wasn't leaving anyone in the lurch. She had just one reservation, linked to the guesthouse: she was concerned about Clarissa. After seeing her father's descent into depression, she didn't want the same thing to happen again. Imogen had asked her mum to check in on Clarissa while she was away, to make sure that she was OK.

There was just one more thing to pack. She got a folder

out of her top drawer and slipped it into her hand luggage. Inside were the letter and photos she'd found, along with the map from the guesthouse, folded up. In Italy she would find out what had happened. She would make some sense of the muddle everything seemed to have become.

She looked over at Finn, still sleeping in bed. The man she loved, but now felt so distant from. A few days and she'd be clearer about everything, she reasoned. She closed her suitcase and checked the time.

Finn stirred. 'Are you going?' he asked, drowsily rubbing his eyes. He looked so adorable like that, still half asleep.

'Yes,' she said. 'The cab's going to be here any minute.'

'Have fun,' he said. 'I'll miss you.'

She bent down beside him and kissed him, then pressed her face into the warm skin of his shoulder and neck. For that moment everything felt all right.

'I'll call you when I get there,' she said.

'Sure. Give my love to Anna and Matteo – and a hug for Bella,' he said. 'Tell them next time I'll be there too.'

A text buzzed through to Imogen's phone announcing that the cab was there. 'Taxi.'

'I love you,' Finn said, simply and clearly.

'Me too,' Imogen said.

The words caught. It wasn't that they weren't true – they were. But it felt as if they weren't the only thing that mattered any more.

Part Three

Chapter 24

That Sunday, Anna smiled with delight as she saw her sister walking into the arrivals hall, in a bright-orange, patterned sarong and strappy black top, her sunglasses perched on top of her head. She dashed over and hugged her.

'I can't believe you're really here,' Anna said, holding her tight.

'Hold up,' Imogen said, laughing. 'You're squeezing the life out of me here. Have you really missed me that much?'

'I have, actually,' Anna said.

'Aw, that's sweet. I've missed you a bit too. How's Bella? Matteo?'

'They're good, thanks,' Anna said. 'Matteo's running the shop today, and Carolina's with Bella. I wanted to have my sister to myself for a little bit. Come and jump in the car, let's get going.'

They loaded Imogen's suitcase into the back of the car, and hit the road back to Sorrento.

'How's the shop?' Imogen asked, tying her hair up into a loose topknot.

'It's doing really well, thanks. Busy. This place is great and we've opened at just the right time of year to build a good buzz around the business, and—'

'So what is it that's making you unhappy?' Imogen asked, studying her sister's face. 'Because I can see something's wrong.'

'Let's stop for a drink,' Anna said. 'I'll tell you all about it.'

They stopped at a bar by the coast, half an hour short of Sorrento itself. Out of earshot of Matteo's family, Anna felt liberated. With Imogen she could say what she wanted without fear of it going back to the wrong (or the right) person. The waiter brought them over two tall glasses of chilled Prosecco.

'First things first: here's to you being here,' Anna said, raising hers.

'Here's to me being here,' Imogen said, chinking her glass with her sister's.

'So what is it? Spill. Is it Matteo's mum still?'

'Yes,' Anna said, relieved to be able to open up about it. 'She keeps meddling in everything. With the business, with Bella . . .'

'Worse than Mum?' Imogen asked.

'Oh, God, she makes Mum look like a saint.' Anna laughed. 'But it's not just her. It's Matteo. When he's with me, he's strong and confident – but five minutes with his mum and he'll roll over and accept whatever she says.'

'Really?' Imogen said, surprised.

'I know. I'm trying to understand, but it's like there's a different side to him that I've never seen before.'

'You should say something,' Imogen urged. 'It doesn't sound like it's going to settle on its own.'

'But she's his mother,' Anna said, shaking her head. 'Family is everything to Matteo. I don't want to make him feel he has to choose sides.'

'So what's the alternative? You keep quiet, and go slowly mad with it all?'

'Don't be dramatic, Imo,' Anna said, smiling in spite of herself.

'I'm serious,' Imogen protested.

'I can't,' Anna said.

'Right. Well, if you really are refusing to get this out in the open, then at least come out with me and let off some steam tonight.'

'That sounds like a perfect compromise,' Anna said, laughing.

Back at the apartment in the late afternoon, Imogen was sitting out on the balcony painting her toenails. Anna stepped outside to join her.

'Good news,' she said, brightly. 'Matteo's looking after

Bella for the night. So I'm officially free to show you some of the local highlights.'

'Great,' Imogen said.

'Nice colour,' Anna said, admiring her toes.

'Thanks. So, what's the plan? Dress code?'

Anna laughed. 'Well, we're starting at Luigi's.' She pointed out of the window at the humble restaurant across the square, currently populated by the lunchtime crowd of flip-flop-clad tourists complete with beach inflatables. 'It does get a little more elegant at night, and there are people out here promenading, but I'd say you'd be just fine in what you're wearing.'

'That's good, because I packed fairly light this time. You know what the budget-airline restrictions are like these days. I was hoping I'd get by on mixing and matching a few separates.'

'You'll be fine. No one's very dressy over here. It's just Capri where you'll have to up your game. You're still planning a trip there, right?'

'Yes, definitely. Just before I leave. Can I tempt you to come too?'

Anna's face fell a little. 'I'd love to, but I can't – what with the shop and everything . . .'

'OK, well, we'll just have to cram in as much fun as possible in my time here, then. Starting now.'

She got out her phone and took a photo of the two of them, faces pressed together, the square behind them.

She uploaded it to Facebook: 'In Sorrento, with the best sister ever.'

That evening, Anna and Imogen were at Luigi's, sitting at an outside table overlooking the fountain. Children played by the water in the pale moonlight, and, as they laughed, Anna remembered what it was about Italian culture that had attracted her to living there in the first place. She couldn't allow the tension with Elisa to take all that positive feeling away.

'What do you think of the linguine?' Anna asked, watching her sister shovel laden forkfuls of the delicious fresh pasta into her mouth.

'Incredible,' Imogen enthused, her mouth still half full. 'God, it's nothing like the pasta you get at home, is it?'

Anna shook her head. 'Luigi's is some of the best around, fresh, locally sourced ingredients, and made to his grandparents' recipes. It's a shame you won't get to meet him tonight.'

'Where is he?'

'He's gone to visit his son's new baby. He's just become a granddad and he's over the moon about it.'

'That's nice,' Imogen said. A granddad. So feasibly the same age as Vivien would have been. Her mind ticked over the possibility that he could be the man who had written to their grandmother. His initial – L. – supported her suspicion. 'Is he as proud as Dad was?'

'Almost. But no one could be quite as proud as that,' Anna laughed.

'What's his surname?' Imogen asked. Her heart raced at the prospect that she might be getting closer to unravelling the mystery.

'I don't know, actually,' Anna said. 'I haven't had reason to ask.'

Imogen felt disappointed, but tried not to let it show. Anna switched the subject back to their parents.

'Are they all right, Mum and Dad, with what we're doing? I feel awful taking Bella so far away from them.'

'They're fine,' Imogen said. 'Obviously they miss her, they miss all of you – but they know that you've made the decision that's right for you as a family. And also that it's something special, what Bella has here – the chance to experience two different cultures.'

'Not boring old English, through and through, like us?' Anna said. 'No wonder you're always seeking adventure somewhere or other, like Dad was in the old days.'

Imogen fell silent for a moment. 'Sometimes I think it would be easier, if I could just accept things as they are. If I was more like Mum, happy with her lot, only really caring about her family, keeping her home nice, the occasional bit of decent gossip to share with the neighbours ...'

'You don't really mean that, though, do you?' Anna asked, raising an eyebrow.

'Not completely,' Imogen said. 'But maybe just a little bit. Because this restlessness, it doesn't make commitment easy. How do you love someone, say that you'll be there for them always, when a part of you is always wanting to get away?'

Imogen looked for the answer in her sister's eyes, but all she saw was concern. Was this how Vivien had felt too, all those years ago?

Chapter 25

The following morning, Imogen was sitting out on the balcony of Anna and Matteo's apartment, sipping coffee as the square slowly woke up around her, people opening their shutters, strolling towards the bakery. Anna would be taking the afternoon off so that she and Imogen could take Bella out – but she had the morning to herself. Normally, she'd want to take her camera out and get some photos of the place, but that morning something else was on her mind. She held up one of the photos of her grandmother in Italy, matching it to the view in front of her – the same buildings, church and fountain. This was it – here in the square. Vivien had been here, decades before, and now her granddaughters were treading in her footsteps. But what exactly had happened here?

She took out the map and looked at the places Vivien had marked. They seemed like the typical tourist stops – nothing unusual there. What had seemed like a catalogue of clues back home now seemed so little to go on, and with Luigi still out of town, she wouldn't be able to follow up that lead either.

That afternoon, Imogen, Anna and Bella took a trip to a café down by the sea. Bella played with some of the local children, and the sisters had time to themselves to talk.

'You know how Granny V used to talk about this place?' Imogen said.

Her sister nodded. 'It must have been such a special holiday for her, coming out here with Evie. Her first real holiday abroad.'

'Yes,' Imogen said, quietly. 'Although sometimes I wonder . . .' She let the sentence tail off.

'What was that?' Anna asked. She had half an eye on her daughter, who was toddling after a red ball, trying to keep up with the older children.

'I'm not sure yet. I just have this feeling that something else happened in Granny's life, something that none of us knew about – not even Dad or Martin. Do you think that's possible?'

'Really? I never thought of her as one for secrets,' Anna said. 'She and Grandpa would tell each other everything. Dad always said that.'

'Who's to say Dad knew the real story, though? Perhaps there was a side to her that none of us knew.'

Bella fell, knocking her head, and let out a wail of pain. The other children ran after the ball, leaving her.

Anna got to her feet and went over to her daughter, sweeping her up into her arms and giving her a cuddle.

'Is she OK?' Imogen asked.

Anna nodded. 'It was just a bump.'

Imogen kissed her niece's head.

It was a good thing that she'd stopped before she said too much. She didn't know the facts yet. Tomorrow she would find out more, and only then would she talk to Anna about it.

That evening, while Anna and Matteo bathed Bella and settled her in bed, Imogen called Finn. She was anxious to hear his voice. She hoped that by talking to him about normal things – what she had been doing, how things were going with his building project – they might be able to return to the good way things had once been. That calm and happy couple they'd been, who laughed together and told each other everything. She didn't know exactly when that had stopped happening, only that it had.

But she got voicemail. She listened to the outgoing message, taking some comfort in hearing his voice. She left him a voicemail saying that she was fine, and that she was thinking of him. When she hung up, she didn't know quite what to do with herself.

Unsettled, she got up and went on to the balcony and looked out at the sea beyond the houses. Out towards Capri, where she'd go at the end of the week; a place she'd often longed to see. She had a feeling she would find what she was missing there. Inspiration, perhaps. That had to be what it was.

The silence out on the balcony left too much space for unsettling thoughts to circle in her mind. She picked up the phone again, and called her mum and dad's landline. Jan picked up.

'Hi, Mum, it's me,' Imogen said.

'Hello, Imogen!' Jan replied excitedly. 'Or should I say *Ciao!* How are you?'

'Really good, thanks. Anna and I have been having a great time. The shop's a gem, and she and Matteo have done wonderful things with it. It's a sweet little square here, where they live. I think you'd like it.'

'Sounds very special,' Jan said. 'I'm so glad you got there OK, and everything's going well. How's Bella?'

'Cute as ever. She's even picked up a few Italian words.'

'Ah, how sweet. I do miss her terribly. But I'm happy that it's working out for them, of course.'

'How's everything with you? Dad?'

'Oh, your father's fine. He's had a couple of new commissions, actually, for a man who lives locally. Quite rich, I think. He has that look of ageing rock star about him.'

Imogen smiled. Jan's gossiping was reassuringly familiar –

she'd always made a habit of keeping tabs on new arrivals in the town.

'And Martin?'

'He's fine. I went to the guesthouse yesterday. Actually I'm glad you called, Imogen, because there's something I wanted to talk to you about. I spoke to her – Clarissa.'

'You did?' Imogen said, Clarissa's face flashing back into her mind for a second. 'How was she?'

'Like you described. Distant, a bit sad. Martin said he found her in the living room the other night, at midnight, so I thought I should say something.'

'You were subtle, right, Mum?'

'Of course I was, Imogen. I asked her about Vivien, the connection. She said her mother had known Vivien, back when she was a teenager. That she'd gone into the shop then, from time to time. That Vivien had been kind to her, when she'd needed it most. And that her mother had been to the house before. That the place meant something to her.'

'Really? She didn't mention that before. Did she say anything else?'

'No, that was it, really. Just that. Then she seemed to shut down.'

'Right. And she seemed OK, in herself?'

'Yes. Just as you'd expect, after what happened with losing her stepfather. She and Martin seemed to be getting on well, and she's been taking Hepburn out for walks. I think that's something she enjoys.'

Imogen smiled as she thought. Hepburn did seem to have an innate capacity to cheer people up.

'Well, thanks for checking in,' Imogen said. 'Is Dad around? Can I say hello?'

'I'll just get him.'

Imogen talked to her dad for a while, filling him in on the trip, and then ended the call to go inside and help Anna get dinner ready. It sounded as if Bella was probably asleep by now.

As she put her phone on the side, she saw a new Facebook notification. She clicked on it, instinctively, to see a new message in her inbox. A face she remembered that conjured up memories of a different time: 'Imogen, I've just seen you're in Sorrento. That's crazy. Come and see me. I'm in Capri.'

Blood rushed to her cheeks. It was from Luca.

Chapter 26

Anna was down in the ice cream shop as soon as the sun was up, her apron on, making fresh batches of lemon sorbet and truffle ice cream for the day. With the shop still in its infancy, she and Matteo needed to do everything they could to get it off to the best start, even if that meant missing out on a morning with Imogen. Thankfully, her sister had seemed happy enough at the prospect of doing some more exploring on her own.

Matteo came in to join her, with Bella in his arms. 'Morning,' he said. They kissed.

'Ah, you're still making the sorbet that way?' he said.

'Yes,' Anna replied. 'That's how I've always made it.'

'Oh.'

'Oh?' Anna said, bristling a little. 'Is it a problem?'

'It's just . . . Don't worry about it.'

'We said we'd introduce some of your family recipes,'

Anna said. 'I'm fine with that. But I never said we'd phase the other things out.'

'Sure. Yes, you're right. But the lemon – it's something that matters a lot to Mamma, that we try that one the Italian way.'

'You want me to start again?' Anna asked, wide-eyed.

'No, sorry, it's fine.'

'OK,' Anna said, relieved.

Bella dipped a finger into a small pot of the truffle, and licked it, giggling happily.

'But perhaps next time?' Matteo said. 'Could we try it my parents' way next time?'

It was sorbet, Anna told herself. That was all. It really wasn't worth falling out over. And yet, every time she gave in to the demands coming from Matteo's side of the family, she felt as if she were growing smaller. She wondered if, like a tiny Alice in Wonderland, she'd keep taking in those family recipes until they found her, just a tiny figure, flailing in a vat of Elisa's famous granita.

It was a welcome relief when, later that afternoon, Imogen returned to the shop.

'Good day?' Anna asked.

'Yes, great, thanks.' Anna noted how distracted her sister seemed, though, as if part of her were somewhere else. She'd been like that ever since she'd arrived.

'I've been thinking,' Imogen said. 'You want to smooth things over with Elisa, right? And I'm only here for a short while too. Why don't we have a cocktail night here at the shop? Just a few friends.'

'A party?' Anna said, lighting up at the idea.

'Yes, cocktails, some canapés,' said Imogen. 'Maybe you could invite Luigi and a few of the locals?' she added, as nonchalantly as she could. Anna had mentioned he was due back soon, and she wasn't going to miss the chance to meet him. 'A celebration. And – a sign to Elisa that you want to include her, even if you don't want to agree to everything she wants you to do. Plus, to celebrate *me*, of course.'

'Sounds good.' Anna said.

'I'm leaving at the weekend, which gives us precisely . . .' – Imogen counted on her fingers – 'three days to get ready – invites, recipes, ingredients. Easy.'

'OK, I'll talk to Matteo. But I'm sure he'll say yes – he's always loved a party. I think it's a great idea.'

Cocktail menu

Sorrento nights – Italian brandy, cinnamon ice cream
Amalfi sea breeze – Limoncello, Prosecco and lime sorbet
The Capri – Grand Marnier liqueur, orange juice
and chocolate orange ice cream

That week, Anna and Imogen worked together to prepare for the party, and on Friday evening the ice cream shop was aglow with nightlights and coloured lanterns. Matteo and Anna were behind the counter making up cocktails and Imogen was ferrying drinks back and forth, chatting brightly in English and using the few Italian words that she knew liberally and loudly.

Elisa had come with Carolina, the two of them smartly dressed and chatting easily to the other Italians. Carolina's short hair was slicked back with a red flower pinned in it.

'Thanks for suggesting this, Imogen,' Anna said, putting her arm around her sister's slim shoulders and bringing her close. 'I guess baby steps is the best way of improving things with Matteo's mum.'

'Look at her: she's having a great time,' Imogen said, pointing to Elisa, who was deep in conversation with one of the locals.

'Maybe you're right,' Anna said, her heart lifting. 'Oh look,' she said, excitedly. 'There's Luigi. Let me introduce you.'

Imogen's heart raced as she looked over to where Luigi was standing. He had his back to them, and was talking to a woman in her fifties.

'Luigi!' Anna called out.

He turned, and Imogen's breath caught. His eyes, hair – a little older, perhaps but he looked just like the man in the photo she'd seen with her grandmother's things.

Anna led her sister over to him. 'Imogen, Luigi. Maria, Imogen,' Anna said, hurriedly. 'Not great at this being-a-hostess business,' she added, with a laugh. Carolina caught her by the arm and led her away. 'I'll leave you to get to know each other,' she said apologetically.

'Imogen, hello!' Luigi greeted her cheerily. 'Anna has told me all about you.'

'She has?' Imogen said, feeling numb.

'Good things, all good things.'

'I know that both of you have made her feel very welcome,' Imogen said.

'Well, as we Espositos always say, you should treat every stranger as a potential friend.'

'Sorry?' Imogen said. The name Luigi had said, and its significance, struck her right in the chest — the only confirmation she needed. *L. Esposito* — the name on the map, and almost certainly the man who'd written to her grandmother. The man her grandmother had been trying to track down. The letter. It hit Imogen with a force that almost made her choke.

'In my family, we always say . . .' Luigi started again.

This is *him*. Imogen made an excuse and left, running out of the shop, into the open air. She breathed in, filling her lungs, but the sensation of deep shock and disbelief stayed with her.

*

At one in the morning, the party drew to a close and the guests emptied out into the square. Anna looked around for her sister, but couldn't see Imogen anywhere. She'd been so busy talking with the guests that she had left Imogen to find her own way mingling at the party, hadn't thought to check up on her until now.

'Have you seen Imogen?' Anna asked Matteo, as he tidied behind the bar.

'I think she might have gone upstairs,' he said. 'Although that was a little while ago.'

Anna went upstairs. The buzz of the party was still with her – but it was mixed now with concern about her sister. She found Imogen upstairs in the bathroom, sitting on the edge of the bath. She looked pale and shaken.

'You OK, Imo? What happened?'

'It's nothing,' she said.

'It can't be nothing,' Anna perched beside her. 'One minute you're the life and soul of the party down there, the next you've disappeared. What happened?'

Imogen bit her lip to stop it trembling. 'You know when you think you know someone, and then you find something out that makes you challenge all of that?'

'Finn?'

She shook her head. 'No. Granny, actually.'

Anna raised her eyebrows, surprised.

Imogen told Anna about the letter she'd found, and how she'd tried to talk to Luigi earlier at the party.

'But . . .' Anna looked as puzzled as Imogen felt. 'Luigi?' She was piecing together the scraps of information, the things that Luigi had told her about his past in their chats together. It had never crossed her mind that he could have been involved with someone she knew – someone so close to her.

'Yes. And the thing is, I don't even know what happened. But from his letter . . . Well, I'll show you.' Imogen got the letter from her bag and brought it over to her sister.

'Wow,' Anna said softly.

'You can tell that he cared about her, can't you? There's real passion there. And for her to get in touch with him again, well, that means something, doesn't it?'

'I can't believe this,' Anna said. 'It's crazy. But, at the same time, I guess it makes sense. There's a reason Matteo and I came here, rather than anywhere else in Italy that we could have chosen to settle. And that's because Granny always spoke about it. She must have had a connection with this place that was stronger than we imagined.'

'I wish I hadn't ever started looking into it,' Imogen said, tears welling up in her eyes.

'Too late for that,' Anna said. 'But we're not having you leave with things like this. When you get back from Capri we're going to go around to Luigi's and find out what really happened.'

Chapter 27

Imogen boarded the boat to Capri in the early morning, the air crisp and fresh, before the heat of the day started to build. She didn't know if she was doing the right thing. She was leaving Sorrento with things unfinished, and Luca's message still fresh in her mind.

But the island jewel that had been glinting at her since the moment she'd arrived had become irresistible. Capri was growing closer as the boat travelled through the water, the hill rising out of the water, bright with bougainvillea. One of the most beautiful places on earth – *everyone* wanted to visit Capri. She'd be mad to let the small fact of her ex-boyfriend being there put her off. Even Finn would understand that.

When the boat docked, she made her way to her hotel. A short walk away, up a winding road, was a little white house with flowers round the door – her room was simple but just right for a night of peace. As she stepped out onto the roof

221

terrace the place came alive – a stunning view out over the sea, and pot plants bright with pink blooms. Imogen sat for a moment, breathed the clean fresh air and felt grateful for the chance she had to see the beautiful place she was in now. After a rest, she freshened up, put on a white strappy dress and wound her hair into a loose plait, slipped into her flip-flops and went out to explore the island.

Taking only her camera, she walked through the town, with its chic boutiques and upmarket restaurants, until she reached a quieter part of the island, with small houses. She kept walking, snapping photos as she went of the vivid pink flowers and the birds that had come to rest on the rocks and cliffs. Zooming in, she captured every colourful feather, the sparkling blue water of the sea behind. Away from the bustle of Sorrento, and the loose threads of her grandmother's story, a clarity had come to her. As she photographed the things she loved most, the natural world that calmed her, she felt her spirit return.

She turned a corner and reached a small fountain. She paused for a moment, sat down and looked back over the pictures she had taken. They may not be the pink dolphins of the Amazon, but there was something here, she thought.

She felt a hand on her arm. Startled, she looked up, and into the eyes of a man she knew well, but hadn't seen for years. His tanned skin was the same, those dark, piercing eyes.

'Luca,' she said, softly.

'I had a feeling I might find you out here,' he said, smiling.

'Hi – I'm sorry, I got your message, I just . . .' she started.

'It's cool. I understand.'

'I wanted to take some photos first of all. It's so beautiful here.'

'Isn't it? No filters necessary,' he laughed.

Imogen remembered the last night she'd spent with him – over four years ago. The two of them had gone night swimming together out in Koh Tao, feeling in that moment that the island was their own. She still had the shark's-tooth necklace he'd given her. Even after the way things ended she hadn't got rid of it. That time – for some reason she hadn't wanted to let go of it altogether.

'What brought you here?' she asked.

'Family,' Luca said. 'I'm staying with my aunt and uncle for the summer, working in a bar. You're here with your sister, right? I saw the photo.'

'Yes,' Imogen said. 'I mean . . . But she's still in Sorrento.' She pointed towards the town on the mainland. 'I'm just here for the night.'

'On your own?' he asked. He glanced down at her hand, and Imogen was suddenly conscious of her bare ring finger.

The question hung in the air for a moment. Luca didn't

have to know everything about her right away, she reasoned. She would tell him about Finn in her own time.

'Looks like it, doesn't it?'

Imogen walked with Luca through the winding cobbled streets. She remembered the promise she'd made to Finn to call, and felt a pang of guilt. She'd ring him later.

'I'm sorry, you know,' Luca said. 'About what happened.'

Imogen remembered how it had stung. When she'd told Luca that she'd have to stay in England longer than planned, to help Anna start up the ice cream shop, he'd been understandably hurt. They'd made no firm decisions about their future together – at least that was what Imogen had thought, until she saw photos online of Luca with her best friend on the island, Santiana.

'Santiana . . .' he said, looking flustered. 'It was a rebound thing. I felt like you'd made your decision to leave me, and I guess it was my way of saving face.'

'It's OK,' Imogen said, reminded of how much time had passed, how different things were for them both now. 'I know that I didn't offer you much incentive to stay with me, not knowing when or where you might see me again. I mean, yes, I was furious at the time – I'm not going to lie. But I don't see the point of overthinking it now.'

'Good,' he said, looking relieved. 'It didn't even last the

summer, you know. I was looking for another you, and she was never going to be you.'

Imogen felt her skin grow hot. This was definitely edging into not-OK territory. No, she was forced to acknowledge it: this had landed them right in the *middle* of not-OK territory. It was time to be honest.

She opened her mouth to confess.

'You don't have to say anything,' Luca said quietly, calmly. 'I'm just telling you what I felt, because maybe I wasn't open enough back then.'

'You ... Luca. Look ...' Imogen ran a hand through her hair. 'I should have said this earlier.'

'You're with someone,' he said.

She looked up at him, disconcerted. 'You knew?'

He shrugged. 'Something about you is different.'

'I'm sorry, I should've been honest.'

'Don't be sorry,' he said. 'You don't owe me anything, Imogen. You didn't then – and you don't now.'

She let his words sink in. 'I suppose it's best if I go,' she said.

But there was something keeping her there, drawing her towards Luca. A sense that here, in Capri, in his company, she could be that young, carefree woman she had been when she'd first met him.

'It's up to you,' he said. 'But, for what it's worth, I'd like you to stay.'

*

Everything about the scene was perfect: the clear blue water, glittering as the last glimmers of light hit it, the chilled Prosecco in long-stemmed glasses, the warmth of the evening, which meant Imogen could sit there on the elegant cliff-top terrace in just her light summer dress. Everything, that was, apart from her being there with the wrong man. Finn was back in Brighton, and here she was with her ex.

'Do you think they bought it?' Imogen said, as Luca hung up the phone.

He shrugged. 'I've never called in sick before, so I'm pretty sure they believed me. If I can't have a night off every once in a while, when it's as beautiful an evening as this – and I've just met someone I haven't seen for years – then I may as well not be here.'

Imogen had wrestled with the decision of whether to leave Luca and continue exploring the island on her own, but in the end she'd opted to stay with him. There was no reason not to see him, she thought. He was a friend, nothing more, and, now that he knew the truth about her and Finn, she didn't have to feel she was hiding anything from him. He'd told her stories about Capri as they'd walked through the cobbled streets.

'Do you think you'll stay here?' Imogen asked him.

He shook his head. 'Another month, maybe two, then I'm going back to San Francisco.'

'Is that your home now?'

226

'Yes. The start-up I was working for in San Francisco folded, but I'm putting together a business plan for a new technology idea, and I want to go out with that soon.'

'Right. And back there – are you living with . . .?' Imogen stopped herself.

'No one,' he said.

When he looked at her that way she couldn't help but recall how it had been in Thailand, the two of them close in his hammock in the evening, as the sun set, sipping from bottles of beer and reading paperbacks before the light went completely. In those early days of their relationship – or what Imogen had thought then were the early days – it had felt as if they really could be something. They'd had a connection – a love of travel, of being free. She felt that way with him now. The pressure to plan for the future, it didn't exist here.

'You haven't told me a thing about you,' Luca said. 'How is your photography going?'

Imogen wished she could give a better answer.

'Still ticking away,' she said. 'I've been doing some underwater photography the past couple of years.'

'Wow, that's cool,' he said, his eyes wide. 'I mean, you've always been so into diving. You make your living that way?' He was clearly impressed.

'Kind of . . .' she started. 'Actually no. Not really. I'm at a bit of a crossroads careerwise right now. I know I should be more settled.'

'Really? Aren't you pretty young for all that?' Luca asked. 'You always said to me you'd be backpacking until you were at least thirty, and that's a way off still. You should stay true to yourself. To the things that you care about.'

His comment hit a nerve. 'I guess.'

'Don't give up. You're talented, Imogen.'

'Thank you.'

'Look, I'm sorry about what happened between us. I feel like we could have been good together. I was too quick to give up, move on.'

'The timing was out. I couldn't leave so soon after my grandma had died, and when my dad was taking the news so badly.'

'Which just shows what a caring person you are. A good person. And back then I guess I made it all about me. I thought if you liked me enough you'd come back to the island. I took it personally, and that was stupid.'

'I would have handled certain things differently, too,' she said.

'Anyway, what does it matter?' Luca asked. 'You're with someone now. You'll probably be married soon enough.'

'I suppose,' she said, numbly.

'But we still have today.'

Chapter 28

Jan cooed over the webcam as she watched Bella come toddling up to the screen. 'Ooh, she's grown so much!'

'Hasn't she?' Anna said. 'I can't get over it. It seems like yesterday that she was just a little baby, and now here she is, starting to chatter away. Her Italian's coming on quicker than mine!'

'What are her favourite words?' Jan asked.

'*Nonna*,' Anna replied. Bella had been saying it all the time to Elisa.

'Oh,' Jan said, seeming a little hurt. 'Well, yes of course.'

'Don't worry, Mum. She hasn't forgotten about her *English* granny – she carries the photo of you and Dad around the apartment, kissing it.'

'That's nice,' Jan said.

'Hello, love,' Tom said, ducking into the screen. 'Did you and Imogen have a good catch-up?'

'It's been wonderful to see her. We had a little party here, and spent some time just the two of us.'

'We just tried to call her, actually – no answer. Is she not with you?'

'She's gone out to Capri; she left this morning. Maybe her phone's out of battery.'

'I told you, that'll be it, Tom. You know what Imogen's like.'

'She'll be back here tomorrow. There were a couple of things we wanted to do together before she flew home.' She thought of Luigi and of what she'd promised Imogen that they'd do on her return. If their suspicions were correct, her dad would most likely be devastated by the news.

'I'm sure she'll fill us in on all your adventures when she gets home. It's good to see you, Anna,' Tom said. 'Are you happy, living out there?'

'Oh, yes,' Anna said, but as she said it she wondered if it was really true. 'It's great. We've got Matteo's mum and sister nearby. They'll be dropping in for tea in a minute, actually, so we'd better go.'

'Of course,' Jan said. 'Give them our best, won't you.'

'Sure.' She brought Bella up onto her lap so that she could see her grandparents again. 'Say bye-bye.'

Bella kissed the screen, and her grandparents waved back. 'We miss you.'

Ten minutes after she'd ended the call, Carolina and Elisa

came into the ice cream shop. Anna greeted them both, and they took a seat with Matteo in one of the booths.

Carolina looked tired, and her shoulders were slumped. As her mother chattered away, Anna noticed how she stayed quiet, coming into the conversation only occasionally to mutter a 'hmm-hmm' and 'yes' – enough so that Elisa didn't notice her lack of attentiveness.

'Carolina,' Anna said gently, sensing her sister-in-law's discomfort, 'do you want to go for a walk, just the two of us? I'm sure Matteo and your mother can manage for an hour or so.'

Her expression lightened, and she nodded. 'Elisa, would you mind keeping an eye on Bella for a moment?' Anna asked. Her mother-in-law responded enthusiastically, as Anna had expected, and with not a moment's hesitation.

The two women walked out into the bustling square. 'Somewhere quieter,' Carolina said.

'There's a cliff walk. It doesn't take long to get there,' Anna said, taking her sister-in-law's hand and leading her away from the crowds.

Ten minutes later, the two women were walking through the grassland on the cliffs that edged Sorrento. 'It's strange, before I got here I always imagined long white beaches,' Anna said. 'But it's not like that at all, at least not right here: you have to travel to get to them.'

Carolina nodded. 'But what you get instead is this: one of

the most spectacular views in the country. It's better than a beach, really, isn't it?'

'I think so, although Bella might disagree. It's not as easy to make sandcastles up here, is it?'

As they walked, Carolina seemed to relax. The muscles in her shoulders, which had been hunched high, loosened, and her warm laugh came more easily.

'Are you OK?' Anna said.

'Not really,' she said, a deep sadness in her eyes. 'Filippo is paying for the summer house because he feels guilty about what happened. And it makes me sick. Mamma still believes he's the golden boy, of course.'

'Couldn't you just tell her the truth? There's no shame in it – he's the one who's done something wrong.'

'The thing is …' Carolina said, her eyes starting to well with tears. 'It's more complicated than that.'

'What is it?' Anna asked, putting a hand on her arm, and drawing them to a stop while they spoke.

'God, Anna. It's such a mess.'

'What's wrong?'

'You can't tell my brother,' she urged.

Reluctantly, Anna nodded her head.

'I'm pregnant.'

Stunned, Anna tried to think of a reply. Carolina continued.

'It's Filippo's. It happened before I found out the truth about him. We were careless.'

'How far gone are you?' Anna asked, her eyes instinctively dropping to her sister-in-law's waist, her loose dress giving nothing away.

'Twelve weeks,' she said.

'How do you feel about it?'

'Confused.'

'Have you told Filippo?'

She shook her head. 'I know I have to.' She looked as if she might cry. 'But I know it won't change things. He's never wanted children.'

'He still deserves to know,' Anna said.

'I guess. But I can't go back to him. I don't want to.'

'You don't have to,' Anna assured her. 'It's your decision.'

'You say that – but wait until my mother finds out. She won't take the shame of me being a mother on my own, Anna. She would insist I went back. She adores him – he can do no wrong in her eyes.'

'She'd have to understand,' Anna said.

'Come on, Anna,' Carolina said, shaking her head. 'You know her.'

'It's your life.'

'I don't know how I'm going to do this alone,' Carolina said, her eyes welling with more tears.

'You're not alone,' Anna said, putting her hand on Carolina's arm.

Chapter 29

Imogen woke up, her limbs tangled in light cotton sheets. The first rays of morning sun were creeping in through the blinds. Her head fuzzy, she turned and burrowed her face into the pillow. She inhaled a scent there: aftershave.

Finn's.

Then she smelled it again. No, she realised, her pulse racing. It wasn't his.

'Oh, crap,' she whispered to herself, fragments of the previous evening coming back to her. She hadn't, had she? She glanced around the room, but there was no one else there. She waited for her memories of the evening before to come back to her, and they did – but they remained piecemeal.

She and Luca had stayed up late on the terrace after dinner, talking and reminiscing about the days they'd spent in Thailand, when there had been nothing more to think about each day than applying sun lotion and arranging diving expeditions. The Prosecco had gone down easily, and they'd ordered more. After the first couple of glasses, Imogen's memories were hazy. She remembered thinking she should call Finn, then somehow never getting round to it.

The door opened and Luca stepped through it, drying his dark hair roughly with a towel. 'Morning,' he said.

Imogen's heart raced. She knew she'd done something wrong. The feeling of guilt in the pit of her stomach was unmistakeable. But she couldn't properly recall what had happened, how far things had gone.

'You OK?' he said, noting the panicked expression on her face.

She nodded mutely, feeling sick with concern and regret.

The smile left his face. 'You're upset about last night, aren't you?'

She remembered it now: the night sky, the heady scent of bougainvillea awakening her senses, Luca's touch, warm and gentle on the skin of her shoulders, the way he had leaned in towards her . . .

'We kissed,' she said, numb.

She'd done it. She'd finally succeeded in messing things up for good. What sort of person was she? How could she have betrayed Finn, when she loved him so much?

Luca shook his head, and there was disappointment in his eyes. 'You didn't do anything wrong,' he said. 'Don't worry. We just hung out.'

'But I remember . . .' she started, piecing together the fragmented memories.

'You said no,' he said. 'And I probably shouldn't have tried. I thought there was a connection.'

'So how come you're still here?'

'It was late. You said it was OK if I crashed here with you.'

She looked at the sheets, where they must have lain together.

'Nothing happened, I promise.'

Had she wanted it to? Did she want it to now? As Luca sat on the edge of her bed, his face so handsome and familiar – a reminder of days when life had been simpler – her mind swam with mixed emotions.

She got up out of bed and moved away from him. 'This shouldn't have happened,' she said, firmly.

'Then it will be easy for you to forget, won't it?' Luca said. He gathered his things together, and left.

A few minutes later, Imogen checked her phone. Two missed calls, three texts she hadn't seen or answered. One from Anna, two from Finn.

She felt empty. She went into the bathroom and splashed her face with cold water. In the hotel mirror she was met with her reflection – tired, and drawn. She looked like a bad person.

She hadn't done anything – but she'd thought about it, hadn't she?

Chapter 30

Anna was putting her freshly made sorbets into the glass cabinet at the shop when the door swung open. In walked Imogen, carrying a small rucksack. Anna went over to greet her.

'Welcome back!' Anna said. When she hugged her sister she noticed the dark circles under her eyes, and her weary expression.

'You OK, Imo?' she asked, concerned. 'I thought you'd come back refreshed. Did something happen out there?'

Imogen shook her head, fighting back tears. 'Not really. I've made a right mess of things, actually.'

'Let's go outside,' Anna said, taking off her apron. 'Sit by the fountain. Matteo can look after things here.'

They walked outside into the square together.

Once they were sitting down, Anna took her sister's hand and squeezed it. 'Go on, spill. It can't be that bad.'

'Can't it?' Imogen said glumly.

Anna waited for her to continue.

'Luca was out there. In Capri. I spent the night with him. I mean nothing happened – nothing at all. But I don't think that makes it OK. Especially as maybe part of me wanted it to.'

'God!' Anna said.

'Thanks. That makes me feel better.'

'Sorry,' Anna said, the story that Imogen had told slowly sinking in. 'I'm just surprised. I mean, Luca? I thought you were over him ages ago, before Finn even came along.'

'I was,' she said. 'I am. I don't know . . .'

'How would Finn feel about this if he knew?'

'He'd be a bit upset. Annoyed. As I would, if the shoe was on the other foot.'

'But if you explained it he'd understand, right? He's a great guy, Imogen, and he really loves you.'

'I know,' she said, hot tears spilling. 'I'm an idiot.'

'You didn't actually do anything – and that's important. But what's going on here, really? Do you care about Luca?'

'I don't know. Maybe,' Imogen said. 'When I saw him, it was like a part of me came back again. I felt alive.'

'You felt alive,' Anna echoed.

'Yes, so I guess maybe I do care about him.'

'You just told me about *you*, not about him.'

'You're right,' Imogen said, shaking her head. 'I guess it was more about that. We talked a lot.'

'Can you imagine being with him, properly?'

Imogen thought it over, then shook her head. 'No. That time's gone.' Anna waited patiently. 'It wouldn't work at all.'

'Did you always know that?'

'No,' she said. 'I guess there was always a what-if. He was my what-if.'

'And now?'

'I feel terrible, Anna. I can't justify what I did. I should've known better.'

'Do you still have a what-if?'

'No. I don't. All I want is to be back with Finn.'

'Then tell him the truth. He's a reasonable man, Imo. He'll understand.'

'OK,' Imogen said. 'I will. I'll tell him and with any luck he'll see that all it's done is made me surer than ever that he's the one I want to be with.'

'You do that. It'll be OK, sis.' Anna put her arm round her sister's shoulders.

Imogen wiped away her tears and nodded.

'And in the meantime there's something else we need to do before you head home.'

Luigi was working in the kitchen when Anna and Imogen got to his restaurant the next day.

'Maybe we shouldn't do this,' Imogen whispered to her sister. 'I mean, where do we even start?'

239

'Just tell him what you told me. About what you found.'

'Hello, you two,' Luigi said, wiping his floury hands on his apron. 'What a pleasure to see you both again so soon. It was a great party the other night.'

'Thanks for coming,' Anna said.

'So, tell me, what can I help you with? It's early for lunch, but I can get you espressos.'

'No, no, don't worry,' Imogen said. 'I was actually hoping ...' The words tailed away and Anna gave her a nudge. She fell silent.

'Is it OK if we sit down?' Anna asked. He joined them, a crease of puzzlement between his brows.

'There's something I wanted to ask you,' Imogen said. 'I tried to, at the party, but I couldn't find the words. You see, our grandmother was here many years ago. And recently I found some things. A letter from you, a photo ... But she died two years ago, so I couldn't ask her.'

'She's gone?' Luigi asked, clearly choked up.

'Yes. And we miss her so very much. We really had no idea that she was in love with you, but I can tell from her letters that she was. We're just hoping that from you we can hear the whole story.'

'Do you have a photo of her?' he asked, a deep sadness in his eyes.

'Yes,' Imogen said. 'I do, in here somewhere.' She flicked through the photos of Vivien that she'd picked up along with the letter, and pulled out one of her and Evie on the seafront, eating ice creams.

He smiled. 'There she is.'

Anna and Imogen exchanged looks, both moved by the love in his eyes. The connection seemed so strong still.

He looked up at them, sadness in his eyes. 'She was a wonderful person.'

'Yes, she was.'

He paused, then looked back at the photo. 'My beautiful Evie.'

Imogen and Anna walked back across the square towards the ice cream shop.

'I should have known,' Imogen said. 'Granny wasn't the type to have an affair. But trying to matchmake her best friend? That's got her written all over it.'

'She did always want to see people happy,' Anna said.

'She must have seen that this was a missed chance for Evie.'

'The look on Luigi's face when he realised she was still alive,' Anna said. 'I thought he was going to cry with happiness.'

'You know we have to do something,' Imogen said. 'We need to make this happen.'

'Imo,' Anna said, sounding a little wary. 'Are you sure?

'It clearly mattered to Granny.'

'I'm not sure we should interfere. And anyway, don't you think you should focus on your own life for a while?'

'No,' Imogen said. 'I'm quite happy for that to stay out of focus right now, thanks. If Granny V thought this guy was right for Evie, then perhaps she was right.'

'You're not going to let this one go, are you?'

'Damn right I'm not.'

Chapter 31

On the flight back to England, Imogen felt dazed. When she got to the baggage hall, she texted Finn to let him know she was almost home. He replied excitedly, with a kiss. The small 'x', so easily given, brought a fresh wave of guilt.

She caught the train to Brighton, and watched through the window as green fields gave way to the pastel-coloured Georgian houses that signalled home. She'd tell Finn that evening, she decided. She'd get straight to the point and explain what had happened with Luca out in Capri.

When she walked into their house in Brighton, the room was rich with the aromas of cooking, Finn singing along to something on 6 Music as he chopped vegetables. 'Hey!' he called out, coming over to her, his eyes bright. She kissed him and held him close.

'Hi, Finn,' she said. In his arms everything felt good again.

'I've really missed you,' he said.

'Me too,' she said. A stab of guilt hit her between the ribs, but she forced herself to blank the feeling out.

They sat down over dinner and Imogen told Finn about Anna's new life and the ice cream shop. As she cleared the plates, he touched her shoulder.

'Leave that for now. I've got a surprise for you,' he said.

'A surprise?' she said.

'Yes. Come outside with me.'

Finn led Imogen around the side of the building and out into the garden.

'Close your eyes.' He stood behind Imogen, putting one hand around in front of her face so that she couldn't see.

'Hey!' she said, laughing. With Finn's strong arms around her, she felt safe, secure, even though one of her senses had been temporarily taken away from her. She felt both a thrill and relief at the temporary loss of control. Walking with him, seeing nothing but darkness and the subtle glow as the sun filtered through the gaps between his fingers, it was as if the time in Capri had never happened. As if there was nothing to think about but the two of them.

'I hope this is a good surprise,' she said. She was walking on the paving stones now; she remembered laying them the previous summer, when everything was still new. When she'd first realised that she didn't have to keep searching for herself, her centre – that it wasn't in the depths of a distant ocean, that she felt most at ease when she was in Finn's arms.

'It's a good surprise, yes. I promise.' He kissed her gently on the delicate skin of her shoulder.

Imogen carried on walking, recognising the scents of the garden that she and Finn had planted together – the fragrant lavender bushes that teemed with bees in the summer, the small herb garden, with mint and thyme, and the rose bushes near to the shed. She could smell them now – a gift from her parents when she'd moved in with Finn. Her dad had come over to plant them. All the things around her, the pieces of her and Finn's life – it all seemed more precious now. She had almost thrown it all away.

The clunk of metal and the jangle of keys. 'Hang on,' she protested. 'Are you putting me in the shed?' The wooden structure could barely be called that – it was little more than a run-down shelter that housed their rake and outside broom, a few garden tools.

'Just be patient,' Finn said. She felt the atmosphere change as she stepped forward. She could tell she was inside somewhere, but it certainly didn't feel like the dank, spider-infested shed she was used to.

'Now, take a look.' He took his hands away.

Imogen opened her eyes to take in the scene, but she couldn't see anything. It was pitch-black in there. She raised a hand up towards her face and could barely make out her fingers. 'I feel like I've gone blind,' she said.

She heard a switch click and the room was cast in a low

red light. It was then that she could see where she was – trays laid out in front of her, vats of chemicals, lines with tiny pegs on them.

'Finn,' she said, as she took in her surroundings. 'A dark-room. My own darkroom.'

In the red light he hugged her closer to him. 'Did I do OK?'

'Yes,' she said. She felt deeply moved, and horribly guilty, at once.

'You'll be able to work in your pyjamas. Or that lion onesie you're so fond of. Whatever you want,' he said, smil-ing.

'I love it,' she said.

'I'm glad you like it. Lauren helped me order some things up, so you should have everything you need.'

'But how did you manage all of this?' Imogen asked.

'I had a bit of help from your dad.'

'But the surf school . . .'

'I kind of got a taste for building work.'

She turned to Finn, lifting a hand to touch the rough stubble on his jaw and drawing him closer to her. She kissed him, softly at first and then more deeply, taking in the salty, outdoorsy scent of him and the warmth of his skin. 'Thank you.'

This is what I have – and it's good, Imogen thought. She wasn't going to risk ruining all this. Some things were better left unsaid – and the time she'd spent with Luca on the island was one of them. She'd learned her lesson. That was what mattered.

The next morning, Imogen was waiting for the kettle to boil. In front of her were two mugs, ready for tea, and two cinnamon bagels, freshly buttered. She was going to take Finn breakfast in bed that morning, part of a vow she'd made to herself that she'd make sure they spent more quality time together.

She checked her phone as she stood at the counter. Her heart raced as she saw a new message in her inbox – from Luca: 'You must be back home by now. Was it so easy for you to forget? It isn't for me.'

Panicking, she closed the message. She thought of Finn, still asleep in their bedroom, and felt acutely aware of what she hadn't told him. She wanted to fix this. She needed to. But now – after she'd missed the opportunity to come clean – she wasn't sure how to.

Later that morning, Imogen was on her own in the house. Finn had been so delighted with the breakfast they'd shared, but it had made her feel even worse. He'd got ready for work, and kissed her, a sweet touch on her lips that still lingered with her. Then he'd left, and all she had was the nagging of her conscience.

When Finn had left for work, Imogen had gone out to the

new darkroom. She had worked slowly but determinedly, printing out the photos that she'd taken on the trip: images of gelato, trees and glistening water. She'd developed a picture of Luigi that she'd taken just before she left. When the time was right to say something to Evie, Imogen would have that to show her.

When she had finished, she came back inside and checked her diary: tea with her mum in Kemp Town before lunch, then two photography sessions in the afternoon. Back to work. A dose of normality after the whirlwind of Italy. This was what she needed.

She cycled into town and met her mother at her favourite teashop, a vintage hideaway in Kemp Town. They hugged hello, and the edge Imogen often felt around her mother wasn't there. So much in her life seemed uncertain that the comfort of family was just what she needed.

'Good to have you back, Imogen,' Jan said. 'So, tell me all about it.'

Imogen told her about Sorrento, the people in the community, the situation with Anna and her in-laws. And about Luigi and Evie. She couldn't resist telling that part.

'Oh, how romantic,' Jan said. 'All these years, and he's still thinking of her. You have to tell her.'

'I will,' Imogen said. 'I just want to find the right time.'

Jan's eyes were bright with the excitement of hearing about Luigi.

'You won't say anything, will you?' Imogen said. 'Please, Mum.'

'No, I won't. I promise,' Jan said.

'OK,' Imogen said. She'd given only a carefully edited version of the story of her time in Italy, of course. There was no way she was mentioning a word about Luca. Before her mum could ask her any uncomfortable questions, she changed the subject.

'Any news from the guesthouse?'

'A group of Japanese tourists have almost filled it this week,' Jan explained. 'All except for Clarissa's room, of course.'

'So she's still there?'

'Yes. She's becoming part of the furniture now. She seems a little happier, I think. And your uncle says there haven't been any problems with night wanderings lately.'

'That's good.'

'She just seems to want to be there. To understand something more about the place. I agree it's odd. But, if your uncle doesn't mind, I don't see the harm.'

'Of course.'

'You know, the funny thing is, when your father saw her, he did a double-take. Said he couldn't put his finger on it, but there was something about her he recognised. He thought perhaps her mother might have stayed there, at the guesthouse, when he and Martin were young. But then I asked him about it, and he . . . Well, you know how he gets. Suddenly vague about the whole thing.'

When Imogen and her mother finished tea, she cycled over to Lauren's studio, letting herself in with the spare key her friend had given her. Lauren had left notes about the sessions Imogen would be covering that afternoon – twin girls, and a dog, Trixie.

By four o'clock, Imogen was starting to wonder if she was losing her touch. The morning session, with unsmiling six-year-old schoolgirls, had felt like an endurance test, as she tried to coax some joy out of them. And now she had Trixie, the world's least cheerful canine.

'Throw Trixie the ball now.' Trixie, an Old English sheep-dog, beloved by her middle-aged owner Samuel, was sitting in the middle of the studio, calmly and quietly, tilting her head only slightly at each command.

Samuel threw the ball and Trixie's eyes moved a fraction, following it, but there was no other movement. She was a sweet-natured dog, but a nightmare in terms of the photography session. Imogen had anticipated an easy afternoon – but this was proving anything but.

'She's not normally like this,' Samuel said, puzzled. 'She's a bouncy dog normally.'

Imogen raised a squeaky toy over her head and squeezed it to get Trixie's attention, but again she didn't flinch.

'Here, girl,' she said, getting down on her knees and throwing some bone-shaped dog treats towards Trixie. She lolloped towards them slowly and without enthusiasm, but Imogen snapped a few shots.

'Maybe I should bring her back another day,' Samuel said.

There was half an hour left. Not ideal, but long enough to get something usable, she hoped. 'Let's give it one more try,' she said.

But it hadn't worked. Imogen brought the session to a close, concerned that there wouldn't be more than a handful of usable photos there. Lauren was not going to be happy about it, but she'd done all that she could.

Later that evening, back in the house, with Finn still out working, Imogen realised that things weren't going to get any better – her mind wasn't going to get clearer – unless she took some decisive action. Luca's email had been on her mind all day, and just the presence of it in her inbox felt like evidence, her guilty conscience returning to it again and again. She had to draw a line under the whole thing. It was the only way to start moving forward.

She took out her phone and replied to his message:

Luca, nothing happened between us. And nothing is ever going to happen. I'm in love with my boyfriend and I want to be with him. I was stupid enough to forget

that for a few days, that's all. Please don't contact me
again.
  Imogen

She sent it. Then she deleted his message, and her reply. It
was done, and now it could be properly forgotten.

Chapter 32

'Imo!' Bella said, running into the living room of Anna's apartment. 'Imo?' Her dark hair was dishevelled from where she'd been sleeping on it but her eyes were bright.

Anna took her daughter into her arms for a hug. 'I'm sorry, sweetie. Imogen's gone. Do you remember when we said goodbye?'

'Bub-bye,' Bella parroted, her face falling a little.

'I guess you're not the only one who's sad that your sister's left,' Matteo said to Anna.

'It was great to see her, wasn't it?' Anna said, smiling at the memory of her sister's visit.

'It was. It feels kind of quiet now, doesn't it?'

'It certainly does.'

'So – I guess it's back to normal for us now,' Matteo said.

'Yes. And I want to make things better, starting today. I'm going to meet your mother later.'

At the cocktail party Anna had seen a glimmer of hope that she and Elisa could find a new balance. And, with what Carolina had told her, she felt she owed it to the family to try to make peace.

'You are?' Matteo said.

'I suggested we have coffee, just the two of us. Talk.'

Matteo said, cautiously. 'I appreciate that. Thank you, Anna.'

That afternoon, Anna walked through the square and down to the summer house, holding a cake that she'd picked up at the bakery.

'Anna! Come in,' Elisa said, when they met each other at the front door.

A few minutes later the two of them were sitting down at the kitchen table, coffee and cake between them.

'I am glad you suggested meeting, Anna,' Elisa said brightly.

'I just thought – there's been so much going on, we don't often get the chance to talk properly, just the two of us. I want to change that.'

'This is true.'

'I know we've had some differences of opinion, about the shop, but hopefully you can see that we've taken on board some of the things you suggested.'

'Yes – it will help you, I'm sure.'

'I appreciate you trying to help.'

'And I know there are some things you need to do yourself,' Elisa said.

Anna felt as if they were finally getting somewhere.

'And, of course, you will have some big decisions to make soon,' Elisa said. 'I want to help you with those.'

'Decisions?' Anna said.

Elisa pursed her lips, then continued. 'We both want the best for Matteo, and for Bella, don't we?'

'Of course,' Anna said.

'And I think we can both see how happy they are here in Italy.'

Anna shuffled in her seat. 'Yes. Things seem to be working out.'

'So you will want to start thinking about making the move permanent, won't you?'

'I don't know about that,' Anna said. 'It's still so early, we need to see how the business goes . . .'

'Follow my advice and you won't have any problems there.'

'And there's my family to think about too, Elisa. I'm not sure I'm ready . . .'

'But you don't have a problem with keeping Matteo from his?'

'That's not true,' Anna said, her voice forceful.

Elisa brought her dark eyebrows together in a frown. 'Well, that's what it looks like.'

'You have Carolina here—'

'And look at her, Anna – she devotes herself completely to her husband. She is not afraid to make compromises for him, for the good of the family. For me it has always been the same. Why is it that you think so differently?'

Anna thought of her conversation with Carolina, how little Elisa knew of what was happening to the family she professed to care about so much.

'You're not being fair,' Anna said.

'My son's happiness matters to me,' Elisa said. 'It should matter to you, too.'

That evening, Anna and Matteo were sitting on the balcony eating by candlelight. People dined and walked in the square below, a buzz of chatter rising up to them.

'So, I went to see your mother today,' Anna said, trying to steady her nerves.

'How did it go?' he said, tentatively.

'Not as well as I'd hoped.'

'What happened?'

'I thought at first we were getting somewhere – but then she started pushing. Trying to get me to commit to us living out here in the long term.'

'Oh dear. I'm sorry.'

'Have you spoken with her about that?'

Matteo frowned. 'I've told her I'm happy to be back. Beyond that, nothing.'

'That was clearly enough for her to think I'm stopping you from living the way you want to.'

'She thinks she's helping,' he said.

'Well, she's not – at all,' Anna said firmly. 'Where we live is a huge decision. It's not down to her.'

Matteo looked wounded. 'And you think I don't know that?' he said. 'I'm not a child, Anna.'

'I feel like whenever she says something you just go along with her.'

'I'm just trying to keep the peace. You make it sound so easy – that we should just do what we want. Well, it isn't that straightforward. I can't just ignore her wishes. She's family.'

'Aren't we your family now? Me and Bella?'

Matteo's expression hardened. 'You want me to turn my back on my mother, my parents?'

'Of course not,' Anna said, frustrated with the turn the conversation was taking. 'That isn't what I meant at all.'

'I want you to be happy, Anna, I really do. But I'm stuck in the middle here.'

'You don't seem stuck in the middle to me at all,' Anna said.

'What do you mean by that?'

'I feel like you're on her side,' Anna said, her emotion spilling over into her voice.

'There aren't sides,' Matteo said, shaking his head. 'That's not how it is at all.'

*

257

That night in bed, Anna wanted to curl in closer to Matteo, to feel the safety of his warm body against hers. But, when she did, he barely responded. She felt she'd broken something in him, by forcing him to choose. And perhaps she'd broken something inside herself, too.

She woke at 1 a.m., and, pulling on her dressing gown, went out to the balcony. Stars filled the sky over the cobbled square – so bright without the lights from street lamps, houses and cars that dimmed the constellations back home in Brighton. A nightmare had woken her, a cold chill running down the back of her neck. Normally, the view from the balcony calmed her, but right then it seemed cold and unfamiliar. All she saw were buildings and landscapes that were so different from the ones she grew up in, and the expanse of sky just made her more aware of the distance, which seemed infinite. Looking out reminded her how far she was from her sister, her family, her flat, everything that felt like home.

The door opened behind her and she turned towards the sound. Matteo came out and joined her on the balcony. 'Hey,' he said, softly. His dark hair was mussed from being in bed, and he was rubbing his eyes. 'What are you doing out here?'

'Couldn't sleep.'

He put an arm around her waist and looked out at the view with her. 'It's beautiful, isn't it?'

'Is it?' she said. As she spoke her voice caught on the emotion and threatened to break.

They were silent for a moment.

'I can't see it any more,' Anna said.

'Is this about today? My mother?'

'Yes, of course it is,' she said. 'I don't feel supported by you. And I don't feel like your mother accepts me for who I am.'

'That's not true,' Matteo said. 'Of course she likes you. It's just her way. Come on. I'll talk to her.'

Anna couldn't hold back the tears any longer. 'I want to go home. I want to be back home with Bella, close to my family. I'm starting to feel like an outsider here.'

Matteo's voice took on a harsher tone. 'And you think I've never felt that way? You know I love living in Brighton. I'm not saying I don't. But when you and your friends are talking fast, making private jokes, or when your family are talking about places I've never been to, or TV programmes I've never watched, don't you think I feel the same way?'

'My family have always accepted you,' Anna snapped.

'I know – but that doesn't mean Britain has always felt like home.'

'I didn't realise you felt that way,' Anna said.

'Not all the time.' Matteo shrugged.

'How do we fix this?' she asked. 'Because when I look at it, wherever we live, one of us is going to be unhappy.'

'I guess you're right,' he said.

'So what, we live apart?' Anna said. As soon as the words were out she wished she could draw them back in.

He shook his head. 'Don't.' He paused. 'We can't do that to Bella,' he said at last, his voice barely a whisper.

Anna pictured her young daughter sleeping in the other room, her face nuzzled into the soft bunny rabbit she took to bed each night, her cheeks a soft pink with sleep. Her home wasn't a country at all. It was her two parents, the warmth of their joint embrace.

Did that home still exist?

Chapter 33

Imogen arrived back at the house, and brought her shopping bags up to the door. She had stopped by a farmers' market on the way home, and picked up some fresh ingredients for dinner that evening: lemon sole with vegetables and sweet-potato fries; Finn would like that. She was looking forward to seeing the look on his face, and to kissing him. Everything felt lighter now that she'd cut ties with Luca completely, and she was even starting to feel a spark of inspiration return.

She opened the door and called out a welcome to Finn. The house was quiet. She looked around, then saw him, over at the breakfast bar. Their eyes met, and he shook his head slightly. There was deep sadness in his expression. Imogen's heart felt heavy. Something was wrong.

'Is everything OK?' Imogen asked. She walked over, and, as she neared the breakfast bar, she saw an expanse of images laid out in front of him. Photos she recognised – ones she had taken herself.

'I found these,' Finn said. 'In your darkroom.'

Imogen's chest felt tight. As she looked at Finn, his brow creased, his sandy hair tousled, regret engulfed her. No words came.

'There was a noise in there, something fell over. That's why I went in. Then, when I did, these were hanging there.'

Imogen's throat was dry.

'These were taken in Italy, right?' he said, pointing to the bright pink flowers and crumbling brickwork.

'Yes, Capri,' Imogen said.

'And this guy?' Finn prompted her, raising his eyebrows. Between them were images of Luca, his dark eyes staring up from the freshly developed prints.

Imogen could have kicked herself for being so careless.

'Who is he?'

'Luca,' Imogen said.

'Luca? Your ex, Luca?' he asked, disbelieving.

'Yes. I met him in Capri. It wasn't planned.'

Finn looked again at one of the photos Imogen had taken with the timer, their faces close, wide smiles beaming out from their tanned faces. She winced thinking how it must look to Finn.

'Nothing happened,' she said, quickly.

'Right, nothing happened,' Finn said, flatly. 'So why did you take these photos of nothing happening?'

'I don't know – I don't even remember taking them, really.'

'And that's supposed to make it better?'

'No ... I meant to explain when I first got back; I don't know why I didn't. Luca and I went out for drinks. Then dinner. Look, I know it doesn't look good, but nothing happened, honestly. We just talked.'

'Explain what, Imogen? That while I was here, waiting for you to call, you were with your ex having a great time in Capri?'

'It was nothing, honestly,' Imogen said, her words spilling out. 'Finn, I would never jeopardise what we have.' She had to put this right. 'I guess I was flattered by the attention. And it felt easy, spending time with him, not having to think about the future. It seems like the two of us have been talking about that so much recently—'

'So that's what this was about?' Finn asked, his eyes widening.

'No ...' Imogen said. 'But yes.' She stalled. 'Well, maybe.'

'Which is it?' Finn said. 'Because I don't get it any more. Do I even make you happy?'

'Of course you do,' she said, desperation creeping into her voice.

'I remember now, you not answering your phone that

night ...' He shook his head. 'Was that you choosing him over me?'

'It wasn't about him or you, it never would be. I finished with Luca for a reason, and I fell in love with you for a hundred things that you are, and that we are together. I just ...' She knew she had to be honest in a way she hadn't been up till now. It was the only way for them to move forward as a couple. 'I thought you might be about to ask me to marry you.'

Finn flinched, surprised. 'And what if I was?'

'It's not that I don't want to be with you, but marriage ...'

'Right,' he said. 'Well, ouch. That kind of hurts.'

'Sorry,' Imogen blundered. 'I was confused about it all ...'

'Wow,' Finn said, rubbing his brow wearily and looking down. 'This conversation wasn't great to start off with, but it does feel like it's hitting a new low.'

'I'm sorry,' Imogen said. She was deflated, unsure now of how she could even start to make things right, to pull them back from this place they'd come to.

'You feel weirded out about the idea of getting married, so this is how you deal with it? Rather than talking to me, you find this guy and spend your time with him instead?'

'It wasn't like that.'

'I think I just need to be on my own for a bit,' Finn said.

'OK,' she said. She felt rooted to the spot but knew that she had to leave. As much as it had become their home, it was still his house, and she was the one at fault here. 'I guess I'll get my things, then.'

He nodded, and gave a reluctant shrug.

Imogen went into their bedroom, and got out her ruck-sack from underneath the bed. She looked around the room, the white bedsheets crumpled from where they'd slept there together, the framed photo of the two of them with their surfboards, on a sandy Devon beach, on top of the dresser.

Her cheeks grew hot and tears spilled down onto them. She stuffed a few of her belongings into her bag and tried not to think about when, and in what circumstances, she might next come back.

Chapter 34

'Banana pancakes?' Anna asked Bella, holding up a banana from the fruit bowl. She needed something to brighten that morning, and pancakes usually helped.

'Yay!' Bella said, clapping her hands together.

'OK, great,' Anna said, getting the ingredients from the cupboard.

Matteo appeared in the doorway to the kitchen, fresh from the shower, towel-drying his hair.

'Pancakes?' Anna asked, softly.

'Yes, please,' he said.

They hadn't spoken since the previous night, and the tension between them was palpable. During their conversation Anna had felt pushed to breaking point, considering things that already, in the light of day, were too upsetting to revisit. It wasn't that she wanted to gloss over it all, pretend that the conversation hadn't happened – and that Elisa's demands hadn't hurt her – but it was her and Matteo's way, she thought, pouring the mixture into the pan, listening to Matteo talking and playing with his daughter. Good food was their foundation, and it helped them get through the days, even difficult ones, like this one.

Matteo took the plate gratefully, and cut some up for his daughter. 'Have you heard from Imogen lately?'

'No.' Anna shook her head. 'It's weird, actually. I got a text saying she'd got back safely, but nothing more.' It had been on her mind. 'I'll call her later.'

'We've got those food bloggers coming in later today,' Matteo said. 'We should put something special together for them. You do remember? The meeting you set up?'

'Yes,' Anna said. 'Yes, of course. I put some things to one side in the freezer, actually, so we're all set for that.'

'And Bella?' Matteo said.

As he said their daughter's name, Anna wondered if Bella was the only thread keeping them together.

'Carolina could probably mind her while the bloggers are there.'

'Sure. Or I can ask Mamma.'

'I don't really want to ask her right now,' Anna said.

'So, what? You have a difference of opinion and now you want to cut her out of our lives?'

'Of course not,' Anna said. 'But after yesterday ... I'd prefer to ask Carolina, that's all.'

'She'll come round in the end,' Matteo said.

'I hope so. Because this is *our* relationship, Matteo. I don't want three people in it.'

Anna took a few moments before the food bloggers arrived to check in with her sister on the phone.

'So, things took a bit of an unexpected turn,' Imogen said. 'Or maybe I should have seen from the start that this was the only way things could go.'

'What happened?'

'Do you really want to know?' Imogen said. Anna could hear the tears in her voice. 'I'm in the van. It's loaded up with my stuff. I've moved out, Anna.'

'You've what?' Anna said, caught off guard. She sat down on one of the seats outside the shop, far from the customers. 'You and Finn ...'

'He found some photos of me and Luca in Capri. I don't know why I was stupid enough to think he wouldn't find out, that I could just keep quiet about it and it would be like nothing had ever happened. As it is, with just the photos to go on, how can I blame him for thinking I was hiding something more serious?'

'Oh, Imogen. I'm so sorry to hear that,' Anna said. 'Have you got somewhere to go? Lauren's? Mum and Dad's?'

'Lauren has her brother staying, and, God, no, I'm not going back to Mum and Dad's. Things are bad, but not that bad.' She laughed wryly. 'I called Uncle Martin and he's got a room free, so I'm driving over to the guesthouse now.'

'It'll work out soon,' Anna said, reassuringly. 'Just give him time.'

'I didn't mean to hurt him, Anna.' Imogen's voice softened. 'I hate that I did. I just wish I could go back and do it all differently.'

At two, Anna and Matteo closed the ice cream shop in Sorrento for an hour, for the bloggers' event – a dozen food writers had arrived, and were chatting to them both over smoothies about how they'd got started.

'We have our own shop in Brighton,' Anna explained, 'but then we were drawn back here to Italy, where Matteo grew up, and it seemed the perfect opportunity to introduce a wider audience to our recipes.'

It helped, Anna thought – having to make a good impression with strangers and present a united front with Matteo. As they talked about happier times, she could almost forget about the devastating conversation they'd had the previous night. Almost.

'The English recipes have actually travelled really well,' Matteo said. 'The gin-and-tonic-and-lemon lolly has been a huge hit here,' Matteo said. 'And our classic Wimbledon ice cream, strawberries and cream.'

The food bloggers took notes, and tasted the samples

Anna had put out for them. They looked around the shop, intrigued.

'It's a real transformation from how it was before,' said one blogger, a woman called Lucy. 'I moved out here from the UK ten years ago and I've been longing to find somewhere that felt like home. As soon as you guys took this place over I knew I'd found it.'

'Thank you,' Anna said. 'That's nice to hear.'

'A few people have commented to me that they find it refreshing to see a mix of different styles on your menu. Obviously, Italy's known for its ice cream for good reason, but there are plenty of places here doing the traditional stuff. I think you're standing out because you're not afraid to try something new.'

Matteo listened and nodded. Anna felt a little vindicated by Lucy's comment – but, then, it didn't seem to matter so much any more. Things had gone beyond that now.

'You're from the Bonomi family, though, aren't you?' Lucy asked.

'You've done your research,' he said.

'Have there been any problems, with you breaking away from the family business like this?' Lucy enquired.

Matteo's and Anna's eyes met, for a fleeting moment.

Anna spoke up first. 'There are challenges in any business, aren't there? What matters is that you try to work past them.'

Lucy smiled, and made a note in her pad.

When Matteo touched her hand behind the counter, warmth spread back through it, and she closed her fingers around his.

When the bloggers left the shop just after three, and things fell quiet again, Carolina arrived back with Bella. She was carrying a new ball – blue with silver stars – and she and Carolina were bouncing it along the floor as they walked.

'You two look like you've been having fun,' Anna said.

'We have been. We went around the local shops and Bella learned how to say "*grazie*". Didn't you, sweetie?'

Bella looked up at them, confused.

'You'll have to take my word for it,' Carolina said. 'So, how did it go here?'

'Really well, actually,' Anna said. 'We seemed to get quite a lot of interest.'

'It's always worth doing these things – ensure that the word spreads. Although you do seem to have been getting plenty of attention already.'

'Yes. How are you feeling, by the way?' Anna whispered. Although she was fairly sure Matteo was out of earshot she didn't want to take any chances.

'Terrible,' Carolina said quietly. 'I thought the sickness was supposed to improve, but mine seems to have got worse. Bella's been a great distraction, though.'

'I'm glad. If it gets too much, though, you must let me know.'

'Don't worry. And I suppose in a way I ought to thank you. Up till now Mamma hasn't stopped bugging me about when Filippo is coming down. Now she's started obsessing about whether you're going to stay here. She seems to have forgotten about Filippo altogether.'

'She's spoken with you about it?' Anna said.

'Yes. I'm sorry, Anna. You know what she's like when she gets an idea in her head. She'll calm down, in time.'

'I hope so. I respect your mother. I really do. I just need this to be our decision.'

'Of course you do. And it should be. Mamma just can't resist making everything her business. You see why I've kept quiet about my own life? How do you think she's going to react when she finds out I'm breaking up with one of the richest men in our region – and about to become a single mother, too?'

'I wish I could help,' Anna said.

'You already have, just by listening. It's my problem,' Carolina said.

'There is one thing I can offer you. It won't fix this – but it might make you feel better. My tried-and-tested morning-sickness solution – lemon-and-ginger sorbet. Light as air. Curative properties almost guaranteed.'

Slowly, Carolina began to smile. 'I thought I couldn't eat anything right now. But that sounds irresistibly good.'

Chapter 35

At the Elderberry Guesthouse, Imogen unpacked her clothes and hung them in the small wardrobe in one of the guestrooms. When she'd arrived earlier that evening, her uncle Martin had welcomed her in, no questions asked, seeming to understand that she needed a quiet place to be.

On the way over, her nerves had felt raw and frayed after the conversation with Finn, but now she drew some comfort from the surroundings – her grandmother's house would always be a haven. It had the power to transport her back to a time when she'd felt nothing bad could or would ever happen, a childhood mostly spent in tears of laughter with her sister and parents, building dens and making potions – mixing things sweet and grimly chemical that they found around the house, pretending to be magicians. Life had been simpler then.

A knock at her door jolted her out of her memories.

Uncle Martin smiled apologetically. 'Your parents are here,' he said.

'What? Why?' she said.

'They just popped in. But, when I mentioned to your mum you were here, she was quite insistent.'

'OK. Don't worry, I'll come down.'

Imogen followed her uncle down the stairs, her heart heavy. She didn't really want to talk to anyone, let alone her mother.

'Oh, Imogen,' Jan said. She was sitting on the sofa in the living room, a cup of tea in her hand. 'Have you left Finn?'

'Something like that,' Imogen said, taking a seat.

'What a mess,' Jan said.

'Thanks, Mum,' she said, flatly. 'That helps.'

'Well, it's just that the two of you were such a good match. I don't really understand how all of this has happened. It was only a couple of weeks ago that your dad was helping him make the darkroom for you.'

'I'm sorry,' Imogen said, turning to her dad, the thought of his work on the darkroom making her feel worse than she already did.

'Oh, don't worry about that,' Tom said. 'Not for a second. It doesn't matter. We just want to know that you're OK.'

'I appreciate that,' Imogen said. 'I think.'

'You sure you wouldn't like to come back home? Just for a little while?' her mum asked.

'No. Definitely not. Sorry, but I don't think that's a good idea.'

Imogen went up to her room, feeling even more deflated. She loved her parents, and knew she was lucky to be close to them, but at times like these she wished that they could stay out of things. When they tried to rescue her like that, it just made her feel like a child.

Up on the top floor, she saw that Clarissa's door was open, and she was sitting on her bed with a book.

On impulse, Imogen went to her own room to pick up the bottle of Limoncello that she'd bought in duty-free. She went back to Clarissa's room and knocked on her door gently.

'Sorry to disturb you. Don't suppose you'd like to help me with this?' Imogen asked.

She'd expected a polite no, and to spend the evening drowning her sorrows alone, but, instead, Clarissa's face brightened. 'Yes. I would like that. Come in.'

Imogen took a seat on the red-velvet armchair near the bed, and cracked open the bottle, pouring two small glasses. She handed one to Clarissa and downed the other herself.

'Like that, is it?' Clarissa asked, kindly.

'A bit. I think me and my boyfriend have just broken up,' Imogen said.

'I'm sorry,' Clarissa said, sympathetically. 'That must be hard.'

'It's my fault. I was an idiot.'

'You still love him?'

'Yes,' Imogen said. The emotions that she'd been working so hard to suppress started to rise to the surface, and her bottom lip trembled.

'Well, then, there's hope, isn't there?' Clarissa's green eyes seemed softer then. 'If something's worth having, it's worth fighting for.'

'Yes,' Imogen said. 'But I don't know how I can expect him to forgive me. I don't think *I* can forgive me. And my mum's already driving me mad, asking about it ...' She caught herself. 'Sorry,' she said. 'Wasn't thinking. I know I'm lucky to have her.'

Clarissa brought the book she'd been holding back into her lap. Imogen saw that it wasn't a hardback but a linen-bound journal, with a satin ribbon keeping her place. 'It's been years since my mother died,' she said. 'And I feel like I'm only just getting to know her.'

Imogen resisted her usual urge to fill the silence. Instead, she waited for Clarissa to go on.

Clarissa's eyes were brimming with tears. 'My stepfather had this all those years, but he only gave it to me just before he died. My mother's diary,' she explained. 'From the time before I was born, and after.'

'Wow,' Imogen said. Her problems seemed to shrink in significance.

'I'm not angry with him. I know he thought about it a lot, what was the right thing to do. Mum didn't throw the diary out, but she didn't leave it for me to find, either. She'd left it somewhere she knew *he* would find it.'

'It must have been a difficult decision for him.'

'It was. I know you must think I'm mad. Still here, barely going out. But in a way it's the closest I've ever felt to Mum. I'm seeing part of her life that she never told anyone about.'

Imogen looked at her, confused.

'And now here I am, talking in riddles,' Clarissa said, with a wry laugh. 'Sorry.'

'What does it say in there?' Imogen asked, motioning to the diary.

'A lot of things I didn't know. I've read it already, of course. But there's only so much I can take in at one time. I go back to it, try and make sense of it little by little.'

'She stayed here, didn't she?' Imogen said.

'Yes. Mum – Emma, that was her name – she grew up in Brighton, with her parents and her brother. When she was a teenager, she'd go into Sunset 99s with her friends, get a drink or an ice lolly when school was out. That was the part she always told me. But in here' – she touched the diary gently – 'is the other part.'

Clarissa took a deep breath before continuing. 'Then Mum started going there on her own, during school hours.

She was only sixteen, so your grandmother felt bound to ask her what was wrong, why she wasn't in classes. Mum told her she'd left school. She was pregnant, with me.'

'Oh dear,' Imogen said. 'That can't have been easy.'

'It wasn't. She'd been up to London with a neighbour, a married man. She'd told her parents she was staying with a girlfriend that night. Anyway, he'd promised to take her to a show – she'd always loved musicals – and she couldn't resist. But when they were there he took her to a hotel instead. She hadn't been willing, not at all, by the sounds of things. But when she got home she couldn't tell anyone what had happened, because of the lies she'd told. When she couldn't hide the pregnancy any longer, her parents got the name out of her. They accused her of trying to break up his family, that they couldn't understand how she could do it. She felt she had no choice but to leave.'

'Where did she go?'

'Her parents gave her some money, and she stayed in a hostel in Hove. But it was squalid, and, the closer she got to the baby arriving, the more anxious she got. Then your grandmother saw her one night, going in there. She insisted Emma came back with her. She came back here, to Elderberry Avenue. Even though your grandparents had their own young family – your dad and uncle – they made space for her. A fortnight later, I was born.'

Imogen took in the story – it still didn't seem quite real.

And yet it did. It was just the kind of thing she could imagine her grandmother doing.

'My mum stayed here for three months, until the two of us were stronger.'

'That's why Dad . . .' Imogen said.

'I think he saw something of my mother in me, when he came round. We looked very alike. He would have been a boy then, but it must have made a mark on him, having us there.

'Anyway, the time came for Mum to move on, so Vivien helped set her up in a flat in Hastings, and put in a good word for her with a couple of local businesses. She ended up working in one of the shops. But it clearly stayed with her – this place, the kindness your grandmother showed her.'

'I can see why you wanted to come.'

'Yes. And maybe now you can see how sorry I am that I was too late. But it's not been a wasted journey. It's been wonderful just being here, in these four walls. Where she was, back then.'

'It's sad, though. That you didn't get to meet. She would have loved to meet you,' Imogen said. Her heart felt heavy from the story she'd heard.

'Sometimes life brings you to a dead end,' Clarissa said. 'You have to turn back around. I'm just stopping here for a little while first.'

Imogen refilled Clarissa's glass, and poured herself another shot. As she drank the sweet yellow liquid, sipping it this time, she thought of something. The diaries Anna used to keep when she was younger. Imogen would sneak a look from time to time, only to be disappointed by the noted-down recipes and snippets of conversations with friends and teachers, very little in the way of romantic gossip at all. She remembered, on the inside front cover, in black biro, the name of the cottage in Hove where they'd lived.

'Could I take a look?' Imogen ventured, pointing to the book. 'I won't read it, I just want to check something.'

Cautiously, Clarissa passed her the diary.

Imogen opened the cover, and there on the marbled end paper was a white space, with writing on it. It had been scratched over in pen until what had originally been there was barely legible. But she could just make it out – 61 Washington Street. She knew it – a friend of hers had lived there once – an ordinary street, a road of small, terraced Georgian houses, in a residential area not far from the Brighton Pavilion.

'Perhaps this isn't a dead end,' Imogen said.

Clarissa looked at her, bringing her eyebrows together.

'Perhaps – without realising it – you might have come here to meet somebody else.'

'Not him, not that man, whoever he was,' Clarissa said, adamant.

'No,' Imogen said, shaking her head. 'It wasn't him I was thinking about.'

*

The next day, with no photography bookings on her calendar, Imogen headed over to the ice cream shop to see Evie. From the doorway, she'd seen that Finn's surf shop was open, and heard sounds of building work coming from the adjacent archway. She'd felt a strong pull towards it – an overwhelming urge to see Finn again, if only for a moment. Even being able to have a look into the building and see how the project was going would have helped her feel a little more connected to him again. When she'd left their home, the fear she'd had about settling, putting down roots, had melted away, and now it was barely there at all. She longed for a feeling of permanence now, when everything around her seemed unreliable and transient.

'Hello, Imogen,' Evie said. 'Well, this is a nice surprise. How was the trip?'

'Good,' Imogen said. 'Good, and not so good. Long story.'

'Your dad mentioned you're living at the guesthouse.'

'Yes. Finn and I have fallen out.'

'Oh, dear. Well, I am sorry to hear that.' Evie paused. 'I just saw him, actually,' she said softly.

'Oh, yes?' Imogen asked, trying to make it seem as if she didn't care.

'He looked about as miserable as you do, if that's any consolation.'

'Not really,' Imogen said, feeling a fresh wave of guilt at the pain she'd caused him. She missed him. The feel of his body against hers, his laughter. The way he'd always supported her in what she was doing, in such an understated way that she hadn't really noticed it until it was gone.

'Go out,' Evie urged her. 'Go and see him. He's working over with Andy, in the shop. Would it do any harm to say hello?'

Imogen felt conflicted, but she was instinctively drawn to seeing him again.

'Give me five minutes,' she said to Evie.

'You take as long as you like,' Evie said, kindly.

Imogen left the ice cream shop, her heart thudding in her chest. She could already see Finn, just a few metres away, working just inside the shell of what had been Evie's shop. In jeans and a T-shirt, his back to her, as he cleared some of the rubble. She stopped, her feet rooted to the spot. She willed them to move, but her body stubbornly refused to cooperate.

Finn was immersed in the task, entirely focused on building something that really mattered to him. When they were still a couple, it had been something he saw as a solid future for the two of them. That had been part of his motivation. Why had that made her want to run? She couldn't even pin it down now. All she could see was that she had been wrong. Luca might have represented freedom to her, in some small way, but, with his flighty lifestyle and grandiose ambitions, he wasn't half the man that Finn was. He never would be.

He turned, seeming to sense her presence, and saw her standing there. His hazel eyes met hers, and her heart skipped.

'Hi,' he said, coolly.

'Hi,' she said back. 'I was just at Vivien's. I thought I'd come and . . .' In that moment it had slipped her mind, why she came, why she had even felt entitled to. If this break was permanent, and the lack of contact between them made it feel that way, then she was nothing to him any more.

He paused, saying nothing.

'I shouldn't have come,' Imogen said, a lump rising to her throat. 'It's too soon, I guess.'

He shrugged. 'Maybe, yes.'

Tears sprang to her eyes and she turned and walked away. She had no right even to be there any more, to talk to him, and it hurt more than she'd ever imagined it could.

On the guest house kitchen table there was some post addressed to Imogen. A postcard from Bella, a scribble in yellow crayon that Anna had turned into a sun. Imogen read the back: 'We miss you Auntie Imo! Love Bella x'.

She felt a tug of longing.

Under the postcard was a slim white envelope with elegant handwriting on it. She flipped it over – the return address was in Sorrento.

Curious, she ripped it open and took out the letter inside.

'Dear Miss Imogen,' it began. 'Please excuse my English. A long time since I write a letter like this.'

She knew right away who it was from, and an image of his face flashed up in her mind.

Would you be kind enough to pass on this letter to Evie?
Because you see since you and your sister met with me, I really
don't think I can stop thinking about her.

Imogen might have messed up her own love life, but she was more determined than ever to make a success of Evie's.

She called her up on the phone. 'Evie, I know it's late, but it's important. Can I come around and talk to you about something?'

Chapter 36

Sirens rang out through the Sorrento square, and Anna rushed over to the window of the ice cream shop to see what was happening, her pulse racing.

'What's going on out there?' she asked Matteo. A police van sped past, closely followed by an ambulance. A crowd of onlookers had formed nearby.

'I'm going to see,' Matteo said, rushing outside. Anna watched as he spoke with a couple of locals, but they were shrugging, and their faces looked blank. He went over to another man by a blue Nissan, and talked with him.

In the time that they'd been in Italy, Anna couldn't recall hearing a police or ambulance siren. For a brief while, she'd felt sheltered from the harsher realities of life. Bella tugged at her skirt, and Anna picked her up and held her close.

'*Nee-naw*,' she said, pointing to the flashing lights, looking confused.

'Yes,' Anna said, working quickly to reassure her. 'There's probably a cat stuck up a tree somewhere. That must be it.' But her heart was still beating fast. She'd lost sight of Matteo in the crowd.

A local, a man in a flat cap, came in and asked for an espresso. Distracted, Anna went back behind the counter and made his drink.

'*Incidente,*' he said.

'What happened?' Anna asked, in Italian.

'On the highway. A moped. These crazy tourists,' he said, shaking his head.

A chill went over Anna's skin.

'Do they know yet, who it was, what happened?'

'I saw them put her in the ambulance. A woman.'

'Was she old? Young?' Anna asked.

The man just shrugged. Anna thought back to the food bloggers they'd had in the shop the other day. A couple of them had left on mopeds. She hadn't thought anything of it at the time.

She walked back over to the window, Bella by her side. The square was quiet now. The emergency vehicles had passed but the area was still full of people. She scanned the crowd for Matteo, but couldn't see him.

Her mobile rang in the pocket of her apron – Matteo's name on the screen. Anna pressed to answer it.

'Anna,' Matteo said, over the noise of traffic. 'I'm in a friend's car, on the way to the hospital.'

'What happened?' Anna said. She realised she was clutching Bella's hand too tightly, and her daughter wriggled free. 'Are you OK?'

'No,' Matteo said, his voice cracking. 'I'm not.'

'What is it? What's happened?' Anna asked, detecting the emotion in his voice.

'The woman – it was a moped crash, on the highway. She got hit by a van at high speed.'

His voice faltered.

'No,' Anna said, knowing the words that were coming. She put her hand up to her mouth. 'Oh, God, no!'

'It was Carolina.'

Chapter 37

Imogen climbed the winding steel steps up to Evie's first-floor flat. Below her was a lush green garden, carefully tended. After all the ups and downs she'd been through, Evie did seem to have found a way of life that made her happy. Imogen rang the doorbell and hoped she was doing the right thing in coming.

'Hi, Imogen,' Evie said, spotting her through the kitchen window and opening the door. 'Come on in.'

'Thanks,' Imogen said, wiping her feet on the mat.

She saw Evie's expression change as she gauged that Imogen had something serious to talk to her about.

'Am I in trouble?' Evie enquired as she gathered the tea things together. 'I feel like I might be.'

'No,' Imogen said, laughing. 'I was just hoping to ask you a few questions, that's all.'

'OK, then. Sounds like we'd better sit down for this one,' she said, getting some biscuits out.

The two women sat down, and Imogen looked Evie directly in the eye. 'You've heard enough about my love life over the past couple of years. Yet you've never told me anything about your own.'

'Oh, Imogen,' Evie said, smiling. 'There's a good reason for that. I'm in my seventies. There isn't a lot to tell.'

'But does it have to be like that?'

'I'm better on my own,' Evie said. 'I'm a stubborn old mule, me. I'm used to my own way of doing things now. I know what I want.'

'But couldn't that work to your advantage?' Imogen enquired gently. 'Not knowing what I want from life is constantly tripping me up. But you, you know so much about what you want, and yet you've just resigned yourself to being alone.'

'You're not going to talk to me about internet dating, are you? I've heard that's what everyone does these days, but, believe me, there are some things I'm absolutely sure I'm too old for.'

Imogen shook her head. 'No. I'm not,' she laughed. 'I'm sure you'd go down a storm, but, no, that's not it.'

'Well, what, then?'

'You always say that no one knew you like my grandma, don't you? That she could almost speak for you, she knew you that well.'

'Yes. That's true. We went through everything together.'

'Did you know anything about this?'

Imogen passed her the letter Vivien had received, along with Luigi's photo.

'Vivien . . .' Evie said, her voice affectionate and irritated at the same time. 'She always was mischief, your grandma.'

'Tell me about him,' Imogen prompted her, gently.

'Luigi?' She looked at his photo. 'He was the only man I ever really loved.'

Evie's face softened as she spoke, and the fine lines around her eyes disappeared.

'He looks the same, you know. More grey in his hair, but the same eyes – you couldn't mistake those.'

'How did you meet him?' Imogen asked.

'I was touring the Amalfi coast on my own, just me and my moped, a year after I first went there with Vivien. I was forty-five. Old enough to know better, some might say. But I'd saved my pennies all year to pay for the trip, and there was nothing to stop me. Your grandfather was getting ill then, so Vivien couldn't get away – she didn't want to, she had everything she wanted in her world here. But travel was always a passion for me; it was what kept me motivated through the long winters in Brighton, looking forward to trips abroad.'

Imogen nodded for her to continue talking.

'He wasn't the kind of man I'd ever gone for before, but, when I met Luigi, I knew I'd been right not to settle for anyone earlier on in life. I'd had offers, but no one I wanted to share my life with, make the sacrifices that come hand in hand with being married. But with Luigi it felt different. We clicked right away. I felt like he understood everything I said. We didn't need to explain things to one another.

'We got to know each other quickly there, over in Italy, and I extended my stay, getting a friend to mind the shop back home. Your grandmother was surprised at first, I think, but very happy for me, too – I told her I'd explain it all when I got back.'

'You fell in love?' Imogen asked.

'Yes. And I felt on top of the world. But that was just the start, before we realised that, in order to be together, we'd have to hurt some of the people Luigi cared about most.'

'Why was that?'

'How are you doing for tea?' Evie asked, peering into Imogen's cup.

'Nearly done,' she said.

'Let's have a top-up. Because this is a long one.'

Evie settled back into her chair and began telling the story.

'Luigi's life was complicated, and I knew that from the start. He'd been married to his childhood sweetheart, a woman from a well-loved local family. They had two young children. Then his wife died at just thirty-four. He was devastated, and so was his whole family – they'd all been devoted to her.'

'Sounds like it would have been difficult to live up to that memory.'

'Exactly, and that's why we decided to keep it a secret. I knew who his family were – I saw them around town, it wasn't a big place – but they had no idea I was part of Luigi's life.'

'That must have been hard.'

'When you're in your forties, fifties, beyond, you accept that most relationships are going to come with some baggage, something extra to handle, and I understood why he made the choice he was making. We agreed that, if things worked out, in time, we would tell people – but he was really close to his daughter, and he didn't want her to think he was betraying the memory of her mother.'

'Then what happened? When you had to come home?'

'I came back to this rainy country, missing him desperately but hoping that after a few weeks the memories would fade and I'd be able to move on with my life. But I couldn't stop thinking about him.'

'Did you stay in touch?'

'Yes, we'd write. And the next summer I took a chance and went back over there.'

'How was it – seeing him again?'

'It was wonderful,' Evie said. 'But, as the week drew to a close, his daughter started to ask questions about me. We decided together that he had to put his family first, concentrate on raising his children. So, after that trip, I never went back.'

'And you never wondered?'

'Oh, I've wondered every day,' Evie said. 'And your poor grandmother got the brunt of it. Which is what got her started with this meddling, I suspect.'

Chapter 38

Matteo and Anna had agreed that she'd stay at home with Bella while he waited for more news on his sister's condition. But Anna couldn't stop thinking of the way he'd sounded on the phone – his voice cut through with desperation and pain. Just after nine in the evening, Anna had a change of heart. She needed to be with him. She called Maria and asked her to babysit, and then got a taxi to the hospital on her own.

She walked the sterile corridors, looking out for Matteo. The first she saw was Elisa, cradled in Matteo's arms, the two of them sitting on plastic waiting-room chairs. Her usually strong, determined face was creased with anxiety, and Matteo was holding her so tight it wasn't really clear who was supporting whom.

'Anna,' her mother-in-law said. 'You're here.'

Anna bent to kiss her and then hugged Matteo. 'I couldn't bear to wait at home. I'm so sorry.'

Elisa shook her head. 'I warned her about that road,' she said. 'I said to her, "Stop being in such a rush, take the long route . . ." But she always was impatient, that is her way.'

'It's a dangerous road, notorious around here,' Matteo said. 'But I guess she thought she could handle it. They say a van caught her on the corner. The moped went off-road and she fell.'

'That sounds terrible,' Anna said. 'How serious is it?'

'It's bad, I think,' he answered. 'Bad enough for her to be in intensive care, damage to her internal organs.' Tears came into his eyes and he hurriedly brushed them away. 'The staff here are incompetent. We've been waiting here for three hours now with no information, not a word from anyone.'

The note of anger and frustration was something she'd never heard in his voice before, and she held his hand tightly, wishing she could ease his grief.

'Did you know?' Elisa asked, looking up at Anna.

'No . . . I had no idea it was her—'

'I don't mean that,' she said. 'Did you know about the baby?'

Anna felt numb with shock. Of course, the doctors would have found that out, and told them. 'Yes, I did.'

Elisa nodded. 'I thought so.' Her expression was tired and pained.

'She was planning to tell you. She wanted time to get used to the idea.'

Matteo looked at his wife. 'You kept this to yourself?'

'I had to,' Anna whispered. 'She made me swear not to tell anyone.'

'Well, I'm glad she wasn't alone with it,' Elisa said, her voice tight with emotion. 'And from what Matteo's just told me about Filippo ... well. I wonder what I knew about my daughter at all. Perhaps that doesn't even matter now,' she said, tears coming to her eyes.

Matteo put an arm around his mother's shoulders. But, instead of feeling as if they were in two camps, as she normally did, Anna had the sense they were all in it together now, with Carolina's wellbeing at the forefront of all their minds.

'I'll get some coffee for us all,' Anna said, checking for change in her purse.

She looked up and Matteo's eyes were fixed on hers. 'I'm glad you came, Anna. I needed you here.'

Anna made herself an espresso and got the ice cream shop ready for the early-morning customers, cleaning down the counters and putting the ices they would sell that day into the glass cabinet. Raspberry, strawberry, lemon ... The bright colours and fresh fruit aromas offered a little comfort in their familiarity. She'd got a call from Matteo saying that Carolina was being taken in for surgery, and he was going to stay at the hospital until she came out. To think of her sister-in-law lying in theatre, unconscious and alone, gave Anna a sick feeling in the pit of her stomach. But they'd decided that the best thing to do was to open the shop. They needed to retain some normality while so much was out of their hands.

Anna closed the shop early that afternoon though, and took Bella with her to the hospital. The taxi pulled up outside the entrance.

Matteo was outside on the edge of the car park, smoking a cigarette and staring into the distance. She'd never seen him smoke in all the time she'd known him. He'd told her he'd given up at thirty. He looked older, and she could see the strain on his face.

She kissed him hello briefly and he reached down to take Bella into his arms; she gurgled as he lifted her up and cuddled her. 'Papi,' she said, delighted to see him again.

'I've missed you, sweetheart,' he said, putting her gently back down onto her feet.

'Have you seen Carolina?' Anna asked.

'Yes. I saw her an hour ago. God, Anna, she looks terrible, her face all bruised, and all these wires.' He motioned to the veins on his hands and arms.

'But . . .?'

He bit his lip. 'She's conscious. It's amazing. I talked to her. She talked back.' Tears sprang to his eyes.

'Sad,' Bella said, pointing at her father's eyes.

He shook his head. 'No, love. Happy.'

Anna took his hand and squeezed it.

'She's out of intensive care. They think she's going to be OK.' He choked on the words.

'That's wonderful news,' Anna said, a wave of relief coming over her.

'And there's more,' he said.

'The baby?' she said quietly.

He nodded. 'The doctor told me – she hasn't lost it.'

'They've told her, too?'

'Yes.'

Anna and Matteo walked with their daughter through to the ward Carolina was recovering on. In the room, Anna saw instantly what Matteo had been talking about. Carolina looked like a shadow of herself, her body seeming more frail somehow. Elisa was at her side.

'Let's play outside,' Elisa said to her granddaughter.

'Is it too much for me to visit her, do you think?' Anna whispered the question to Matteo.

'No,' he said, firmly. 'You're family. You go in and visit her. She'll want to see you.'

They closed the door, leaving the two women alone in the room.

Anna stood for a moment, taking in the scene. Carolina, normally so immaculately made up, was barely recognisable, dark bruises all over her face and chest.

'I look a mess, right?' Carolina said, a trace of her familiar warm smile on her lips, the skin around them swollen.

'The swelling will go down soon, I'm sure,' Anna said, attempting to comfort her.

'It sounds like they did quite a job on me. My lung had collapsed. Urgh! Anna, when I think about it — if my fall hadn't been broken by that tree . . .' She shook her head but only a millimetre, and even then the movement made her wince in discomfort.

'You're here now,' Anna said. 'That's what matters.'

'And the baby is still here, too.' Carolina's expression softened.

Anna held back, giving her space to continue. After a pause, she did.

'We both got a second chance,' Carolina said.

'You're feeling more ready?'

'Yes. I know it's going to be difficult. And the whole thing is crazy, really. But I've never felt more certain about anything. I'll make it work.'

Anna looked at her sister-in-law, bruised but stronger, and felt honoured to know her.

'I should leave you to rest,' Anna said, touching her arm gently. 'But we're all so happy to see you getting well, and we'll be here for you every step of the way.'

'Thank you,' Carolina said. 'And thank you, Anna. For listening.'

Chapter 39

It was a hot August day and Evie and Imogen were sitting together eating lemon sorbets in the ice cream shop. The morning rush had passed, and there was only one regular there, an older man immersed in his newspaper.

'What on earth am I going to write to Luigi?' Evie said, quietly. 'His letter was lovely. But it's been such a long time.'

'Just tell him what you're doing,' Imogen said casually. 'Talk to him about this place. Or tell him about the last book you read, the swim you went for this morning. It doesn't really matter – he'll just want to hear back from you.'

'Do you really think so?' Evie said, smiling with a hint of shyness.

'I know so,' Imogen said.

'Well, he says he's still running the restaurant, so perhaps he doesn't expect me to've changed the world too much.'

She fell silent for a moment. 'What did you think of him, Imogen?' she asked softly.

'I liked him. Warm. Funny. Honest.'

'That's just how I remember him. Devoted to his family, of course.'

'Let's put some photos in. He loved seeing the one of you and Granny.'

'Oh, I'm not surprised: that one was ancient. But I'm an old lady now. I don't think I even have any photographs of me from the last few years.'

'Well, perhaps it's time we fixed that.'

Imogen tidied a lock of Evie's hair and shifted the chair she was sitting on slightly so that her face caught the light.

'There we are,' Imogen said. She stepped back and set up her camera. It hadn't taken long to get her equipment, and the post-lunchtime lull afforded them the perfect opportunity.

'Think back to Italy,' Imogen said. 'Let's try and capture some of that same Evie.'

Evie laughed. 'Oh, Imogen, I was so much younger then.'

'That's it – perfect,' Imogen said, snapping photos.

Sensing some action, Hepburn bounded over to Evie and leaped up into her lap.

'Hepburn!' Evie reprimanded him. Unconcerned, he settled into her lap comfortably.

'OK. Well, we can work with this. A couple of shots with the dog, too,' Imogen said, taking a few more.

She then zoomed in for some more close-ups.

'Right, all done,' Imogen said.

'Finished already?' Evie said.

'Yes. You were the ideal model. Now, let's take a look and see what we've got.' She pulled up a chair beside Evie.

'That one's rather nice, isn't it?' Evie said, pointing at the screen. 'I think that's the one where I look most like me.'

'Great. I'll edit that one and a couple of others this afternoon and print them for you.'

'Thank you, Imogen. You are kind to do this. Then I suppose I'll put one in with my letter to Luigi. Send that out.' Evie's natural confidence seemed to waver for a moment. 'What if he . . .?'

'He will love getting your letter and your photo,' Imogen said. 'I just know it.'

The bell that announced the arrival of new customers rang out, and Imogen looked over to the door. Clarissa came in; her dark red hair was swept up into a pleat and she wore a knee-length flowered dress and sandals. It was the first time Imogen had seen her outside of the rooms in the guesthouse. She looked energised and her cheeks were prettily flushed.

'Hello,' Imogen said, as Clarissa came in. 'This is a nice surprise.'

'Do you mind if I join you?' Clarissa asked. Imogen introduced her to Evie, and she said hello politely, but there was a slightly wild excitement in her eyes.

'I'm sorry, this is so rude of me to interrupt,' Clarissa said to them both. 'But I had to come down here and talk to you. The most unusual thing has happened, and I can't bear to have it all just sit here in my head.'

Evie went to make them all some tea, and Imogen led Clarissa over to one of the booths to sit down. By the time that Evie returned, with a large red teapot and cups, Clarissa was gradually getting her breath back.

'Washington Street,' Clarissa said. 'I've been thinking about it ever since you showed me that address, Imogen.'

'Oh, dear, I guess I opened Pandora's box with that one,' Imogen said, biting the inside of her cheek. She hadn't properly thought through how it might leave Clarissa feeling.

'Yes. I suppose you did,' Clarissa said. 'I've not been able to stop thinking about it, who might be living there now – after all, it's over forty years since my mother left it. I even got so far as to reach the end of the road, only to turn back around again.'

'I'm sorry – perhaps it was insensitive of me to suggest it,' Imogen said.

'No,' Clarissa said. 'You didn't push me into anything, did you? Just put the idea out there, for me to make up my mind. But then I started to think that maybe I wasn't brave enough. I wondered if they – these strangers – would even be alive, let alone whether they would be open to talking to me.'

Evie quietly poured the tea, staying out of the conversation, but not moving to leave, either, her presence quietly calming.

'So what did you decide?' Imogen asked.

'That I wouldn't be able to go back to London, never knowing. That I didn't want to think on it too long, only to find I'd left it too late, like I did with your grandmother. So I went,' Clarissa said. 'I went there today. To the house.'

'And?' Imogen said, barely able to contain her curiosity.

'They're still alive, both of them,' Clarissa said. 'Vincent and Catherine.'

She paused, and when she started to talk again, her voice was unsteady. 'And it seems they did want to see me. Very much so, in fact.' Tears filled Clarissa's eyes, balancing on the lower rims of her eyes.

Evie passed her a handkerchief, and she dabbed them away.

'They were so vibrant,' Clarissa laughed, her tears still falling. 'That's one plus of Mum having me so young, I suppose. I was expecting to see these elderly people, if indeed there was anyone still alive at all, and instead there's Catherine, who volunteers in the library, and Vincent, who's fit and healthy too. They're both full of energy still. Not that it matters, but ...' She dabbed again at her eyes, taking a moment to compose herself.

'You spoke to them?' Imogen asked, reaching out a hand to touch Clarissa's shoulder. 'About the past?'

'Oh, yes. There was no stopping us, really,' Clarissa said.

'Had they ...?' Imogen started.

'Ever looked for me?' Clarissa asked. She nodded. 'Yes, they'd looked. They feel terrible about what happened, what they did. So much so that, when I first explained who I was, and they asked me in, we all just sat there in silence in their living room. Complete silence. I realised they were waiting for me to say something, to be angry. But when I saw their faces – they were about to cry, both of them – that wasn't what I felt, not at all.

'They told me they'd always assumed that Mum would come back, in time. They realised they were wrong almost as soon as she left – I think it had sunk in that whatever choice their daughter had made wasn't worth losing her for. My father's wife had found out and was distraught, calling Mum every name under the sun, and they had felt so shocked and humiliated that they acted before thinking, they said.'

'Did you tell them, about the way things really happened? The fact your mum didn't consent?'

Clarissa frowned, and there was pain in her eyes then.

'No,' she said. 'No. I couldn't face it. What an awful thing to know. I find it hard enough – but they've been living next door to that man all these years. But I will, in time. I think it's important that they know the truth.'

Evie put an arm around her, instinctively, and she seemed to welcome it.

'Of course. It's a horrible situation. So they did search for you?' Imogen asked.

'They came to Elderberry Avenue, looking for Mum, but Vivien didn't tell them anything about where we were – she'd sworn to Mum that she wouldn't. The only thing she told them was that the baby – I – was a girl. She'd taken pity on them, by the sounds of things, and told them that.'

'But they never tracked you down?'

'Mum married again the next year, and I took my stepfather's surname. I wonder now if she wasn't glad to be rid of the name, anyway: it sounded from the diary as if her heart was broken by it all. Then she died. They knew about that, somehow. Perhaps they – my grandparents, although it seems so strange to say that – perhaps they could have looked harder, I don't know. Maybe they respected that she'd not wanted to be found.'

'And, now that you've found each other, do you think you'll meet again?' Imogen asked hopefully.

'Oh, yes,' Clarissa said, brightly. 'It's already in the diary. I'm meeting them for tea next week. Then they're going to come and see me in London, at the start of September. I think it's about time I went home, don't you?'

Imogen smiled.

'I can't thank you enough, Imogen,' Clarissa said. 'You helped make this happen and I'm so very grateful.'

Chapter 40

'*Buongiorno*,' Maria said brightly, coming into the ice cream shop.

'*Buongiorno*,' Anna replied, comforted by seeing her Italian teacher's face. 'Can I get you a drink?'

'I can't stay long. I came in to see how Carolina is doing,' Maria said. 'Have you had any more updates?'

'She's much better, thank you,' Anna said. 'In fact yesterday we got some very good news. Carolina's well enough to come home.'

'I'm really happy to hear that,' Maria said. She laid a box of chocolates on the counter. 'These are for her. Not much, of course, but I find chocolate often helps.'

'Thank you, that's really kind,' Anna said, taking them and putting them with the cards that regulars from the small town had presented her with.

That week, it felt as if things were slowly returning to normal at the ice-cream shop. Matteo, so pale and drawn over the preceding days, was even starting to look more like his old self. He'd spent lunch hours and evenings with his sister, taking her in fresh fruit and her favourite puzzle books. He said she was seeming better with each visit.

'It must have been a very difficult time for you all,' Maria said, gently.

'It has been, yes, but they're a strong family,' Anna said.

'No arguments, you're staying with us,' Matteo said, loading Carolina's things into the back of the taxi. 'Isn't that right, Anna?'

'Absolutely,' Anna said. 'We won't take no for an answer. You need time to rest and recover. You'll be back to the summer house soon – I know you're eager to go there again, but for the next few days what you need is looking after, and that's what your family are here for.'

'You two go in the taxi,' Elisa said. 'I'd like to speak to Anna alone for a moment.'

Matteo looked over at Anna and their eyes met. 'You go,' Anna mouthed silently to him. Elisa led her away from the hospital building and into a park. They sat down together on a bench. Anna's heart beat fast.

Elisa took her hand. 'I'm sorry, Anna,' she said, quietly.

Strain showed in the deep creases around Elisa's eyes. Those brown eyes – so much like Matteo's – seemed more open, trusting, than before.

'For what?' Anna asked.

'You know what for,' she said, shaking her head. 'You don't need to be polite. I haven't made your life easy.'

'I know you love Bella, and you've always shown that.'

'I do – and I have. But what I haven't shown enough, my dear, is that I also care about you.'

Anna felt emotion well up inside her. She'd become so used to her encounters with Elisa – fraught with unspoken resentments. This felt different.

'We won't ever agree on everything,' Elisa said. 'And I still can't understand how you can put your wishes before—' Anna's mouth tightened, and Elisa reacted, putting a hand up. 'Sorry, this is not what I mean. What I'm saying is, perhaps these things don't matter quite as much as I thought. Because you have shown you are family, Anna.'

She looked Anna directly in the eye.

'You were there for Carolina. You listened to her when she needed someone to talk to.'

'I was honoured that she trusted me enough,' Anna said, honestly.

'Times have changed. And that is difficult for me sometimes. Carolina has chosen to leave her marriage, and Matteo tells me I need to accept that. I was wrong about Filippo. I can see that now. Yet still, if she'd come to me, told me she was pregnant, I would have insisted she went back to him.'

Anna nodded, listening.

'That's why she didn't tell me,' Elisa continued, glancing down, her pain evident. 'I thought I knew my daughter. I thought I was close to her, but she kept this a secret. And, while that hurts, I am more grateful than you can imagine that she is still here. That she is OK. And that she had someone to talk to about this, someone who gave her good advice. That someone was you.'

'She loves you,' Anna said. 'She was just worried you would judge her.'

'And she was right,' Elisa said, frankly. 'I wish it could be another way, but it's not. And what I've seen is it's not her who needs to change, it's me.'

In the time since Carolina had been injured – the long, caffeine-fuelled hours of waiting at the hospital, united in their desperate need to hear positive news from the doctor about the person they all loved dearly – something had shifted inside Anna. Matteo's family had gone from being Matteo's family to being – truly – *her* family. And somehow, in that moment, the distance that she'd thought could break her and Matteo up seemed to disappear.

Back at the apartment, Anna set up the sofa bed in the living room for herself and Matteo.

'Your mother apologised to me just now,' she explained to him.

'She did?'

311

'Yes. She was very kind, actually,' Anna said. Since talking to Elisa she felt that a weight had been lifted from her shoulders, that she had been accepted, that she could be part of the Bonomi family after all.

'I'm glad,' Matteo said, taking her hand. 'I know you've had to be patient, Anna. And that part of that was my fault. You've been so good to us all.'

'It's because I love you, that's why,' Anna said, a smile coming to her lips. 'And I'm annoyed with myself that I let anything get in the way of that.'

He squeezed her hand, and for a moment there were just the two of them, standing there.

'I'd better get Carolina's room ready,' Anna said, reluctantly pulling away.

'Yes,' he said. 'Thank you.'

She went through to put fresh sheets on the bed in the room where Carolina would be sleeping. She plumped up the pillows. Carolina sat in the chair by the window, a citron pressé freshly made by her brother in her hands.

'Thank you for this, Anna,' she said softly. Her bravado was gone now, and instead Anna saw a piercing vulnerability.

'I spoke to him, you know,' Carolina said. 'Filippo called. While I was in the hospital. He didn't manage to actually come and visit.' She shook her head, a wry smile on her face. 'Of course not. That would have been far too much for him ... Don't worry. I won't go there,' Carolina said. 'If the last week has taught me anything, it is that I have to look forward, not back. I cannot be angry any more. He's not worth the energy – and, God, I don't even have the energy even if I wanted to spend it on him.' She laughed in spite of her obvious distress.

'I have got no time for bitterness,' she continued. 'I know now just how short life really is – I can feel it. I think I even saw the white light, back there, Anna. Can you believe that? It's been the most insane thing. To know that I was so close to death. So close I could almost have chosen it. I could have reached out, and let go of being here on earth. And, believe me, there were times when I was with Filippo, dark times when I would have done that. Even before the accident I knew I had the power to choose life or to choose the opposite. Anyway, what I am saying – and I know it's a long, rambling way in which I am saying it – is that I was that close to death, Anna. I should have felt alone. But I didn't. Not for a moment.' She put her hand on her abdomen and looked at Anna. 'So I told him – Filippo – what was going on.'

'You did? How did he react?'

'I think he's in shock. He says he needs time to think about it – but he's never wanted children; he's hardly going to change his mind about that now.'

'And you're all right with that?' Anna said.

'I think so, yes. It's me and the baby now. And it may not be perfect, but that's OK. Having him in my life wasn't healthy, Anna. And I don't think the baby would benefit from it, either.'

Anna sat down on the edge of the bed and looked her sister-in-law in the eye.

'You're not going to be on your own,' she said. She'd felt compelled to say it, and knew as the words came out that it was the right thing. She felt torn – of course she did. But this wasn't just about her. Matteo would want to be here for his sister, to give her whatever she needed. 'I don't know where we'll be living in the long term, here or back in England – but, either way, we'll be here for you.'

'Thank you, Anna,' Carolina said, laying her hand on top of Anna's, her olive skin dark against Anna's pale fingers, the turquoise stone in her chunky silver ring bold even in the dimmed light of the bedroom.

'I appreciate that. And of course I'll have my parents back in Siena. And while my mother might be many things' – she gave Anna a knowing smile – 'she is certainly a devoted grandmother. Yes, she would rather the circumstances were different, but I know she and Dad will be there for us.'

'I'll talk to Matteo. I know he'll want ...' Anna started. She couldn't make any promises. It was still too early for that.

'You need to do what's right for both of you, not base your future on me,' Carolina said. Anna nodded. She could see that Carolina was getting tired.

'Listen, I'll leave you to sleep,' Anna said gently. She

reached over and stroked Caroline's hair. 'If you need anything just let me know.'

Anna and Matteo sat together on the terrace, the square
bustling in the early evening, but their flat, finally, calm. Bella
was asleep and Carolina was reading in her room.

'It feels good to have her here,' Matteo said. 'To be able to
watch over her and know that she's safe.'

'She's very strong,' Anna said. 'The doctors said they were
expecting her to recover quickly. Although, of course, with
the baby she'll have to take things slowly.'

'The baby. I'm still getting used to that. Carolina, a
mother. But I know she's going to be a wonderful mum.'

'The best,' Anna agreed.

'She's always been so caring. She'll manage fine – better, in
fact, without Filippo around. I don't know what his plans are
but she's told me to stay out of it, and she's probably right. If
it were down to me, well ...' His expression took on a
harsher edge as he thought about the man who had broken
his sister's heart.

'She's perfectly capable of fixing her own life. You know
that, don't you?' Anna asked.

'Yes,' he replied. 'But I guess old habits are hard to break. She
might be older than me, but it's still my job to look after her.'

'We're all here to look after her. That baby is going to be
very loved.'

Chapter 41

With her feet up on the sofa, Imogen typed out an email to her sister.

To: annalovesamaretto@gmail.com
Subject: Don't youuuu forget about me
Hey Anna,

SO happy to hear that Carolina is recovering OK, and that it's all going well with her pregnancy. You must all have been very worried. I hope Bella is keeping you all smiling and dishing out her best cuddles. Oh, how I miss those.

I've sent B a little parcel – something for you to play with on the beach. Do you remember how we used to go down to the beach with Granny V and fly kites? Well, I thought she should have a go too – it's a McAvoy tradition, after all.

You asked how things are going here. With a little nudge from me, Evie's written to Luigi ... and sent some photos I took of her looking HOT. So it's now down to you to follow the progress at your end ...

In other news, the guesthouse is still fully booked. Amazing, eh. Uncle Martin's over the moon. And that's even without Clarissa – she's gone back to London now, but is still coming down at weekends to see her grandparents. They all came to the guesthouse last week – Clarissa wanted them to see it how it is now, and to meet me and Martin. It was all pretty emotional! I even saw Martin welling up. Vincent and Catherine are warm, lovely people, and Clarissa seems so much happier since she met them.

And me? Well, I've also moved out of the guest-house. Something came up. I'm getting back on my feet.

Imo xx

'We're all out of tea,' Lauren said to Imogen shaking the empty box of PG Tips.

'Right, I'll go out and get some,' Imogen said, swinging her legs off the sofa and slipping her flip-flops on.

'Like that?'

Lauren eyed her pyjama bottoms and hoody.

Imogen shrugged. 'Why not? I'm only going across the road.'

The two of them were up in the flat above the photography studio that she shared with Lauren. Imogen was renting her box room, setting up the sofa bed at night, and it was working out – Lauren needed the extra cash, and Imogen needed somewhere to live that wasn't her family's guesthouse, with her parents coming round every few days to check up on her.

'Could you grab a newspaper at the same time?' Lauren asked. 'There's a bacon sandwich in it for you.'

'Sure,' Imogen said. They'd been out at a bar the night before and were both feeling worse for wear that morning.

Outside, the cobbled lanes were bright with sunshine. Imogen ducked through the early-morning shoppers and across to the newsagent, picking up a newspaper and a large box of PG Tips. She grabbed a packet of jammy dodgers for good measure.

As she left the shop, she saw Finn walking past outside. He glanced towards her and their eyes met. He came over to her. Imogen's heart raced, and she desperately hoped he wouldn't glance down at her pyjamas.

'Jammy dodgers for breakfast?' he said at last.

'Lauren's favourite,' she said, pointing up at the flat. 'We've got a lot of editing to do this afternoon. Figured we could use the fuel.'

'Is that where you're living now?' Finn asked.

'Yes. Lauren's got a spare room. It's working out OK.' She shrugged.

Finn's eyes seemed to glaze, and he looked down. 'There are still a lot of your things at my place. Clothes. DVDs, kitchen stuff. Do you want me to drop them round – now that you've got somewhere more permanent?'

She wondered if it was sadness she'd detected in his voice, or just an air of finality. Without seeing the look in his eyes she couldn't tell.

'Sure,' she said, her voice cracking a little. 'Thanks. I'd appreciate that. How has everything been going with the surf school?'

'Well, actually,' Finn said, 'it's all ready. The shop opened last week.'

'Really? You got everything set up quickly.'

'Fewer distractions I guess,' he said, with a shrug.

The words were gently spoken, but crushing to Imogen. He had started to see the positives in a life without her, free from the ups and downs and drama that seemed to follow her.

'Look, I—'

He shook his head. 'Let's not go over what happened,' he said.

'OK. Sure.' Imogen nodded. 'Well, if you're in this evening, I'll come round for my stuff.'

'I'll be there, yes,' Finn said.

As she put her key in the door to Lauren's flat, hot tears fell onto her cheeks. This was it. A new stage for them both. She and Finn were really over.

'Come over here, beside the rose tree,' Imogen said, leading the bride and groom over. It was Saturday, a week after she'd collected her stuff from Finn's house.

Sarah, the bride, tripped up on something and her new husband Joe helped her get her balance back, gently holding her waist. Their eyes met; Imogen saw the trust and care that was there between them.

'That's good,' she said, capturing the photo.

They carried on laughing together and Imogen took photo after photo. Away from the wedding guests, their love came to life. It was as if she weren't there, exactly what she wanted. When she'd got the photos, she walked with the couple back to the wedding group.

'How did you two meet, if you don't mind me asking?'

They exchanged a glance, and, without a word, seemed to decide who would tell the story.

'At Brighton General Hospital.'

'Do you work there?' Imogen asked.

'I do. I'm a nurse,' Joe said. 'Sarah was just visiting.'

'You could call it that,' she said, with a smile. She turned to Imogen and said directly, 'I'd just found out I was very ill.'

Imogen felt her cheeks colour. 'I'm so sorry. I shouldn't have asked.'

'Don't be sorry,' Sarah said, taking her husband's hand. 'I met Joe when I was at rock bottom, and he pulled me right back up.'

'We got her happy again.'

'And, two years later, I'm still here. And we're married.'

Imogen looked at them, content and at peace in each other's company. 'You have a lot to celebrate,' she said softly.

'That's how we see it,' Sarah said.

That afternoon, Imogen photographed Joe and Sarah's family and friends in the gardens of the Brighton Pavilion. They were taking the chance of happiness they'd been given and running with it. A wedding wasn't just a show, she thought to herself. It was so much more than that.

Chapter 42

'Two tangerine sorbets coming up,' Matteo said, passing the ices over to the customers waiting at the counter.

'They look delicious,' the woman said, pushing her sunglasses up on top of her head and taking a scoop. 'You're the talk of the Amalfi coast, you know. We stayed at a hotel up in Positano and the guests were all on about how we must come here.'

'Thank you. And that's good to hear,' Anna said. 'We're very new around here still, so it's always nice to get feedback.'

'We've only heard wonderful things.'

She sat with her friend at an outside table, and the shop fell quiet. Anna turned to Matteo. 'Do you think things might finally be settling down?'

'Don't say it!' Matteo said, putting his arms around her waist and kissing her on the neck playfully. 'Let's wait until we get to the end of the day.'

'It was nice of your mum to take Bella out to the market today. Certainly makes it easier to run things here.'

'You know it makes her happier than anything.'

'Well, I appreciate it. I feel like it's getting a lot easier between us now. She's a very generous woman.'

'And she respects you a lot. I wish she had been better at showing that from the start – but at least you two got there in the end.'

'Good things take time, I guess,' Anna said. 'I had to talk Carolina out of joining them, you know. Now there's a woman who really can't handle the concept of rest.'

'Well, she's going to have to learn how: the doctors said she needed to take it easy for a month at least, possibly longer depending on how the pregnancy progresses.'

'I'll get her some good books. She's always saying she wants to read all of Jane Austen and now she's got no excuse.'

Matteo drew Anna near and brushed a hair away from her face. 'I'm glad I met you, Anna McAvoy.'

'Me too,' Anna said. 'Partly because you make the finest cappuccino gelato I've ever tasted. But a few other things, too.' She kissed him, and the drama of the last few weeks that had consumed them so completely seemed to drift away.

'So, how's it going at your end?' Anna asked. 'I don't know what you've been up to, but Luigi's been grinning from ear to ear these past few days.'

'Excellent,' Imogen said. 'I'm just supporting Evie in her communication, that's all.'

'Well, it certainly seems to have kick-started something. Luigi gave me and Matteo a free carafe of his best wine last night at dinner.'

'She was a bit reluctant at first. I guess she's settled into her own ways over time. I think she was scared of reopening old wounds, getting hurt again. But when she got the first reply from Luigi she came into the ice cream shop and it was obvious she was delighted.'

'I got her on Skype with him too. I set her up and then—'

'Spied through the crack in the door?' Anna said.

'Noooo ... Anna, come on. I tactfully withdrew to the kitchen. Where I just happened to be able to overhear some of the conversation.'

'Ha! Go on, then, spill.'

'Well, let's just say I think there's still a whole lot of feeling there. I've never heard Evie laugh like that before.'

'That's lovely. So, what's the next step?' Anna asked.

'Getting her out there, of course.'

'Right. Yes. I don't think Luigi's going to need any persuading. I get the impression he can't wait to see her.'

'I just happened to stumble on some reasonably priced flights to Naples,' Imogen said, 'and have printed out the details for her. So, perhaps you should tell Luigi to clear a space in his diary.'

Chapter 43

Imogen and her parents were sitting in the guesthouse living room on a Sunday afternoon, sun rays falling through the bay window onto the Persian rug and Vivien's beloved green-velvet chair. Hepburn was curled up on the sofa with Imogen and she was tickling him gently behind his ears.

'So is it really true, what I hear about Evie heading out to Italy?' Jan asked, her eyes wide.

'Straight out to Sorrento, first class,' Imogen said. 'She didn't want to leave the shop, but I wasn't going to let her get out of it that easily. I'm doing a couple of days, and Lauren's boyfriend Callum is doing the others.'

'Well, I do hope it all goes well for her,' Jan said. 'How exciting, don't you think, Tom?'

'I've always got that sense from her, that there are more adventures to come. Perhaps this is the next one,' Tom said.

'I'm very hopeful,' Imogen said. 'And there does seem to be a fair bit of love in the air at the moment.'

Imogen nodded over to the kitchen, where Clarissa and Martin were laughing together as they prepared tea for the family.

'She's moved out, as you know – back to London,' Imogen whispered. 'Not that you'd notice, of course – she's down here every spare minute. I'm pretty sure it's not just to see her grandparents.'

'She seems nice, doesn't she?' Jan remarked, glancing over at Clarissa.

'She's lovely,' Imogen said. 'He's done well for himself. And look at him – he can barely stop smiling. She's a vast improvement on Françoise, obviously.'

'Oh, Imogen. Be nice,' Tom chided her.

'It's true, though, isn't it?' Jan said, cheekily.

'You're as bad as each other,' Tom said, shaking his head.

'He didn't deny it,' Imogen said. Her mum laughed. 'So, what's next for you two? How are you planning on filling your days now that things have settled down here?'

Jan considered a moment before answering. 'Well, your dad's got his sculptures, and I have a bit of charity work . . .'

'Oh, come on!' Imogen scoffed. 'That can all wait. Evie's flown off at the blink of an eye, and Anna's dropped everything to go to Italy. When are you two going to have your big adventure? Or were you working all those years for nothing?'

'She's got a point,' Tom said.

'It wasn't for nothing: it was for our family,' Jan said.

'I know, I know,' Imogen said. 'And we're very grateful and all that. But Anna and I are both grown up now. You deserve a proper break.'

Tom and Jan glanced at each other. 'Well, I hadn't really thought about it,' Jan said. 'I've always been a homebody. You know that, Imogen.'

'Life is short, Mum,' Imogen said. 'It's never too late to change.'

Evie walked into the ice cream shop, in a summer dress and sandals, pulling a suitcase along behind her. There was a glow in her cheeks, and she looked younger than when she'd left.

'You're back!' said Imogen, excitedly laying down the ice cream scoop she'd been holding.

'Here I am,' Evie said. 'And what a trip it was.'

'Come in and tell me *all* about it,' Imogen said, pulling out a chair for Evie.

Since the day Evie had left for Italy, Imogen had barely stopped thinking about her. 'I tried to get updates from Anna, but she insisted I should wait and let you tell me everything yourself.'

'It was wonderful to see your sister out there,' Evie said. 'She and Matteo were so welcoming, and the ice cream at their new place was delicious. Little Bella has settled right in, hasn't she?'

'Yes.' Imogen said. 'That's all nice, but—'

Evie laughed at Imogen's evident impatience. 'I get the sense there's something else you're more interested in.'

'Of course there is,' Imogen said. 'My mind's been on overdrive.'

'Well, I'd better put you out of your misery then. I met Luigi, and it went well. Very well, in fact.'

'Excellent,' Imogen said, unable to restrain a huge smile.

'I think Luigi was even more nervous that I was, if that's possible. But the moment we saw each other – well, something came back.' Evie had a sparkle in her eyes. 'It didn't feel like so long ago all of a sudden. And the fact we'd chatted on the computer beforehand – thanks to you – made the whole thing more relaxed.'

'Was he how you remembered him?' Imogen asked.

'He's older and greyer, of course, but the years suit him. I must admit I was wondering what he'd make of me, the way I am now – but, well . . .' She blushed slightly. 'I needn't have worried.'

'That's amazing,' Imogen said, full of excitement. 'I'm so proud of you for going out there.'

'I don't know if it's the craziest or the most sensible thing I've ever done, Imogen,' Evie said. 'But it's one of the two. In any case, it was worth it.'

'Were you tempted to stay longer?'

'I was, actually,' Evie said.

'So why didn't you?'

'I wanted to come home and see how I felt. It's a lot to take in all at once, a reunion like that. It's all felt a little too good to be true – how we have a proper chance to be together now, in a way we didn't back when we were younger.'

'You want to be more sure.'

'Exactly. It's such a beautiful place, the Amalfi coast, it's easy to get swept up with the romance of it all, the landscape, the delicious food and good wine.'

Imogen had a flash of how it had been with Luca, how easy it had been to get caught up in the moment out in Italy. But she could already see from the content look on Evie's face how different the situation was for her.

'I'm not one for rushing. I don't want to be an old fool, Imogen.'

'I don't think there's any chance of that,' Imogen reassured her. 'And he seems very genuine.'

'Yes – he does, doesn't he?' Evie said. 'Kind. And charming. And we have fun together. A lot of fun. I know in my head that we need longer to get to know one another . . .'

'But your heart says you want to get back over there as soon as you can.'

Evie nodded her head, laughing. 'Tell me again I'm not an old fool?'

'You *love* him,' Imogen said confidently. 'That's brilliant!'

There was a new light in Evie's eyes. 'Calm down, Imogen,' she said. 'You're getting rather too much like your grandmother these days.'

Chapter 44

'Here,' Matteo said, passing Anna a cone laden with chocolate ice cream and raspberry sorbet. 'Your favourite.'

'Thank you,' she said, taking it from him gratefully. They'd had a long evening of clearing the shop, and cleaning, making plans for the week ahead, and the thought of an ice cream at the end of it was what had been keeping her going.

He picked up his drink, a gin cocktail with a scoop of lime sorbet. 'It's such a beautiful night. Let's go outside.'

They walked out into the square and sat on the edge of the fountain. It was nearly midnight and, it being a Monday evening, the square was quiet. A faint glow came from the back room of Luigi's, but the other bars and restaurants, like their own, were closed.

Anna ate her ice cream in silence for a while, relishing the peace of the square. Being there, beside Matteo, appreciating his closeness, his calm. With him she felt complete.

Matteo said, softly, 'It hasn't been easy this summer, has it?'

'No.' She shook her head. 'Not quite the holiday we both imagined.'

'And yet it's been amazing too,' he said.

She nodded. She followed his gaze over to the ice cream shop, but saw that it was fixed higher, at the small room their young daughter was asleep in.

'Every moment,' she agreed.

'It's taught me a lot,' he said.

'Like what?'

'That, whatever we go through in life, I want you by my side,' he said. 'I already knew it, of course. But I feel it now, so deeply.' He reached over and took her hand. 'I've made you cry,' he said, brushing away a tear on her cheek.

'They're happy tears,' she said.

'Promise?'

'Yes,' she said. 'And how could I not be happy when I'm eating the best ice cream in the world?' she added, taking the final lick of chocolate.

'I love you, Anna,' he said, kissing her.

She pulled away, looking deeply into his brown eyes and running a hand over the stubble on his jaw. 'I love you, too.'

She returned to her ice cream, taking a bite of the waffle cone.

'You know you might not want to eat that right down to the bottom,' he said.

She glanced down into the waffle cone in her hand. Something inside caught the light.

'You didn't!' she said, laughing. She turned the cone upside down onto her hand. A platinum ring with a solitaire diamond twinkled in the light of the moon. Her breath caught. 'Matteo!' she whispered.

'Shall we make it official?' he asked. 'Say you'll make me the happiest man in Italy.'

'This isn't . . .' Anna said, hesitantly.

'It's nothing to do with my mother, if that's what you're thinking.' He laughed, gently. 'It's about you and me, our family. No one else. Nothing else.'

Flashes of the previous two years came to Anna – the days spent in Florence, their emails, the moment Matteo arrived in Vivien's Heavenly Ice Cream Shop, filling her life with happiness. Yes, they'd had their rocky times, too, but all she could see now was that he was the man for her and she wanted to be with him for ever.

'Yes,' she said. '*Sí, sí* and *sí*.'

He laughed. 'You're sure?'

'Absolutely,' she said.

He put the ring on her finger and kissed her. 'Thank you,' he said.

The next day, Anna and Matteo called through to her family on her laptop.

'Have you got any plans for October?' Anna asked them coyly.

Imogen wrinkled her nose. 'I haven't got any plans beyond next week,' she said, sounding glum.

Jan and Tom shrugged. 'Nothing we can't rearrange,' Jan said. 'Why do you ask?'

'I think you'll all need to book some plane tickets,' Anna said cheerily.

'Anna's agreed to marry me,' Matteo said, a warm smile on his face. 'And we very much want you all to be there with us.'

'Wow!' Imogen said, brightening immediately. 'That's amazing! Congratulations!'

'Thanks. I nearly ate the ring,' Anna said, laughing and holding it up to the camera. 'He'd stashed it in my ice cream cone.'

'Very romantic,' Jan said, laughing. 'We're thrilled for you both. Will Bella be a bridesmaid?'

'Yes,' Anna said. 'And Imogen ...' She hesitated. This moment was one she'd often imagined, and she wanted to savour it. 'I'm hoping you will be one too?'

'Just you try and stop me,' Imogen said.

'I promise I'll go easy on the peach taffet,' Anna promised her.

'It's all happening rather quickly, isn't it?' Jan said. 'Are you sure you don't want to give yourselves a bit longer to plan everything?'

Anna shook her head, and turned towards Matteo. 'We're pretty sure it's what we want,' he said, smiling. 'And we want to get on with being married as soon as possible.'

'I think it's great,' Tom said. 'Never understood these long engagements. And you've made the commitment already, haven't you, with Bella?'

'That's the way we see it, yes,' Anna said.

'Well, count us all in,' Tom said.

'And you don't mind,' Anna said, cautiously, 'that we're having it out here rather that at home?'

'Of course not,' Jan said. 'We'd come to the moon to see you two get married if we had to.'

'We'll set you up in a beautiful hotel,' Matteo explained. 'We've booked out one just a few minutes from the venue. Swimming pool, spa ... the works. I'll send you the details.'

'You too, Imogen,' Anna said. 'Just let us know ...' she started.

'A single will do me,' she said flatly. 'And thank you – the place sounds great.'

'They still haven't made it up,' Jan whispered into the screen.

'Mum!' Imogen snapped.

'Well, she needs to know,' Jan said, defensively. 'They'll have things to plan.'

'It's all flexible,' Anna said, embarrassed on her sister's behalf for her mother's reaction. 'Don't worry.'

'We'd better get booking our tickets,' Jan said.

'Congratulations again,' Tom said. 'Hope you'll be having some bubbly tonight.'

'Absolutely,' Matteo said.

'Bye,' Imogen said, waving.

Anna and Matteo shut the laptop and looked at one another. 'That went well,' Matteo said. They kissed excitedly.

'It feels even more real now,' Anna said.

'One family down, one to go,' Matteo replied.

Chapter 45

Imogen was at her parents' cottage in Lewes, sitting with her mum and dad in the kitchen. Three weeks had passed since Anna and Matteo had announced their engagement – and thinking about the wedding was just the distraction that Imogen needed. Yes, she was still photographing babies, but with the steady income, she was on track to save enough for her plane ticket out to Italy.

'Me and your dad have been thinking about it, and we're going to take the bike.'

Imogen's mother's face was bright with excitement.

'You're kidding,' Imogen said. 'Mum, you've barely even been on that thing before.'

'Well, I thought it was about time,' Jan said, proudly. 'It's not often we have such a good excuse to get out to Italy. Your dad's motorbike's been sitting idle in that shed for far too long. And, given those trips he did out in Asia in the

337

sixties, I reckon Europe should be a breeze. Dad's going to take me to get kitted out with some leathers this weekend.'

'She wants a silver helmet,' Tom said. 'So we'll have to go shopping for that.'

'My God! I never thought I'd see the day,' Imogen said, laughing.

'We'll be making quite a few stop-offs as we travel down through France,' Jan said. 'Make a proper holiday of it. We've been waiting a long time to be retired, after all.'

'Brilliant idea,' Imogen said.

'It's going to be fun, isn't it, Tom?' Jan said, squeezing her husband's hand. He nodded happily.

Imogen was happy for them. She also couldn't help feeling a pang of nostalgia laced with regret. She remembered how it had felt to leave the country with Finn, setting out on the adventure in Thailand that cemented their relationship and the time from which she had dozens of gilded memories. They may have had youth, but what they were missing was what her parents had proved time and time again: that their relationship was rich in staying power.

'Be careful,' Imogen said to her mum.

Their eyes met and Jan smiled. 'Feels funny this way round, doesn't it? You worrying about me for once.'

'It does. Something tells me I might have to start getting used to it.'

*

Imogen was sitting in the living room in Lauren's flat when her mobile rang. She answered it, smiling when she saw Anna's name. 'Hello!'

'You sound cheery,' Anna said.

'Don't I always? It's nice to hear from you, that's all. How are the wedding plans coming along?'

'Really well, actually. I've found a couple of options for bridesmaids' dresses and I'm going to email them over to you now . . . Right, done. Yes, it was funny trying to find something that would suit both you and Bella, but hopefully you'll like them.'

'Colour?'

'Pistachio.'

'Summery *and* one of my top ice cream flavours. I'm sure it will be perfect. You've heard what Mum and Dad are up to, right?'

'Yes, Mum called me. She seems really excited about it. We think it's a great idea.'

'I guess after all these years she's finally curious enough to see what Dad's been going on about.'

Anna laughed, then the line was silent for a moment. 'Listen, Imo, there's another reason I'm calling.'

'Sure. What?'

'Look, you're my priority and if this isn't cool with you then we can just forget it.' Imogen detected a certain nervousness in her sister's voice. 'But Matteo was wondering if we could invite Finn to the wedding. If it's awkward, then, like I say, forget I ever mentioned it. But he is one of Matteo's best friends from the UK, and we'd like to have him there.'

Imogen's chest tightened. She pictured Finn – his broad shoulders, the smile that she'd once seen every day. And now? Well, she didn't deserve to see it directed at her again. It was right that she had to make this decision: today was the day she moved on, properly.

'Of course,' she said, as breezily as she could. 'As long as he doesn't mind seeing me, that's fine.'

'You're sure?'

'Absolutely,' Imogen said, nonchalantly, trying to dismiss the tug at her heart.

Chapter 46

Anna ran a hand over the pale-green satin of Bella's bridesmaid's dress. Bella was twirling from side to side, looking in the mirror. 'It's beautiful, Elisa. You've done a wonderful job. Thank you.'

'It's a pleasure,' Elisa said. 'It fits her well, doesn't it? She's growing so quickly at the moment that I wasn't sure.'

'It's a perfect fit.'

Autumn leaves drifted down from trees in the cobbled square outside, and the change in seasons, coupled with the way her daughter had grown and changed, reminded Anna that she'd been in Italy almost a half a year. And, in just a couple of weeks, she'd be getting married.

'How is your wedding dress?' Elisa asked.

'I think it'll be fine,' Anna said. 'The dressmaker that Carolina recommended is doing a final fitting this week.'

Elisa clasped her hands together in front of her in excitement. 'My Matteo – and you. Getting married at last. It's going to be a fantastic day.'

Anna allowed herself to enjoy the moment. Elisa's enthusiasm was contagious, and, as much as she must have been tempted to during the wedding preparations, she hadn't interfered at all.

Bella was scrabbling around now trying to pull the dress off, so Anna bent down and carefully unzipped it. 'We'll keep this nice now until next week.'

Carolina put her head around the door. 'Anyone for cake?' she said. 'I've got a lemon-drizzle fresh from the oven.'

'Perfect,' Anna said.

They went into the kitchen, and Bella sat up in her high chair at the table with them.

The three women murmured appreciatively as they tried the cake, and Bella banged her spoon on the table in delight.

'If there's one thing to be said for being a pregnant invalid,' Carolina said, 'it's certainly improved my baking skills.'

Carolina leaned back in her chair, one hand resting on the small bump. In a black flowery dress, it was barely visible, but there was a distinct glow in her cheeks. 'One more week and then the doctors will hopefully give me the all-clear to start exercising again. I cannot wait.'

'Go slowly, Caro,' Elisa urged her. 'We're lucky to have you two safe and sound, and I want to keep you that way.'

'We'll be fine, Mamma. I just want to at least have a swim

before the wedding, something to make me feel like a normal human being again. I've been cooped up here being a burden on this young couple for far too long.'

'Not for a minute,' Anna said. 'We've loved having you, and you've both helped us so much – with this little one and to get the shop going.'

'And now you are doing so well,' Elisa said. 'Even I have to admit that the peppermint-and-orange sorbet is quite delicious. One of my favourites, in fact. You'll have a job convincing Matteo's father, of course. But let's see: he'll be here at the weekend so he can sample some of the ice creams for himself.'

'The wedding's come around so quickly,' Anna said. 'But I can't wait to have everyone together again. Imogen's coming out tomorrow, and we'll be having drinks here at the shop the night before the wedding so that everyone has a chance to catch up with each other.'

'Is she coming out with her boyfriend?' Elisa asked. 'That handsome young man who we met at Christmas?'

'No, sadly not, although he'll be here too. They broke up.'

'I'm sorry to hear that,' Elisa said.

'I'll dance with her,' Carolina said brightly. 'Life without men can be a whole lot better than being stuck with the wrong person,' she said. 'I feel like leaving Filippo was the smartest thing I ever did.'

'That's good. Well, I bet he's kicking himself,' Anna said.

'Not really – he's wasted no time filing for divorce, so he can marry the other woman.' She shrugged.

'Good riddance,' Elisa said. 'He should be ashamed of himself for the way he's behaved.'

'He's done me a favour, Mamma. And anyway, I'm ready. We both need to move on, and I've got a busy year ahead of me. Starting with watching my beloved brother marry this brilliant woman.'

'Don't make me blush,' Anna said, laughing.

'I mean it, Anna,' Carolina said. 'You've been with us all through thick and thin – and cared for both Matteo and Bella so well. He's a lucky man.'

Chapter 47

Imogen strode out onto the runway in Naples. The Italian sun warmed her bare shoulders. Here she was again, for the second time in a matter of months. But this holiday would be different – she wasn't here looking for answers, that part of her life was over now. This trip was all about her sister's wedding, and she couldn't wait to be part of it. As she waited for her baggage to come out onto the conveyer belt, she checked her parents' blog.

Day 12
By Jan

Leaving Verona. Tom and I are so sad to go! It's been like a second honeymoon, lots of good food, wine and we even splashed out on a lovely hotel. But it's back on the bikes today. I'm getting used to it, and we were

really speeding down through France on our way
here.

We've got so much to look forward to – tomorrow
night we'll be staying with our soon-to-be son-in-law
Matteo's father in Siena, and trying out the ice creams
there, at one of the most famous gelaterias in the
country. Here are some photos!

All being well, they'd arrive the day before the wedding.
Imogen scrolled through the photos Jan had posted of the
two of them in Verona and smiled. She was so proud of her
parents for taking a chance.

'You're here!' Anna squealed as Imogen walked into the ice
cream shop.

'Again!' Imogen said, laughing. 'Come here and give me
a hug.' They hugged each other, with Matteo and Bella joining them.

'Excited yet?' Imogen asked her sister.

'God, yes,' Anna said, smiling. 'Well, that and a bit of the
obligatory panic ... I can't stop thinking about it, dreaming
it, breathing it ...'

'Not to mention eating,' Matteo said. 'This wedding has
called for extensive research in that area.'

'I'm so pleased you're here,' Anna said, squeezing her sister
more tightly.

'And Mum and Dad are hot on my heels, by the looks of things – one more stop in Siena with your dad, Matteo, and then they'll be heading over.'

'Great. It feels like there's still so much to do,' Anna said. 'Did I mention we're having a party here on Friday, the night before?'

'Yes. Well, that's easy enough,' Imogen said. 'I've done that before.'

Matteo led Bella away and Imogen and Anna had a moment to themselves to talk.

'You look so happy today, Anna.'

'I *am* happy,' Anna said. 'I never thought I'd be getting married in a place as beautiful as this, even less that I'd be living here.'

'Have you made any decisions about that? About the future?' Imogen asked.

'We've decided that we can't decide,' Anna said, with a wry laugh. 'At least not yet.' She glanced over at her hus-band-to-be.

'Well, wherever you end up, you know now that you're stuck with us,' Imogen said. 'It really isn't that far to come and visit.'

'And I'll always come back and see you – I'll need to keep an eye on Vivien's,' Anna said.

'Yes, of course. The great thing about you being a control freak is that I know you'll never let go of that place.'

*

347

On Friday, Evie and Imogen were in the ice cream shop as Anna rushed to get things ready for the pre-wedding party.

'Right, what can we help with?' Evie asked brightly, rubbing her hands together.

'These,' Anna said, passing her some old maps of the Amalfi coast. Imogen furrowed her brow. 'Can you cut them up and make them into heart-shaped decorations for us? And, Imogen, can you round up some jam jars from the kitchen and put tea lights in all of them?'

Evie and Imogen got to work, chatting merrily as they prepared the decorations.

'So, you've been here for a week, and I've been here in Sorrento three days and I've barely seen you,' Imogen said. 'I'm taking that as a good sign.'

'Yes, it is.' Evie said. 'Luigi and I have been travelling around a fair bit.'

'Getting on well?'

'Oh, yes. We slipped straight into chatting and catching up.'

'You look really happy, Evie.'

'You know what? I think I am. And of course I have you to thank.'

'My pleasure,' Imogen said. 'Although I can't really take the credit. Vivien was the one who got this all started.'

'Yes, I suppose this is all her doing, really. That woman, meddling in my love life even from up there.' She glanced up at the cloudless blue sky.

'She cared about you so much, Evie. And she always was a romantic – she might have pushed the issue, but she was right, wasn't she? You and Luigi were meant to have a second chance.'

'Yes, she was right,' Evie said. 'She always was. Maddening most of the time, but, on this occasion, I'll admit I'm grateful.'

'So how's it been, meeting all of the family?' Imogen asked.

'It's been wonderful. Better than I'd dared to hope. We went to visit his daughter in Naples last week, and then yesterday went out to the country to meet his son and the new baby. I was wary at first: I didn't want to intrude at such an important time. But they really welcomed me in, Imogen. It was a perfect day. My Italian's coming back to me slowly, so at least I can talk to them a little bit now.'

'That's great. You should talk to Anna about it. She's been working hard on her Italian too.'

Anna poked her head out of the kitchen and checked the wall clock. 'Imo – any idea where Mum and Dad are? They should be here by now.'

Anna checked her phone for messages, and the blog still had her parents located around Siena, hours away. 'They'll be here,' she said, feigning confidence. 'Just keeping you on your toes, that's all.'

*

That evening, Anna and Matteo's friends and family gathered at the ice cream shop for amaretto cocktails, Prosecco and canapés. Imogen moved among the guests, introducing people and topping up their glasses. She could see Anna glancing around, looking out for their parents. Imogen had called them three times now, but got no reply.

'Luigi, you look like you could do with a refill,' Imogen said, topping up his glass.

'Oh, be gentle with me,' Luigi said. 'We've got a whole day of partying tomorrow, too – and I'm a grandfather these days.'

Evie looped her arm through his. 'Don't listen to him. He can handle it,' she laughed. 'And while you're offering ...' She lifted her glass and Imogen filled it. Her and Imogen's eyes met, in silent understanding.

As she looked away, Imogen's gaze fell over by the counter. *Finn.* He must have arrived when she wasn't paying attention. He looked up for a second, and nodded in acknowledgement, then went back to talking to Carolina. He seemed immersed in conversation with her, as if they were old friends rather than virtual strangers. It stung a little bit. But it wasn't her place to care, or to say anything. Imogen didn't want anything to detract from Anna's big day.

A mechanical roar followed by revving came from the square, and Anna raced outside to see, Bella in her arms. Once she'd got a good look she turned back inside and called out to the guests, 'My God, it's them. My parents are here!'

Everyone filtered outside as Tom and Jan parked up their motorbike. Jan took off her helmet, revealing her normally perfectly coiffed hair pointing in all directions. Glowing with excitement, she didn't even seem to notice or care.

'Here we are!' she called out.

'We got sidetracked by a wonderful restaurant on the way, but I hope you knew we'd never miss this,' Tom said, giving his elder daughter a big hug.

Matteo's extended family seemed to engulf her parents with greetings and kisses, helping with their things and bringing them drinks and snacks.

'Hey,' came a voice, soft at Imogen's shoulder.

She turned and saw Finn there, in jeans and a grey T-shirt that showed off his arms, tanned from working outside all summer.

'Hi,' Imogen said. It was achingly hard to be this close to him, yet unable to touch him, kiss him, curl up towards him in the way that she wanted to.

'Quite the entrance,' he said.

'Yes. And they kept us waiting, too. It's been on my mind all evening. And after what happened to Carolina ...'

'She was just telling me,' he said.

'Yes,' Imogen said, biting her lip and trying to fend off the jealousy. 'She's very brave.'

'Anyway, everyone's here now,' Finn said.

Imogen wanted more than anything to erase the distance that had grown between them, to undo what she'd done, and make it all right again. 'It's good you could come. I know how much Anna and Matteo wanted you here.'

'I wouldn't have missed it,' Finn said. 'I know it would be hard seeing you again though, and it is.'

Imogen nodded, and tears sprang to her eyes. They stood like that for a moment in silence, then he reached a hand up to brush the tears away from her cheeks.

'Don't cry,' he whispered.

'I've been an idiot,' Imogen said.

Finn looked away, over at the crowd, for a moment. Then he turned back and said, 'You're not going to hear any arguments from me on that one.'

The silence between them stretched out, and even with the buzz of the party it seemed as if everything was quiet.

'I've thrown away the best thing that ever happened to me,' Imogen said.

'You haven't,' Finn said, shaking his head.

'But after everything . . .'

'You haven't,' he repeated, softly.

Jan and Anna walked together through the party at the ice cream shop.

'Me and your dad have been so excited about all of this,' Jan said. She looked around the room and marvelled at the décor. 'The shop – I can see what attracted you to this place. It all looks fantastic.'

'Well, I'm glad you arrived in one piece. And you're one person I've never had to worry about before.'

'I've never done much that's adventurous, that's why – I mean besides raise my family, which was an adventure of sorts – but now, with this bike trip. It's opened my eyes, Anna. We've met the most interesting people, and it's brought me and your dad back to our best, being in all these romantic places.'

'That's great. There's something about Italy, isn't there?'

'Yes. It's very special. And Matteo's father was so generous showing us around. He and your dad got along famously – much better than at Christmas.'

'Oh, good.' Anna lowered her voice to a whisper, even though the hum in the room was already loud enough to mask anything she was saying. 'They take a little while to warm to, but they're very good people.'

'I can see that. And also what it was that attracted you to living out here.'

'It's been a rollercoaster, but I'm glad we came.'

'I hope you'll come back – of course I do. But if you choose to make your life here, you know that the two of us will understand.'

Anna put her arm around her mum and brought her in towards her for a hug.

'Thank you, Mum.'

*

At the end of the night, as the guests headed back to their apartments and homes, Matteo and Anna were standing in front of their shop, waving goodbye. Bella had gone upstairs with Carolina a few hours before, after being passed around the relatives for most of the evening.

'And we'll be doing all of this again tomorrow,' Anna said.

'We'll be doing more than this. We'll be getting married too – or did you forget about that part?'

'I didn't forget,' Anna said, taking his hand. 'That's the part I'm looking forward to most of all. So I guess this is it – our first night apart in over two years.'

'It'll be strange, won't it?'

Anna nodded. 'I've got kind of used to having you around.'

'It won't be for long. So who would have thought it? The two of us. Two ice cream shops and a little girl later, and here we are, ready to get married.'

'You're not getting cold feet, are you?' Anna said. 'Because, if you are, there is going to be an awful lot of tiramisu for me to get through on my own tomorrow . . .'

'Don't worry about that,' he said.

'The town hall. Twelve o'clock. None of this Mediterranean timing, either.'

'I'll be there.'

Chapter 48

Anna turned to Imogen, and Imogen adjusted one of the white flowers in her hair. 'There. Perfect.'

Anna, Imogen and Bella were standing just outside the doors of the town hall, in the centre of Sorrento. Anna's hair was loose, falling in dark-brown waves around her shoulders, with two small sections twisted and pinned back with flowers. Her makeup was subtle – the summer in Sorrento had already given her a warm hazelnut glow, and Imogen had just added some shimmer and mascara to her eyes, and a touch of lip gloss. Her dress was ivory satin, with spaghetti straps and a low back, and it fell to just below her knee. Matching satin heels showed off her long, tanned legs.

'You look beautiful,' Imogen said.

'Thank you. I feel like I might cry.'

'Don't you dare smudge that mascara,' Imogen said. 'Now, are you ready?'

'Yes,' Anna said, a trace of nerves in her voice. 'I think so.'

Imogen looked down at her niece. In her pistachio satin dress, with its wide bow, Bella looked like a mini version of her. Imogen squeezed her tiny hand. 'Bella, how about you?'

She pointed through the gap in the doors. 'Daddy!' she called out, spying her father waiting.

'I think we'd better go before she beats you to the top of the aisle,' Imogen said, laughing.

'OK.' Anna took a deep breath. 'This is it, then.'

'Yes,' Imogen said. 'It is. Let's do this.'

Imogen and Bella followed Anna down the aisle, passing Anna's and Matteo's families. Imogen kept her eyes focused on her sister, and led Bella past the relatives, all of whom she wanted to play with.

At the top of the aisle, Imogen brought her restless niece up into her arms as they watched Anna and Matteo say their vows. This was it. Things were changing. Anna, the elder sister she'd always adored and idolised, was making official her commitment to Matteo, and to their small family. Imogen was close enough to see Anna's tears, and hers started to fall too. Matteo – with his easy smile and ability to roll with the ups and downs of life – was the right man for Anna, and a great father to their daughter. To see them promise to always be there for one another, whatever happened, didn't seem like either of them making a compromise, or a sacrifice. It simply seemed like the most natural thing in the world.

As they exchanged rings, a cheer went up from the crowd, and Bella leaped into her father's arms.

Imogen looked out at the guests: Jan and Tom, whooping and calling out; Carolina, linking arms with her parents, who were both smiling broadly; Martin and Clarissa, holding each other close. And there, on the third row back, was Finn. She tried not to let her gaze linger there too long.

As Matteo and Anna pulled away from one another, Imogen brought her sister in towards her for a hug. 'Congratulations!' she said.

'We did it!' Anna said, her smile irrepressible. 'We actually did it, Imo.'

After the ceremony, a procession of hooting cars, led by Anna and Matteo in a white Cinquecento, headed up to a nearby cliff-top village. There, they trooped out towards the marquee and bar set up with a breathtaking view of the coast.

Imogen looked out at sunshine on pastel-coloured, picture-book houses, and the coastal road snaking out of view. The bride and groom were chatting and laughing, Anna's hair blowing gently in the sea breeze, Matteo's hand clasped tightly in hers. This was better, thought Imogen. Much better, than watching a wedding from the outside.

'Dreaming?' Imogen turned to see Carolina by her side. In a navy empire-line dress, her dark curls pinned up loosely, she looked elegant and serene.

'I guess I was,' Imogen said. 'Your brother and Anna look happy, don't they?'

'He's got excellent taste, Matteo,' Carolina said with a smile.

'Anna, too, of course. Have your parents enjoyed the day?'

'Oh, everyone's had a wonderful time, yes.'

Tom chinked a glass, and announced that everyone should take their seats for dinner. Imogen's eyes drifted over the crowd, and came to rest on Finn, who was leading Bella up to the top table.

'You should talk to him, you know,' Carolina said, kindly.

'I don't know. It's complicated.'

'There's something about weddings,' Carolina said, with a wink. 'It's a different set of rules.'

Anna and Matteo danced their first dance together as the sun set on the sea.

The dance floor filled: Tom led Jan up there by the hand; Evie and Luigi swayed gently to the music; and Carolina danced with Bella, their laughter ringing out. Elisa and Matteo's father were up there, too, Elisa's high heels lay on the ground, kicked to one side, as her husband twirled her round. Carolina was right, Imogen thought: when there was so much love in one place – people united regardless of blood ties – there was a different set of rules.

She saw Finn standing by the edge of the dance floor, a glass of wine in his hand. Steeling herself, she approached him and stood by his side. 'Have you got a minute?' she asked.

He smiled, confused. 'I suppose so. I don't have anywhere in particular I need to be.'

She took his hand, leading him away from the crowd and towards the ocean. They sat on a bench there.

'I've really missed you,' she said. 'I know when we bumped into each other I acted like everything was OK, but it's not. I still think about you – about what we had – every single day. I was so stupid to risk it all by not being honest with you.'

Finn looked at her, then glanced away. 'Don't say this stuff unless you mean it, Imo. We've been through so much this year and I don't think I can have my head messed with any more.'

'I do mean it,' Imogen said. 'And the one thing I've always wanted is to be with you. Nothing happened with Luca, and he knows that nothing ever will. You're the only one I've ever wanted to be with. It's just that ... that it scared me, I guess. The idea of marriage, settling down.'

'I get that,' he said. 'And there's no hurry. Really there isn't. I just wish you'd given me a chance to say that to you at the time. I can't help the way I feel, that I was so caught up in loving you I couldn't wait to propose. But I always knew you might not say yes. I never wanted to settle down for the sake of settling down – it was because I loved every day with you and didn't ever want there to be a day when things were different.'

'Instead, it was the thing that broke us up,' Imogen said.

'Yep. Perhaps I should have seen that coming. I knew it was never going to be the easiest path being with you. But you know what? I don't care. I don't care about easy – I care about you.'

'I love you, Finn,' she said, tears rising to her eyes. 'I've learned my lesson, I really have …' The words gushed out, uncontrolled. 'If you give me another chance, I'll be honest – one hundred per cent.'

'Promise?'

'I promise.'

He held out a hand and drew her in towards him. She relished the warmth of his skin.

Imogen bit her lip, tears rising to her eyes. 'I do want the same things as you, Finn. I know I haven't made that clear. But I want to be with you. For the long haul.'

'Do you really mean that?' Finn said.

'Of course I do. I wouldn't be here begging for you to take me back if I didn't,' she said, reaching out her hands, which he took in his.

'Hang on, did you say begging? I don't think I heard that part . . .' Finn said, smiling.

'Please,' she said, playfully. 'Please.'

'OK, then. Move back in with me, then. Because you know what? I've really, really missed you. The house is empty and quiet, and God knows I'd never find another use for the darkroom. You know I'm rubbish at taking photos.'

She started to laugh, then moved closer to him. He touched her hair gently, tucking a loose strand back behind her ear. Their eyes met and he brought her in towards him and kissed her.

Strains of music drifted over to them through the night sky. Italy had taught Imogen so many things that summer, but what she was looking forward to, more than anything, was going back home.

Acknowledgements

Three years ago I met with my editor, Jo Dickinson, and we got talking about the joys of ice cream. From there came the idea for *Vivien's Heavenly Ice Cream Shop*, and then this Italian sequel. Thank you Jo for all your brilliant support as an editor and a friend.

To the wonderful team at Simon & Schuster – Carla Josephson, Sara-Jade Virtue, Rumana Haider, Eleanor Fewster and Matt Johnson.

To Caroline Hardman, the best agent there is.

To my mum, Sheelagh, expert in both toddler-juggling and spotting continuity errors and tirelessly committed to both.

To James – we made it through this whirlwind year together. Thank you for your love, patience and for all the laughter.

Finally, to my son Finn, I hope you don't mind being in this story. It turns out OK for you in the end.